# DAY OF RECKONING

**Jack Higgins** lived in Belfast till the age of twelve. Leaving school at fifteen, he spent three years with the Royal Horse Guards, serving on the East German border during the Cold War. His subsequent employment included occupations as diverse as circus roustabout, truck driver, clerk and, after taking an honours degree in sociology and social psychology, teacher and university lecturer.

*The Eagle Has Landed* turned him into an international bestselling author, and his novels have since sold over 250 million copies and have been translated into sixty languages. In addition to *The Eagle Has Landed*, ten of them have been made into successful films. His recent novels include *The Wolf at the Door*, *The Judas Gate*, *A Devil is Waiting* and *The Death Trade*, which were all *Sunday Times* bestsellers.

In 1995 Jack Higgins was awarded an honorary doctorate by Leeds Metropolitan University. He is a fellow of the Royal Society of Arts and an expert scuba diver and marksman. In 2014 he was awarded an Honorary Doctorate of Literature by the University of London. He lives on Jersey.

# ALSO BY JACK HIGGINS

# JACK HIGGINS

## Day of Reckoning

HARPER

*Harper*
An imprint of
HarperCollins*Publishers*
1 London Bridge Street,
London SE1 9GF

www.harpercollins.co.uk

This paperback edition 2015
1

First published in Great Britain by HarperCollins*Publishers* 2000

A catalogue record for this book is
available from the British Library

ISBN: 978-0-00-812489-2

Set in Sabon by Born Group using Atomik ePublisher from Easypress

**MIX**
**Paper from**
**responsible sources**
**FSC**
www.fsc.org **FSC C007454**

FSC is a non-profit international organization established
to promote the responsible management of the world's forests.
Products carrying the FSC label are independently certified
to assure consumers that they come from forests that are managed
to meet the social, economic and ecological needs
of present and future generations.

Find out more about HarperCollins and the environment at
**www.harpercollins.co.uk/green**

*When you have sinned grievously,*
*the Devil is waiting.*

Sicilian Proverb

# HELLSMOUTH

# 1

It was the rat, in a way, which brought Blake Johnson not only awake, but back to life. Sitting on the stone seat in the darkness, up to his waist in water, it was astonishing that he'd drifted into sleep at all, and then he'd come awake, aware of something on his neck, and had sat up.

The light in the grilled entrance behind him gave enough illumination for him to see what it was that slid from his left shoulder. It splashed into the water, surfaced, and turned to look at him, nose pointing, eyes unwinking.

It took Blake back more than twenty-five years to when he'd been a young Special Forces sergeant at the end of the Vietnam War, up to his neck in a tidal swamp in the Mekong Delta, trying to avoid sudden death at the hands of the Vietcong. There had been rats there, too, especially because of the bodies.

No bodies here. Just the grille entrance with the faint light showing through, the rough stone walls of the tunnel, the strong, dank sewer smell, and the grille forty yards the other way, the grille that meant there was nowhere to go, as he'd found when they had first put him into this place.

The rat floated, watching him, strangely friendly. Blake said softly, 'Now you behave yourself. Be off with you.'

He stirred the water, and the rat fled. He leaned back, intensely cold, and tried to think straight. He remembered coming to a kind of half-life in the Range Rover, the effects of the drugs wearing off. They'd come over a hill, in heavy rain, some sort of storm, and then in the lightning he'd seen cliffs below, a cruel sea, and above the cliffs a castle like something out of a fairy tale by the Brothers Grimm.

When Blake had groaned and tried to sit up, Falcone, the one sitting beside the driver, had turned and smiled.

'There you are. Back in the land of the living.'

And Blake, trying hard to return to some kind of reality, had said, 'Where am I?'

And Falcone had smiled. 'The end of the world, my friend. There's nowhere else but the Atlantic Ocean all the way to America. Hellsmouth, that's what they call this place.'

He'd started to laugh as Blake lapsed back into semi-consciousness.

Time really had no meaning. His bandaged right shoulder hurt as he sat on the seat, arms tightly folded to try and preserve some kind of body heat, and yet his senses were alert and strangely sharp so that when there was a clang behind him and the grille opened, he sat up.

'Hey, there you are, *Dottore*. Still with us,' Falcone said.

'And fuck you, too,' Blake managed.

'Excellent. Signs of life. I like that. Out you come.'

Falcone got a hand on the collar of Blake's shirt and pulled. Blake went through the opening and landed on his hands and knees in the corridor. Russo was there, a smile on his ugly face.

'He don't look too good.'

'Well, he sure as hell stinks. Wash him down.'

There was a hose fastened to a brass tap in the wall. Russo turned it on and directed the spray all over Blake's body. It was ice cold and he fought for breath. Russo finally switched off and draped a blanket round Blake's shoulders.

'The boss wants to see you, so be good.'

'Sure, he'll be good,' Falcone said. 'Just like that nice little wife of his in Brooklyn was good.'

Blake pulled the blanket around him and looked up. 'You did that?'

'Hey, business is business.'

'I'll kill you for that.'

'Don't be stupid. You're on borrowed time as it is. Let's move it, the man's waiting,' and he pushed Blake along the corridor.

They climbed two sets of stone steps and finally reached a black oak door bound in iron. Russo opened it, and Falcone pushed Blake through into a baronial hall, stone-flagged, with a staircase to the left and a log fire burning on a stone hearth. Suits of armour and ancient banners hung from poles. There was a slightly unreal touch to things, like a bad film set.

'What happened to Dracula?' Blake asked.

Russo frowned. 'Dracula? What is this?'

'Never mind.' Two men were lounging by the fire. Rossi and Cameci; he'd seen their faces on the computer, more Solazzo family hoods.

Falcone pushed Blake forward. 'Hey, I'm with you. Christopher Lee was the best. I loved those Hammer movies.'

Russo opened another black oak door. Inside was a room with a high ceiling, another log fire on a stone hearth, candlelight and shadows, and behind a large desk shrouded in darkness, a shadowy figure.

'Bring Mr Johnson in, Aldo. By the fire. He must be cold.'

Falcone took Blake to the fire and pulled a chair forward. 'Sit.'

The man in the shadows said, 'Brandy, I think. A large one would seem to be in order.'

5

Blake sat there while Russo went to a side table and poured brandy from a decanter and brought it to him. It burned all the way down and Blake coughed.

'Now give him a cigarette, Aldo. Like all of us, Mr Johnson is trying to stop, but life is short, art long, and experiment perilous. There's Latin for that, but I forget how it goes.'

'Oh, didn't they teach you that at Harvard Law School?' Blake took the cigarette and light from Falcone.

'As a matter of fact, no. But clever of you. You obviously know who I am.'

'Hell, why carry on like this? Of course I know who you are. Jack Fox, pride of the Solazzo family. So why don't you turn up the light?'

A moment passed, and it did go up and Fox sat there; the dark hair, the devil's wedge of a face, the mocking smile. He took a cigarette from a silver case and lit it.

'And I know you, Blake Johnson. You came out of Vietnam with a chestful of medals, joined the FBI, and saved President Jake Cazalet from assassination when he was still a senator. Shot two bad guys and took a bullet. Now you run the Basement, downstairs at the White House, as a kind of private hit force for the President. But unfortunately, Blake' – he paused to take a puff – 'I don't think Cazalet can save you now.'

Blake snapped two fingers at Falcone. 'Another brandy.' He turned to Fox. 'There's an old Sicilian saying, which you might appreciate, since I know you have a Sicilian mother. When you have sinned grievously, the devil is waiting.'

Fox laughed. 'Would your devil be you or Sean Dillon?'

'Take your pick. But God help you if it's Dillon,' Blake told him.

Fox leaned closer. 'Let me tell you something, Johnson. I *hope* it's Dillon. I've been waiting a long time to put a bullet in his brain. And in yours.'

Blake said, 'You killed my wife.'

'Your ex-wife,' Fox said. 'But it wasn't personal. She got too close, that's all. I wish you could have understood that.' Fox shook his head. 'You've caused me a lot of grief. Now you'll have to pay for it.' Fox smiled. 'I hope Dillon *is* stupid enough to come. Then I'll have you both.'

'Or we'll have you.'

Fox said to Falcone. 'Take him back.'

He turned down the light, and Russo punched Blake in the belly. Blake doubled over and they took him out between them, feet dragging.

# NEW YORK
# IN THE BEGINNING

# 2

It was a wet March evening in Manhattan when the Lincoln stopped at Trump Tower, the snow long gone, but replaced by heavy, relentless rain. Jack Fox sat in the rear, Russo at the wheel, Falcone beside him. They pulled in at the kerb and Falcone got out with an umbrella.

Fox said, 'You're okay for a couple of hours.' He took a hundred dollar bill from his pocket. 'You two go and eat. I'll call you on my mobile when I need you.'

'Sure.' Falcone walked him to the entrance. 'Please convey my respects to Don Solazzo.'

Fox patted him on the shoulder. 'Hey, Aldo, he knows he has your loyalty.'

He turned and went in.

The maid who admitted him to the top floor apartment was very Italian, small and demure in black dress and stockings. She didn't say a word but simply took him through to the enormous sitting room with its incredible view of Manhattan, where he found his uncle sitting by the fire reading *Truth* magazine. Don Marco Solazzo was seventy-five years of age, a heavyweight in a loose-fitting linen suit, his face very calm, and his eyes expressionless. A walking stick with an ivory handle lay on the floor beside him.

'Hey, Jack, come in.'

His nephew went forward and gave him a kiss on each cheek. 'Uncle, you look good.'

'So do you.' The Don offered him the magazine. 'I read the piece. You look nice, Jack. Very pretty. Savile Row suits. Big smile. They talk about the hero stuff, decorated in the Gulf War, that's all good. But then they have to mention the other stuff. That in spite of a name like Fox your mother was Maria Solazzo, the niece of Don Marco Solazzo. God rest her and your father. That isn't good.'

Fox waved his hand. 'It's innocuous stuff. Everybody knows I'm related to you. But they think I'm legit.'

'You think so? This journalist, this Katherine Johnson, you think "innocuous stuff" is all she's after? Don't delude yourself. She knows who we are, in spite of our Wall Street interests. So we're respectable – property, manufacturing, finance – but we're still Mafia, that's what gives us our power. That side is not for people such as her. No, she's after something – and you . . . you're a good boy. You've done well, but I'm not a fool. I know, beside the family business, that you have this factory in Brooklyn, the one that processes cheap whisky for the clubs.'

'Uncle, please,' Fox said.

The Don waved his hand. 'A young man wanting to make an extra buck I understand, but sometimes you're greedy. There's nothing I don't know. Your dealings with the IRA in Ireland, for instance, that underground dump they have for the weapons they won't hand over. The weapons you supply them. Your trips to London to the Colosseum.'

'That's our flagship casino, Uncle.'

'Sure, but while you're there, you organize armed robberies with our London connection. Over a million pounds cash two months ago from a security van.' The Don waved him back. 'Don't annoy me by denying it, Jack.'

'Uncle.' Fox tried to sound contrite.

'Just remember your true purpose. The drug business is no longer growing in America. You have to encourage its rise in Russia and the Eastern European countries. That's where growth lies. Prostitution, leave to our Russian and Chinese friends. Just take a percentage.'

'As you say, Uncle.'

'Anything else is okay, but Jack, no more doing things behind my back.'

'Yes, Uncle.'

'And this reporter, this Johnson. Have you gone to bed with her? The truth, now.'

Fox hesitated. 'No, it hasn't been like that.'

'Then like what? Why should she be interested in making you look good? She's in it for more. I'm telling you, she's hiding something. This piece, it's not so bad, all right, but what's next? What's behind the front?' The Don shook his head. 'She flattered you, Jack, and you fell for it. You better find out what she really wants.'

'What would you advise, Uncle?'

'Turn over her apartment. See what you can find.' He reached for a pitcher. 'Have a martini and then we'll eat.'

Terry Mount was very ordinary-looking, small and wiry, the kind of youngster who could have been a delivery boy for some deli. He was, in fact, a highly accomplished burglar and boasted that there was no lock he couldn't open. He'd served time only once, and that was as a juvenile. His very ordinariness had saved his hide on many occasions.

A nice touch two nights before had netted him fifteen thousand dollars, which he'd just picked up from his fence, so he was feeling good, sitting in a bar, relishing the whisky sour the barman was creating, and then a heavy hand touched his shoulder.

13

Terry turned and his stomach churned. Falcone smiled. 'Terry, you look good.'

Russo leaned against the bar, his usual dreadful self, and Terry took a deep breath. 'Aldo, you want something?'

'Not me, but the Solazzo family would like a favour. You would never say no to the Don, would you, Terry?'

'Of course not,' Terry gabbled, reached for the whisky sour and swallowed it in one gulp.

'Only in this case, it's Jack Fox who wants the favour.'

Which was enough to almost give Terry a bowel movement. 'Anything I can do.'

'That goes without saying.' Falcone patted his cheek and said to the barman, who was looking wary, 'Give him another. He's going to need it.'

The barman said, 'Now, look, I don't want any trouble in here.'

Russo leaned over the bar, his face full of menace. 'Make him the fucking drink and shut up. Okay?'

Hurriedly, the barman did as he was told, his hands shaking.

Jack Fox was in the sitting room of his Park Avenue townhouse, on the second floor, enjoying a light lunch of champagne and smoked salmon sandwiches, when Falcone brought Terry Mount in.

'Why, Terry, you look worried,' Fox told him. 'Now why should that be?' He bit into a sandwich, then Falcone took a wad of money from his pocket. 'Aldo, have you won the lottery or something?'

'No, Signore, but I think Terry has. There's fifteen grand here.'

Fox nodded to the champagne bucket and Falcone poured him another glass. 'Terry, I think you've been a naughty boy again.'

'Please, Mr Fox, I'm just trying to make a buck.'

'And so you shall.' Fox smiled. 'Two grand, Terry.'

Terry's eyes rolled. 'And what do I have to do for that?'

'What you do best.' Fox pushed a piece of paper across that had been lying on the table. 'Katherine Johnson. Ten Barrow Street. Just on the edge of the Village. You'll toss her place this afternoon.'

'But that doesn't give me time to prepare.'

'For what?' Fox said coldly. 'It's a small townhouse. She won't be there. You boast that you can break in anywhere.'

Terry licked his lips. 'What do I do?'

'She's a magazine reporter, so you'll probably find an office, a computer, a VCR, all that stuff. Bring whatever disks you find. Bring the videos on her business shelf.'

Terry said, 'People keep videos all the time. I mean, do I bring all of them?'

'Be sensible, Terry,' Fox said patiently. 'I'm not looking for *Dirty Harry* or *She Wore a Yellow Ribbon*. Just use your brain, such as it is. The boys will take you, they'll wait and bring you back. Anything you've got, I want by five o'clock. I'm sure you won't disappoint me.'

Terry's feet hardly touched the ground as Falcone pushed him outside.

He went to Barrow Street wearing a bomber jacket that said 'Smith Electronics' on the back. He didn't bother with the front door, after three rings got no reply, but went down to the basement. There were double deadlocks, but they both responded to his touch.

He found himself in a laundry room and moved upstairs to the entrance hall. There was a parlour, dining room and kitchen, so he tried the stairs, the only sound disturbing the quiet the grandfather clock ticking in the hall. The first door he tried was the study. He saw shelves crammed with books and videos, a computer next to two video and disk machines, and a multiple tape recorder. He switched them all on and removed everything he found in them, placing his haul in the carry bag that hung from his left shoulder. He opened drawers and found more disks and cassettes, which he also took.

The rest really was frustrating. Rows of movies on video, rows of instructional tapes. He was sweating now and swung at the shelves and scattered videotapes across the floor.

Okay. So he'd done what Fox wanted. Time to go. There were some bottles on a side table, and glasses. He poured some bourbon, savoured it, and left by the same route, locking the basement door before returning to Falcone and Russo.

When they arrived at the Park Avenue townhouse, Fox was waiting eagerly. He took the disks and tapes Terry Mount offered and said to Russo, 'Look after him.' He turned to Falcone. 'You stay. It could be bad.'

'Then it's bad for both of us, Signore.' They had been friends since boyhood.

Fox started checking the disks, mostly work notes, letters, accounts, and quickly discarded them. Then he started on the tapes Mount had found in the tape recorder, and on the second struck pure gold.

At first, the sounds were of an innocuous conversation about family business and so on. The woman's voice was very pleasant and intimate, and the man's . . .

Falcone said, 'Jesus, Maria, Signore, that's you.'

There were restaurant sounds in the background, a little music. Fox said, 'She was recording us.'

Suddenly, the tape changed. Now, the woman was clearly making notes to herself.

'There can be little doubt that Jack Fox, in spite of the war hero and Wall Street image, is nothing less than the new face of the Solazzo family and the new Mafia. I'll lull him to sleep with the first article in *Truth* and then hit him hard with the rest. There might even be a special on the Truth Channel in this. I've just got to take it easy, and flatter him. His vanity should take care of the rest.'

Fox switched off the machine. 'The bitch.'

'So it would appear, Signore. What should we do?'

Fox got up, went to the sideboard, and poured a glass of Scotch. He turned. 'I think you know, old friend.' He went to the telephone and punched in a number. 'Katherine Johnson, please. Hello, Kate? Jack Fox. Would you be free for dinner tonight? I was thinking about that piece, and, what the hell, there's some more you might be interested in . . . You are? Terrific. Listen, don't bother going home. I'll send a car. You come on over to Park Avenue and pick me up. We've just bought this new restaurant in Brooklyn, and I'd like to check it out. Will you help? . . . Great! I'll send Falcone to pick you up.' He put the phone down, surprised at the genuine regret he felt.

In that evening of dreary rain, darkness already descending, she sat in the rear of the Lincoln, a small, pretty woman of forty, with dark hair and an intelligent face. Russo was at the wheel and Falcone beside him. They reached the Park Avenue house and Falcone called Fox on his mobile.

'Hey, Signore, we're here.' He turned. 'He'll be right down.'

She smiled and took out a Marlboro. Falcone gave her a light.

'Thank you.'

'Prego, Signora.'

He closed the glass divide between them, and a moment later, Fox arrived, wearing a black overcoat. He scrambled in and kissed her on the cheek.

'Kate, you look good.'

The Lincoln took off.

'You look pretty good yourself.'

He smiled amiably. 'Well, here's to a good night.'

At that precise moment, Terry Mount was swallowing another whisky sour in a downtown bar, aware of the bulge that seventeen thousand dollars now made in his right-hand breast pocket. He went out into the street, drew up his collar as rain dashed in his face, started along the pavement, and sensed someone move in behind him, and then a needlepoint going through his clothes.

'Just turn right into the alley.' He did as he was told, and found himself shoved against a wall. A hand searched. 'Hey, seventeen grand. You were right.'

'Who are you?'

'I'm a big black mother named Henry, and you wouldn't want to meet me in the showers on Rikers Island.'

Terry was terrified. 'I just did what I was told.'

'Which means you know too much. Regards from the Solazzos.'

The knife went up through the breast bone and found the heart, and Terry Mount slid down the wall.

It was early evening and March dark on Columbia Street, Brooklyn, as the Lincoln turned right and pulled on to a pier where a few coastal ships were tied up. Russo switched off the engine. Suddenly alarmed, Katherine Johnson said, 'What is this? Where are we, Jack?'

'This is the end of the line, Signora. You sure played me for a sucker.'

She managed a smile. 'Come on, Jack.'

'Come on, nothing. I've had your house searched. Found your little tape recordings of us. Not that I said anything, but you sure did. Just take it easy and flatter me, huh? You shouldn't have done that to me.'

'For God's sake, Jack, you've got to listen to me.'

'No, I'm done listening. And talking.'

A limousine pulled up behind. Fox got out and said to Falcone, 'Aldo, you make this good.'

'At your order, Signore.'

Fox got in the rear limousine and was driven away.

Katherine tried to open the door, but Russo was there, his great hand raised. Falcone cried, 'Leave it. I don't want bruising.'

He found her neck and yanked her forward on her knees on the rear seat. Her skirt rose up.

'Go on, get on with it.'

He held her as she struggled. Russo took a box from his pocket, opened it, and produced a hypodermic. 'You'll like this, girlie. Best heroin on the market.' He jabbed her left thigh, then injected her again, this time in the right buttock. 'There you go.'

She cried out and slumped forward.

Russo patted her. 'Hey, she's not bad looking. Maybe I could do myself a little good here.'

He turned, reaching for his zipper, and Falcone gave him a shove. 'You stupid bastard, that'll blow the whole thing. Come on, give me a hand.'

Grumbling, Russo picked up her feet while Falcone took her arms, and they carried her to the edge of the pier.

'Easy now,' and she was in the water.

'Come on, let's go get a drink.' They walked back to the Lincoln, and a minute later they drove away.

Neither of them noticed Katherine Johnson's purse, where it had fallen out of the car, in the shadows beside a packing case.

The following morning at six o'clock, rain drove in across the East River, rattling the windows of the old precinct house. Harry Parker, brought out of bed only an hour before, drank coffee from a machine and made a face as a woman detective sergeant named Helen Abruzzi came in.

'This is disgusting,' Parker told her. 'Reminds me of why I switched to tea. Okay, what have we got?'

'This kid is called Charlene Wilson. She was working a strip bar not far from here.'

'And doing business on the side?'

'I'm afraid so.'

'What happened?'

'A man called Paul Moody took her home. When we found her, she'd been raped orally, half-strangled, her wrists tied.'

Parker frowned. 'That sounds like those two murders in Battery Park.'

'That's what I thought, Captain, and that's why I phoned you to come here. Charlene got away because he got drunk and fell asleep and she managed to loosen her hands.'

Parker nodded. 'Okay, let me know when the line-up's ready.'

She went out and Parker went to the window, the rain driving against it, and found a Marlboro, having long since stopped pretending to have quit. He lit it and looked out at the river morosely, a huge black man who had started life in Harlem, earned a law degree at Columbia, and then decided to join the police rather than a law firm. He'd never minded seventy-hour weeks, although his wife had, and had divorced him for it.

For three years now, he'd been captain in charge of a special homicide unit based at One Police Plaza. Sometimes he got depressed dealing with one killing after another, in a never-ending series, and when you were close to fifty you began to wonder if there was something better to do. He wondered if Blake had really meant what he'd said that there might be room for him in that special intelligence unit of his in Washington . . .

The door opened and Helen Abruzzi called, 'Show time, Captain.'

The girl in the viewing room was in a bad way, a blanket around her shoulders, her face swollen, one eye black, bruise marks on her neck. Helen stood behind her, a hand on her shoulder, while Parker read the file. He finished, nodded, and she pressed a buzzer. A light flared and five men appeared on the other side. The girl cried out.

'Number three. That's him,' she said and then she broke down.

Compassion didn't come easy at six o'clock in the morning on the East River, but Parker put an arm around her.

20

'Hey, take a deep breath. I know it isn't easy, but I'll make you a promise. I'm going to take this fuck out.' He squeezed her shoulder and nodded to Abruzzi. 'Take her away, then bring that bastard in.'

He stood at the window, looking down at the water, and after a while the door opened and Helen Abruzzi came in, followed by Paul Moody, cuffed between two police officers.

'And who the hell are you?' Moody demanded.

'Captain Harry Parker. Sergeant Abruzzi's got quite a list of charges against you, Moody, beginning with aggravated sexual assault.'

'Hey, the bitch wanted it. She was into sadomasochism, all kinds of stuff. I mean, I was shocked, man.'

'I'm sure you were, and I was forgetting physical assault on a minor.'

There was silence. Moody said, 'What's this minor crap?'

'Didn't Sergeant Abruzzi tell you? The girl, Charlene Wilson, was fifteen two weeks ago.'

Moody's face paled. 'Now, look, I didn't know that.'

'Well, you do now,' Helen Abruzzi told him.

'Another thing,' Parker said. 'There've been two killings in Battery Park within the last three months, using the same technique you prefer, Moody. Girls tied up, abused, beaten, and young.'

'You can't pin those on me.'

'I don't need to. We have good DNA samples retrieved from Charlene Wilson. We've got the DNA of the Battery Park killer. I'd bet my pension we'll have a match.'

'Fuck you, nigger bastard.'

Moody lunged at him and the two officers restrained him.

Parker said, 'Why, Paul, you should conserve your energy. You're going to need it to keep you going for the next forty years in prison.' He nodded to the officers. 'Get this piece of shit out of here.'

He turned to the window as the door closed. Helen Abruzzi said, 'It's a bad one, sir.'

'They're all bad, Sergeant.' He turned. 'I need air. I'll take a walk if you can find me an umbrella. I'll come back to sign the papers later.'

'Fine, sir.'

He smiled, and suddenly looked charming. 'You've been doing a good job here, Sergeant. I've been noticing. There's an inspector's job coming up, if you'd like a posting to Police Plaza. You deserve it. I can't promise, mind you.'

'I know, sir.'

'Fine. I'll see you later, but ring the front desk and get me that umbrella.'

It was raining hard on the waterfront. Parker had borrowed a police raincoat with caped shoulders, and carried the umbrella Abruzzi had organized. The rain actually made him feel good, cleared the head. He lit another cigarette, and then an old man was running towards him in a panic.

Parker got his hand up. 'What is it? What's your problem?'

'I need the police!'

'You've found them. What's the problem?'

'My name's Richardson. I'm a night watchman at the old Darmer warehouse there. I was coming off shift and I went to the edge of the pier to toss my butt in the water, and . . . and there's a woman in the water!'

'Okay, show me,' said Parker and pushed him forward.

Katherine Johnson was a couple of feet under dark green water. Her arms floated to each side, her legs were open, the eyes stared into eternity. There was a look of surprise on her face and she was achingly beautiful in death.

Harry Parker took out his mobile and called the precinct. 'This is Captain Parker. I've got a Jane Doe in the water only three hundred yards from you. Let's get an ambulance and back-up out here.' He stood there, holding his mobile phone, then handed it to Richardson and took off his raincoat. 'Hang on to those.'

He went down a flight of stone steps, waist deep in water, and reached for her. It was stupid, because that was the recovery team's job, but he couldn't leave her there. In a strange way, it was personal.

She was covered for a moment by flotsam, and he went chest deep and pulled her in and above his head. Above him, he heard the sound of vehicles grinding to a halt as the recovery team arrived.

Parker went home, changed, had breakfast at his corner coffee shop – eggs, bacon, English breakfast tea – and returned to his office. But the dead woman's face, the open eyes, wouldn't go away as he phoned Abruzzi.

'What's happening with the Jane Doe I found?'

'She's at the morgue. They've brought in the chief medical examiner. I believe he's doing the post-mortem himself later this morning.'

'I'll be down. Tell him I'm coming.'

When Harry Parker arrived at the office of the chief medical examiner, Dr George Romano was eating a sandwich and drinking coffee.

'Harry, my man, what's new?'

'This Jane Doe from the river. I took her out.'

'So you're feeling personal about it, right?'

'Something like that.'

'I'm about to finish the post-mortem. I was just taking a break. What do you want to know? Did she fall or was she pushed?'

'Something like that.'

'Okay, Harry, join me, 'cause this one stinks.' Romano drained his coffee and led the way out.

They went into the post-mortem room, where two technicians waited, suitably gowned. Romano held up his arms and

23

one of them helped him into a robe. He went and scrubbed at the sink.

'There she is, all yours, Harry.'

Katherine Johnson lay on a slanting steel operating table, her head on a wooden block. She was naked, the Y cut of the preliminary vivid against her pale skin. Romano held up his hands and one of the technicians pulled on surgical gloves for him. There was a cart loaded with instruments and a TV video recorder on a swivel.

Romano said, 'Tuesday, March 2, resuming post-mortem Mrs Katherine Johnson, 10 Barrow Street, Greenwich Village.'

'Hey, what is this?' Parker demanded.

'Didn't you know?' Romano looked surprised. 'The guy who found her, Richardson? He was hanging around and discovered her purse. She must have dropped it when she went over the pier. Plenty of ID.'

'Okay. Fine. Let's get on with it. Why did you say this stinks?'

'She's a nice lady, well nourished, good condition, about forty years of age.'

'So?'

'So she died of a massive heroin overdose. Enough to kill her twice over. It doesn't fit. Someone like her, in her condition? Plus, someone on that stuff at a high level would have needle sores all over. She only had two – the recent ones. One in the left thigh, the other in the right buttock. And what was she doing in the water?'

'Accidentally overdosed and fell in?'

'Maybe. But I doubt it. Like I said, she wasn't an addict. And another thing. Her medical insurance card was in her purse and I checked it out. She was a lefty.'

'So?'

'Harry, with the greatest will in the world, I can't see a left-handed person injecting herself in the side of the right buttock. It's possible but unlikely.'

He reached for a De Soutter vibratory saw.

'So you're saying she was stiffed by someone?'

'Harry, like you, I've spent years in the death business. You get a smell for it. Yes, I'd say someone wasted her.'

'Which means I've got a murder case on my hands.'

'I'd say so. Now I'm about to take off the skullcap, so if you're not too happy about that, I'd leave.'

'Excellent advice. I'll take it,' said Harry Parker, and he turned and left.

He found his way to Abruzzi's office. She was seated at her desk, working away.

'I hear you turned up ID on the Jane Doe,' he said. 'Let me see.'

'It's an interesting one. She's a reporter for *Truth* magazine, named Katherine Johnson. I did a computer printout. Divorced, no children. Her husband was a guy called Blake Johnson, FBI.'

Parker's mouth went dry. 'Blake Johnson?'

'That's right. You know him?'

'We've worked together. Except he isn't FBI anymore. He works for the President.'

'Jesus, is this a hot one, Captain?'

'I'd say as hot as they come. You zip your mouth tight, Sergeant.'

'If you say so.'

'Jesus,' he said again. He looked at her. 'You wouldn't happen to have a bottle of anything here, would you, Sergeant?'

She hesitated, then took a half-bottle of Irish whiskey from a drawer in her desk. 'For medicinal purposes,' she said.

'And sometimes we need it. Sergeant, you're working for me now. I'll take care of things with your lieutenant. The first thing I want you to do is call the White House and ask for a woman named Alice Quarmby. Got that? That's Johnson's assistant. I need to talk to her.'

25

He turned to the window, stared out, and took another swig from the bottle. Abruzzi called to him, he turned and took the phone.

'Alice? Harry Parker. Is Blake there?'

'He's with the President, Harry.'

'Damn.'

There was a pause. 'Is it important?'

So he told her.

In the Oval Office, President Jake Cazalet sat at his desk, Blake Johnson on the other side, as they reviewed the latest intelligence reports on the Irish peace process. The President's favourite Secret Service man, Clancy Smith, a tall, black Gulf veteran, stood by the door. The phone rang and Cazalet picked it up.

'Alice Quarmby, Mr President.'

'Hello, Alice, you want Blake?'

'No, Mr President, I need you.'

He straightened, aware from the tone of her voice that something was very badly wrong.

'Tell me, Alice.'

She did, and a minute later he replaced the phone and turned to Blake, genuine pain on his face, for this was a man he liked more than most, a man who had helped save his beloved daughter's life, who had saved the President himself from assassination.

Blake, sitting there in shirtsleeves, papers in front of him, said, 'What's the problem, Mr President? What did Alice say?'

Cazalet stood up and walked to the window, watching the rain drifting across Capitol Hill. He summoned up all his strength and turned.

'Blake, you're a true friend and one of the finest men I've known, and I'm going to hurt you now in the most terrible way. At least, thank God, it's me.'

Blake looked puzzled. 'Mr President?'

And Cazalet gave him the dreadful news.

When he was done, he ordered, 'Whisky, Clancy, a large one.'

Clancy was at the sideboard at once and back within seconds with a crystal glass half-filled with bourbon. He handed it to Blake, who stared at it, frowning, then swallowed it whole. He put the glass down on the desk.

'I'm sorry, Mr President. This is quite a shock. Although my wife and I were divorced, we've always stayed close, and now I . . . May I phone Alice back?'

'Of course. Use the anteroom for privacy, then we'll talk.'

'Thank you.' Clancy opened the door and Blake went out.

'Clancy,' Cazalet said, 'I need a cigarette.'

Clancy found a pack, shook one out, and gave it to him. 'Mr President.'

Cazalet inhaled deeply. 'These got me through Vietnam, Clancy. Blake, too, I suspect. What about you? In the Gulf?'

'Long days of boredom, broken by moments of sheer terror? Yes sir, a cigarette came in handy now and then.'

Cazalet nodded. 'Old soldiers, the three of us.' He sighed. 'He doesn't deserve this, Clancy. If there's anything we can do for him, I'd appreciate it.'

'My privilege, Mr President.'

Twenty minutes later Blake returned, his face grey, eyes burning.

'Is there anything I can do to help, Blake?'

'No, Mr President, except with your permission I need to get to New York now.'

Cazalet turned to Clancy Smith. 'Make the call and get the Gulfstream ready to take Blake to New York immediately.'

'You got it, Mr President,' and Clancy went out fast.

Cazalet turned to Blake. 'My friend, do you have any kind of idea what happened?'

'No, Mr President.' Blake pulled on his jacket. 'But I intend to find out. And with Harry Parker helping me, that's just what I'll do.' He held out his hand. 'Many thanks, Mr President, for your understanding.'

He turned and went out.

# 3

In Parker's office at One Police Plaza, Blake listened to the whole story. When the police captain was finished, Blake nodded.

'I'd like to hear what Romano said from his own mouth, then I'd like to see where it happened.'

'Be my guest.' Parker picked up the telephone. 'Have my car at the front entrance in five minutes.'

Shortly thereafter, still in the rain, that bad March weather, they stood on the edge of the pier with umbrellas and looked down into the water covered with scum and flotsam.

'She was there by the steps,' Parker told him. 'The night watchman saw her. I happened to be walking along.'

'And you pulled her in.'

'I couldn't leave her.'

Blake nodded. 'Let's go and see Romano.' He turned and walked away.

At the morgue, Romano was in the chief medical examiner's office, drinking minestrone soup from a plastic cup and eating French bread. Parker made the introductions.

Romano said, 'I'm really sorry.'

'Just tell me what you told Harry.'

Romano did.

'So she was murdered?'

'In my opinion, and for what it's worth, yes.'

'But why?' Parker demanded. 'And what would a nice middle-class lady with an apartment in the Village be doing in Brooklyn under these circumstances?' They sat silent for a moment. 'You never had any children, did you, Blake?'

'No.' Blake shrugged. 'It wasn't possible. She was sterile, so she concentrated on her career, and I concentrated on mine. We just kind of drifted apart. But though we got divorced, we never lost touch. We were always concerned friends.' He turned to Romano. 'I'd like to see the body.'

'No, you wouldn't.'

'Yes, I damn well would.' At that moment Blake looked every inch the Vietnam veteran.

Parker put a hand on Romano's shoulder. 'George, I'd say we should indulge the man.'

'Okay, let me phone down.'

She lay on one of the tables under the hard white light. There were enormous stitched scars where Romano had opened her up, the same scar around the skull.

Blake felt incredibly detached. This creature had been the love of his life, his wife, his support in many bad times, and now . . .

He said, 'I was never all that religious, but human beings are pretty remarkable. Einstein, Fleming, Shakespeare, Dickens. Is this what it ends up as? Where's Kate? This isn't her.'

'I can't give you an answer,' Romano told him. 'The essence, the life force – it just goes. That's all I can say.'

Blake nodded slowly. 'I'll tell you one thing. She deserved better, and someone should pay for this.' His smile was the most terrible thing Parker had ever seen when he said, 'And I'm going to see that they do.'

Back at Parker's office, there was a message for him to phone Helen Abruzzi.

'What's new?' Parker asked.

'Well, we checked out Katherine Johnson's house, and it's been burgled.'

'Damn,' Parker said. 'Okay, we'll be right there.' He turned to Blake and explained. Blake said, 'Let's take a look.' Helen Abruzzi was already there ahead of them when they arrived.

'There's no sign of forced entry, but the study upstairs has been ransacked. It's hard to tell what's been taken.'

She led the way, opened the study door, and entered. The scene of devastation was evident, videotapes scattered all over the place.

Parker said, 'Anything in the machinery?'

'Not a thing. No disks, no tapes, no copies, nothing in the computer.'

'That smells, for starters.'

Blake said, 'Somebody was after something, Harry, that's obvious, and probably found it. The thing is, what and why?' He turned to Abruzzi. 'Have the crime scene people finished here?' She nodded. 'Then could you get your people to look at these tapes littering the floor, Sergeant? You never know. You might turn up something.'

'I'll see to it, sir.'

Blake started down the stairs, and Parker said, 'Now where?'

'*Truth* magazine. I want to see Kate's editor, find out what she was working on. You don't have to come. You've got other cases on your hands, Harry. I can handle this on my own.'

'Like hell you will,' Harry Parker told him. 'Let's get going.'

The editor of *Truth* magazine, Rupert O'Dowd, was the kind of middle-aged journalist who'd seen it all, been there, and done that, and he had little residual faith in human nature. Nevertheless, sitting in his office in shirtsleeves, he reacted with horror to the suggestion that Katherine Johnson had been murdered.

'Please, tell me, what can I do to help?'

'You can tell us what she'd been involved in lately,' Johnson said. 'Was she working on anything special, anything dangerous?'

O'Dowd hesitated. 'Well, there's a question of journalistic ethics here.'

'And there's the question of my wife being murdered by the administration of a massive heroin dose, Mr O'Dowd. So don't play around or I'll make you wish you'd never been born.'

O'Dowd put up a hand. 'Okay, okay, you don't have to come down hard.' He took a deep breath. 'She was working on a big Mafia exposé.'

There was silence. Parker said, 'Isn't that old stuff?'

'Only because the Mafia wants you to think that. Let me explain. The ruling power in the Mafia, the Commission, right? It called a halt to mob killings in New York in 1992 because of the bad publicity.'

'So?'

'So they started again last year. Five stiffed in Palermo a month ago, three in New York, four in London. But it's all different, all back-room stuff you can't connect to them. They've gone legit. They don't figure in *Forbes* magazine, but they're easily the biggest company structure in Europe. The drug market in America is saturated, so they've moved to Eastern Europe and Russia, but now they do it behind an elaborate façade.'

'So what are you saying?' Blake asked.

'That the days of men in gold chains have gone. Now they wear good suits and sit next to you in the Four Seasons or the Piano Bar at the Dorchester in London. They are into construction, property development, leisure, TV. You name it, they do it.'

There was a pause. Blake said, 'So where did my wife fit in to all this?'

'As I indicated, these days the new image is everything. The most influential Mafia group right now is the Solazzo family. Don Marco is the old devil who runs things, but he has an extraordinary nephew named Jack Fox. Fox's mother was Don Marco's niece, so the good Jack is half and half, though he sounds very Anglo-Saxon. He was a young Marine in the Gulf, a decorated war hero, Harvard Law School, and now he's the respectable face of the Solazzos.'

'And how does this affect Katherine?'

'She managed to get into a relationship with Fox. She was intending to produce a devastating series, not only for *Truth* magazine but also for our TV side.' There was silence, then O'Dowd said, 'She wanted to get behind that acceptable face of the Mafia and expose it.'

'Which meant showing the reality behind Fox,' Parker said.

'And he couldn't have that.' Blake nodded. 'So now we know.' He stood up and said to O'Dowd, 'Play this down. Trust me. Give us time and you'll get the story Kate wanted.' He held out his hand. 'A bargain?'

'It sure as hell is.'

On the way downstairs, Parker's mobile rang. He answered and nodded. 'We'll be there.' He turned to Blake. 'Abruzzi. She's sorted out the videotapes. Wondered if you'd like a look.'

'Why not?' Blake said.

The study at Barrow Street was much more ordered now, the videotapes arranged neatly on the shelves.

Helen Abruzzi said, 'I've put the movies on the top two shelves, the language courses and self-help tapes on the bottom two shelves.' She turned to Blake. 'There is one that refers to you, sir. That's what I thought you'd want to know.'

Blake said, 'What do you mean?'

'The label says: Blake's parents.'

Blake was silent for a moment. 'My parents died when I was very young. I never knew them. And my wife knew that better than anyone. I'd appreciate you turning that tape on, Sergeant.'

He sat down, Parker stood behind him, and the screen flickered.

'This is just a fail-safe, Blake, my darling, in case anything goes wrong. As someone who was the pride of the FBI and whatever you get up to there at the White House, I know you'll find this one way or the other.' She smiled at him. 'These are bad people that I'm trying to expose, the Solazzo family. Don Marco's like Brando resurrected for *Godfather IV*, cold, calm, and businesslike, even while he seems like your favourite grandfather.'

'Jesus!' Harry Parker said.

'But Don Marco is old-school. Jack Fox is different. The genuine all-American hero and Wall Street golden boy. You'd think he was some Boston blue blood, but instead he's a cold-blooded psychopath, the worst of them all. Get in his way and you're dead. Well, I'm going to get *him*. Lull him to sleep with the first article, then wham! He'll never know what hit him.'

Blake hammered a clenched fist on a coffee table and Helen Abruzzi stopped the tape.

'What in the hell are you doing?'

'I'm giving you a chance to breathe deeply. I'm also finding you a drink. Trust me, sir.'

Parker put a hand on his shoulder. 'She's right, Blake.'

Helen Abruzzi returned with a glass. 'Vodka, it's all I could find. It was in the freezer.'

'That's what she liked, cold vodka.' Blake drank it down. 'Okay, let's get on with it.'

The screen flickered again. 'I was real lucky. I found a guy called Sammy Goff, who used to do accounting work for Jack Fox. Nice guy, very gay and very ill. AIDS, which is why Fox threw him out. I was having lunch with Fox in Manhattan one day. He left early, and Goff came up to me.

"You look like a nice lady," he said, "so watch it. He's not good for you.'"

A telephone sounded in the background and she went to answer it and returned.

'Okay, Goff was dying and bitter. I cultivated him, and with three martinis in him he sounded off good, and what he told me was special. Here's the lead. Fox is front man for the family. Smart, very clever, but he's always pushing for more. He's played the market with family money and lost, particularly with the Asian crisis. How much the Don knows about this is unknown to me. He's getting by because he's responsible for the Solazzo flagship casino in London, the Colosseum. The cash flow from that is critical to him. He can't milk the family's large interests, the drug market in Eastern Europe and Russia, for example, but he has personal cash flow that helps keep him afloat. There's a warehouse in Brooklyn called Hadley's Depository. The one thing they store there is whisky. Cheap liquor. The booze is watered down and then sold to the clubs at a huge profit margin.'

Parker said, 'I can't believe the Don doesn't know.'

Blake waved a hand and Katherine continued. 'Another side-line in London is he's been involved with some heavy gangsters called the Jago brothers. Armed robbery, that kind of stuff, Sammy Goff said, always a source of instant cash. Fox's bad investments in the Far East are draining him. More serious, he's been into arms dealing, too, specifically for the IRA. He helped somebody called Brendan Murphy, a real hardliner who didn't like the peace process, not only to buy arms but to build a concrete bunker in County Louth in the Irish Republic. There's everything there from mortars to the kind of machine gun that can shoot down an Army helicopter. Oh, and lots of Semtex.'

'My God,' Helen Abruzzi said softly.

'Goff told me there was also some link with Beirut via Murphy. Arms for Saddam, that sort of thing. He didn't have many details on that. The other thing he told me was that Fox doesn't own a London house. He usually stays in a suite at the Dorchester, but he does have an indulgence. An old castle and estate in Cornwall, in England. Very rural, very remote. Believe it or not, it's called Hellsmouth. Somewhere near Land's End.'

A telephone sounded in the background again. There was some confusion. She was off-screen, then back quickly.

'It's a hell of a story, thanks to Sammy Goff. However, although I'd like to expose it, Blake, life is uncertain, and the other day poor dying drunken Sammy was the victim of a hit-and-run driver. Now, was that an accident? I don't think so. He just knew too much.'

The screen seemed to jump and her voice scrambled for a moment. Things returned to normal. She smiled brightly.

'So there you are, my darling Blake. I'd like to believe the good guys win, but life can be such a bitch. If you're watching this, that probably means that the bad guys won this time.' The smile slipped for a moment, then came back, a little more tentative this time. 'Take care, and remember, in spite of everything, I've always loved you.'

Helen Abruzzi switched off. Blake sat there, eyes dark. 'I'd appreciate you running that back, Sergeant.'

'It's evidence, sir.'

'Just get the man a copy,' Parker told her.

Blake got up and walked to the window. After a moment, he turned. 'Okay, Harry, arrange a meeting with the bastard.'

'I'll have to check with the District Attorney.'

'Try the Pope if you like, but I want to face Jack Fox.'

'Maybe you should take time, sir,' Abruzzi told him.

Blake took a document from an inside pocket and unfolded it. 'You've never seen one of these, Sergeant. Harry has. It's a Presidential warrant. You belong to me, not NYPD, and so does he. Now let's get moving.'

It was the following morning when Parker picked up the Buick at the Plaza Hotel. The woman in the rear of the police car was very personable, around forty and smartly dressed, a briefcase on the floor beside her.

Blake sat in front and Parker said, 'Assistant District Attorney Madge McGuire.'

She shook hands as they drove away. 'I understand you're FBI, Mr Johnson.'

'Used to be.' He turned to Parker. 'Did you tell her?'

'How could I?'

Blake took out his Presidential warrant and passed it across. Madge McGuire read it. 'Jesus Christ.'

She handed it back and Blake put it in his pocket. 'So, what do you think?'

'We're wasting our time. Dammit, Mr Johnson, we all know the reality, but we can't prove it. You'll see – Fox will be all sweetness and light: any way he can help, he will, but when we finish we'll be no better off than when we started. His attorney, Carter Whelan, will be there, by the way. That one is a serpent.'

'Fine by me.'

'Okay. I'm bound by that warrant, but let me do my job, Mr Johnson.'

'Be my guest.'

When they got there, Fox was sitting behind a desk, wearing an excellent navy blue suit, his hair swept back from his handsome face. The man who sat beside him, Carter Whelan, was small, balding, and wore a black suit.

'I'm Madge McGuire, Assistant District Attorney, and this is Captain Harry Parker.'

'Pleased to meet you, Miss McGuire. I'm sure you know my attorney, Carter Whelan. And you are aware, I'm sure, that I'm an attorney myself. May I ask who this other gentleman is?'

'Blake Johnson, also an attorney,' Blake told him. 'I believe you knew my wife.'

Whelan said, 'He's no right to be here.'

Fox cut in. 'I've no objection. I was distressed to know of Katherine Johnson's untimely end. You have my sympathy.'

Parker said, 'Evidence would suggest that Mrs Johnson's death was no accident. Could you assist us in that matter, sir?'

Whelan said, 'Jack, you don't need to answer any of this.'

'Why not?' Fox shrugged. 'I've nothing to hide. I knew Katherine Johnson, gave her interviews, and she did an article about me for *Truth* magazine. It's in the latest edition. Quite flattering, actually.'

'Except for the references to the Solazzo family.'

'Just how well did you know her, sir?' Parker asked.

Fox said, 'I knew her well.'

'How well?'

Fox seemed to struggle with himself. 'All right, we had a brief affair. It only lasted a few weeks, and I didn't want to mention it, because I didn't want to damage her reputation in any way. For God's sake, the lady is dead.'

It was an impressive performance.

Madge McGuire said, 'Did you ever know her to use heroin?'

Fox struggled with himself again, got up, went to the window, turned, face working. 'Yes, once. I caught her at her apartment. I was shocked, tried to remonstrate. She said she'd only just started and promised to stop, but . . . I guess she didn't.'

Whelan said, 'She was obviously not very practised with it and must have accidentally given herself too much, or had a particularly lethal batch.'

'Still, there are certain anomalies,' Parker told him.

'Which have nothing to do with my client.' Whelan turned to Madge McGuire. 'Are we finished here?'

'Yes,' Madge said. 'That'll do for now. Thank you for your cooperation.'

She stood up, and Fox said, 'Hasn't Mr Johnson anything to say?'

Blake stood up, face pale, eyes very dark. 'Not really. It's all pretty clear,' and he turned and walked out.

In the car, Madge said, 'There's no case, people. It's not even worth trying to bring one. He just gave the explanation for the lack of track marks – she'd just started shooting and didn't know what she was doing.'

'But if she'd shot up before, wouldn't there be *some* tracks?'

'If it was only a few times, not necessarily. Whelan would laugh it out of court, Mr Johnson. There's evil here and we don't know the half of it, but there's nothing we can do,' Madge told him.

'It gets harder the older I get.' Parker shook his head. 'I've been a cop long enough to know when something stinks, and this surely does.'

Blake lit a cigarette and leaned back. 'But what about justice?'

'What do you mean?' Madge asked.

'What happens if it isn't done, and the law doesn't work? Is someone entitled to take the law into his own hands?'

'Well, I know one thing,' Parker told him. 'It wouldn't be the law they were taking.'

'I suppose not.'

'What will you do, Blake?'

'Go back to Washington. See the President. Arrange a funeral.' The car pulled in at the Plaza. He shook hands with Parker and turned to Madge. 'Many thanks, Miss McGuire.'

He got out and went up the steps to the hotel. As the car moved away, Madge said, 'Are you thinking what I am, Harry?'

'If you mean, God help Jack Fox, yes.'

At the office, Fox waited for a computer printout he'd ordered on Blake Johnson. It finally appeared and he was reading through it when there was a knock on the door and Falcone entered.

'Just checking, Signore. Is there anything I can do?'

Fox passed him the printout. Falcone read it. 'Quite a record.'

'It sure as hell is. War hero, FBI, took a bullet saving the President. But there's a block there. What's he been doing lately? I'll have to get my top people to work on it.'

'Is he a threat?'

'Of course he is. He didn't believe me for a moment about his wife. Aldo, I've stared at the face of the enemy in Iraq, and I know what I saw in Blake Johnson's eyes. There was no rage in them, only revenge. He'll be coming, and we must be ready.'

'Always, Signore.'

Falcone went out, and Fox went to the window as a flurry of sleet brushed across Manhattan. Strange, he wasn't afraid. He was excited.

# 4

Fox had an impeccable source when it came to computer-accessing: an ageing lady named Maud Jackson, who was a retired professor in communication sciences at MIT, seventy years old – and a confirmed gambler. A nice Jewish widow who lived in Crown Heights, she was always chronically short of money, because she was an easy mark and liked the game anyway.

Fox met her in a local bar by appointment. She sat there, sucking on a cigarette and drinking Chablis, while he told her about Blake Johnson.

'The thing is, there's a block on the guy.'

'Like any roadblock, Jack, it's made to be gone around.'

'Exactly, and who better than you to do it?'

'Flattery will get you everywhere, but if this guy used to be FBI and there's a block, this is serious stuff.'

She took out another cigarette and he gave her a light, revolted by the thinning dyed red hair, the cunning old eyes, but she was a genius.

'Okay, Maud, I'll pay you twenty thousand dollars.'

'Twenty-five, Jack, and happy to oblige.'

He nodded. 'Done. There's only one problem. I want it, like, yesterday.'

'No problem.' She swallowed her Chablis and stood up and nodded to Falcone. 'Now, if this big ape will take me home, I'll get on with it.'

Falcone smiled amiably. 'My pleasure, Signora.'

It took her no more than three hours of devious double play to make her breakthrough and there it was: Blake Johnson, ex-FBI, now Director of the Basement for the President, and what a treasure house that turned out to be. The President's personal hit squad, and such an interesting cross-reference to London. It seemed that Johnson was very cosy with the British Prime Minister's personal intelligence outfit, led by one Brigadier Charles Ferguson, its muscle supplied by an ex-IRA enforcer named Sean Dillon. It was all there, past exploits, addresses, homes and phones. She telephoned Fox and asked to be put through.

'Jack, it's Maud.'

'Have you got something?'

'Jack, I don't know what's going on, but what I've got is pure dynamite, so don't screw with me. Just send Falcone round with thirty thousand in cash.'

'Our deal was for twenty-five, Maud.'

'Jack, this is better than the midnight movie. Believe me, it's worth the extra five.'

'All right. I'll have him there in an hour.'

'And, Jack, no rough stuff.'

'Don't be stupid. You're too important.'

An hour and a half later, Falcone returned with the printout. What Fox didn't know was that Falcone had stopped on the way and had the printout copied.

Fox read the printout – Johnson's background, the London end of things, Ferguson, Dillon, the computer photos – and shook his head.

'My God.'

'Trouble, Signore?'

'No, just rather startling information. The old bitch did well. Read it.'

Falcone already had, but pretended to again. He nodded and handed the printout back, face impassive. 'Interesting.'

Fox laughed. 'You could say that. This Dillon.' He shook his head. 'What a sweetheart. Still, it's always useful to know what you're up against.'

'Of course.'

'Good. You can go. Pick me up at eight for dinner.'

Falcone left, and was at Don Marco's apartment at Trump Tower half an hour later, where the old man read the copy of the printout with interest and checked the photos.

'You've done well, Aldo.'

'Thank you, Don Marco.'

'Anything else you find out, tell me at once.'

He held out his hand and Falcone kissed it. 'As always.'

Brigadier Charles Ferguson's office was on the third floor of the Ministry of Defence, overlooking Horse Guards Avenue in London. He sat at his desk, a large, untidy man in a crumpled suit and Guards tie, working his way through a mass of papers.

The buzzer rang and he pressed a button. 'Is Dillon here?'

A woman's voice said, 'Yes, sir.'

'Good. Come in.'

The door opened. The woman who entered was perhaps thirty, wore a fawn trouser suit and horn-rimmed glasses, and had cropped red hair. She was Detective Superintendent Hannah Bernstein of Special Branch and allocated to Ferguson as his assistant. Many people had underestimated her because of her looks, and they'd come to regret it. She'd killed four times in the line of duty.

The man behind her, Sean Dillon, was no more than five feet four or five, with fair hair almost white. He wore an old leather jacket, dark cords and a white scarf. His eyes held no colour, but his mouth was lifted with a perpetual smile that said he didn't take life too seriously. Once an actor, and later the most feared enforcer the IRA had ever had, he had been working for what had become known as the Prime Minister's Private Army for several years.

'Anyone heard anything?' Ferguson asked. 'We keep getting rumours about secret IRA gun caches, but no specifics. Sean?'

'Not a peep,' Dillon told him.

'So what's next, sir?' Hannah Bernstein asked.

The phone rang on Ferguson's desk. He answered it and his face showed considerable surprise. 'Yes, sir. Of course . . . well, would you like to talk with him directly? He's right here . . . Just one moment.' He held the phone out. 'Dillon? President Cazalet would like a word.'

Dillon frowned in surprise and took the phone. 'Mr President?'

'This is a bad one, my fine Irish friend, involving Blake Johnson. Just listen . . .'

A few minutes later, Dillon relayed the news to Ferguson and Hannah Bernstein. He walked to the window, looked out, and turned.

'The funeral's the day after tomorrow. I'm going, Brigadier.'

Ferguson raised a hand. 'Sean, the three of us have all been to hell and back with Blake Johnson. We'll all go. We owe him that.' He turned to Hannah. 'Order the plane.'

Katherine Johnson's funeral at the crematorium two days later was singularly unimpressive. Taped and fake-sounding religious music played, and a minister who looked as if he'd hired his costume from a TV wardrobe company threw out platitudes.

Ferguson, Dillon and Hannah arrived halfway through the ceremony, just in time to see the coffin slide through the plastic curtains. The only other people there were the funeral staff

44

and a couple of people from *Truth*. Blake distributed dollars, turned, and found his friends. His face said it all.

Hannah Bernstein embraced him, Ferguson shook hands; only Dillon stood back, very calm. He inclined his head and walked out.

They stood on the step, the rain driving in, and Dillon lit a cigarette. 'I've heard what the President had to say, now I want it from you. You've saved my life on a number of occasions and I've saved yours. There are no secrets between us, Blake.'

'No, Sean, no secrets.'

'So let's collect the Brigadier and Hannah and go and sit in the limousine and we can all hear the worst.'

Blake told them everything, including all that Katherine had relayed to them on the videotape. Afterwards, they all sat silent for a moment. 'From my point of view, the arms-dealing with the IRA, the Brendan Murphy business, that's the worst,' said Ferguson, shaking his head. 'And the Beirut connection, working for Saddam. We've got to do something about that.' He turned to Hannah. 'What are your thoughts, Superintendent?'

'That Fox has problems. He's skimmed money from the Commission, he's fiddling from the London casino, the Colosseum. Beirut and Ireland are desperate attempts to make cash.'

'And those hits with the Jago brothers are even more desperate,' Dillon said.

'Do you know them?' Ferguson asked.

'No, but I'm sure Harry Salter does.'

'Salter?'

Hannah said, 'You know him, sir. A London gangster and smuggler. Owns a pub at Wapping called the Dark Man.'

'Ah, I remember now,' Ferguson said.

'He's into warehouse developments by the Thames, also running booze and cigarettes from Europe.'

'But no drugs and no prostitution,' Dillon reminded her.

'Yes, an old-fashioned gangster. How very nice. He only shoots his rivals when absolutely necessary.'

Dillon shrugged. 'Well, they shouldn't have become gangsters then. I'm sure he'll help us with the Jago brothers and with Fox, though. He has a good team – his nephew Billy Salter, Joe Baxter, Sam Hall.'

'Dillon, these people are real villains,' Hannah said.

'Compared to Jack Fox, they're sweetness and light.' And then Dillon smiled. 'Except that if you push them hard, they'll be Fox's worst nightmare.'

There was a pause. Ferguson said, 'Yes, well, we'll see. We'll talk about it more on the way back to London.'

Dillon said, 'Not me, Brigadier. I haven't had a vacation in two years. I think it's about time I took one.'

Ferguson said, 'Sean, you're not getting into one of your moods, are you?'

'Now, do I look that kind of fella, Brigadier?' He kissed Hannah on the cheek. 'Off you go. I'll see you in London. I'll drive back with Blake.'

She frowned. 'Now, look, Sean . . .'

'Just do it,' he said, turned and walked towards Blake Johnson's limousine.

Driving back to Manhattan, Dillon closed the sliding window partition.

'I take it we're going to take Jack Fox to the cleaners.'

'You say we.'

'Don't mess with me, Blake. If you're in, I'm in, for more reasons than we need to state.'

'Nobody should die like she did, Sean. Can you imagine? A dark, rainy night on the waterfront? Forced into taking that massive overdose?' He shook his head. 'I'll see Fox in hell, and don't talk to me about the law and all that kind of crap. I'm going to take him down in whatever way I have to, so my advice to you is to stay out of it.'

Dillon pulled open the panel and said to the driver, 'Pull over for five minutes and pass the umbrella.'

The man did as he was told, and Dillon got out and opened the huge golfing umbrella as Blake joined him. They stood by the wall and looked out at the East River. Dillon lit a cigarette.

'Listen, Blake, you're one of life's good guys, and Jack Fox is one of life's bad guys.'

'And you, Sean, what are you?'

Dillon turned, his eyes blank, face wiped of all emotion. 'Oh, I'm his worst nightmare, Blake. I was engaged in what I saw as war for twenty-five years with the Brits and the IRA. Fox and his fucking Mafia think they're big stuff. Well, let me tell you something. They wouldn't last five minutes in Belfast.'

'So what are you saying?'

'We take this animal out, only we do it my way. It's too easy to shoot him on the street. I want this to be slow and painful. We destroy his miserable little empire bit by bit, until he has nothing left. And then we destroy him.'

Blake smiled slowly. 'Now, that I would like. Where do we begin?'

'Well, according to Katherine, there's this place called Hadley's Depository in Brooklyn where they process cheap liquor.'

'So?'

'So let's take it out.'

'You mean that?'

'Sure. Just the two of us.'

Blake's face was pale with excitement. 'You really mean this?'

'It's a start, me old son.'

'Then you're on, by God.'


Hadley's Depository was beside a pier close to Clark Street on the river in Brooklyn. It was eleven o'clock that night, black rods of March rain falling, as Dillon and Blake drove up in an old Ford panel truck and parked at the side of the road.

They stood by a wall and Dillon lit a cigarette as they looked the place over. 'This shouldn't be hard,' he said. 'You, me, and no one else. An in-and-out job.'

'There's just one thing, Sean. I don't want any victims here.'

'No problem. If there's a night shift, we leave it. If there's just security, we'll handle them. There'll be only one victim here, Blake: Jack Fox and his income from the booze business.' He laughed and hit Blake on the shoulder. 'Hey, trust me. It'll work.'

The following day, Blake went through files and accessed city and police records to find out everything he could about the Hadley Depository. When he saw Dillon for lunch at a small Italian family restaurant, he was quite strong again, probably because he had an end in view.

'It's funny, but this place has no record. Not even a hint with the police.'

'So Fox is a clever bastard. Do you have any details on how it operates?'

'I know the security firm who handles it. Two men guard the place. On the other hand, since the warehouse is not what it seems to be, who knows? They could have a night shift.'

'We'll see.' Dillon smiled, looking like the Devil himself. 'No waiting, Blake. We go in and stiff the place. Give Fox something to think about.'

'When?'

'Tonight, for God's sake.'

Blake said, 'You're right. To hell with him.'

It was midnight when they drove up to Hadley's Depository in the old Ford. Blake was driving and pulled into a side turning. Both he and Dillon wore dark trousers and sweaters. Now, as they sat there, they pulled on ski masks, and Dillon took a Browning out of a handbag and stuffed it into the waistband of his trousers at the rear.

'Bring the other bag,' he told Blake. 'The Semtex pencils. Let's move it.'

There was a nine-foot wall. He cupped his hands, helped Blake over, then passed the bag, reached for an outstretched hand, and scrambled over himself. They crouched on the other side, as it started to rain.

'Okay, let's do it,' Dillon said.

There were indeed two security guards in a small, lighted office off a courtyard. Dillon and Blake moved in through factory doors which, surprisingly, had been left open. Inside the main building, they saw an extensive range of equipment, obviously all of importance to the racket that was going on there. Great vats, stacks of bottles, many with exotic labels.

Dillon pulled one up. 'Highland Pride Old Scots Whisky.'

'Believe that, you'll believe anything,' Blake told him.

'Okay, so let's get on with it.'

Dillon opened the bag that hung from his shoulder. He took out several Semtex primer pencils Blake had obtained for him, ran round the main area, and placed them.

'How long?' Blake asked.

'Ten minutes. Let's get those guards out and move on.'

The two security guards were playing Trivial Pursuit when the door opened and the men in hoods slipped in. Dillon relieved them of their guns.

'If you want to live, move fast and make it to the street.'

They didn't argue, did exactly as they were told, and a few moments later were out of the front gate. Just after that, the Semtex timers exploded and the whisky in the vats caught fire.

Dillon caught the nearest guard by the collar. 'Listen, here's a message. It isn't for the police. It's for Jack Fox. Tell him, this is just the beginning, for Katherine Johnson. Got that? Okay, now run for it.'

Which they did.

Dillon and Blake drove some little distance away and parked, watching the flames and waiting for the fire department.

Blake said, 'Funny, but I didn't feel guilty.'

'Why should you? Fox is a murdering bastard.'

'I work for the President, Sean. You work for the Prime Minister.'

'I don't care about that. One way or another, Fox goes down.'

The following morning, Jack Fox was at Trump Tower, summoned there by a phone call from Don Marco. The old man sipped coffee by the fire.

'A bad night, I hear, Jack.'

Fox hesitated, then decided that at least some sort of truth was the best way to handle it.

'Yes, Uncle. The whole place was destroyed by fire. Thank God there is the insurance.'

'But only the equipment, Jack, not on a couple of million in booze.' The Don shook his head. 'It's very unfortunate. Still, these things happen. Have you anything to add? Anything you wish to tell me?'

Fox hesitated, then said, 'No, Uncle.'

'Fine. I'll see you again.'

Fox went out. After a while, Falcone looked in. 'Don Marco.'

'Has he gone?'

'Yes.'

'Good. Bring the security guard in. My nephew failed to mention him, Aldo.'

'A matter to be regretted, Signore.'

'But you did, Aldo, and I'm grateful.'

He poured another cup of coffee, and a moment later Falcone brought in the security guard.

'Your name?' Don Marco asked.

'Mirabella, Signore.'

'Good, a fellow countryman. Now tell me what happened.'

Which Mirabella did.

Don Marco said, 'Tell me again what he said, the man in the hood.'

Mirabella clutched his cap in his hands. 'He said, this isn't for the police. Tell Jack Fox, it's just the beginning. For Katherine Johnson.'

'Good, thank you.' Don Marco looked at Falcone. 'Take care of him, then come back.'

Perhaps twenty minutes later, Falcone returned. The Don stood at the window, fingering a Cuban cigar. Falcone offered a light. Don Marco smiled.

'You're a good boy, Aldo. Your father was one of my most trusted people until those Virelli swine murdered him on that Palermo trip. He was always loyal, and loyalty is everything.'

'Absolutely, Don Marco.'

'So where does loyalty lie? You and my nephew, you were boyhood friends.'

'Please, Don Marco.' Falcone held up a hand. 'My loyalty is to you, above everything else.'

Don Marco patted his chest. 'You're a great comfort to me. You will attend to Jack's requirements, that goes without saying, but you will tell me everything that goes on, won't you, Aldo?'

'Always, Signore.'

'Good. Now be on your way.'


Jack Fox, in the Grill Room of the Four Seasons, sat with the great and the good and the not-so-good, drank champagne, and tried to come to terms with what had happened the previous night. The interview with Mirabella had been particularly unnerving, and he hadn't mentioned it to his uncle, for obvious reasons. Falcone and Russo stood against the wall.

A waiter appeared. 'Sir, your guests are here.'

'My guests?' Fox looked up, and Dillon and Blake appeared. Falcone stepped forward and Fox waved him away. They sat down, and Dillon reached for the champagne bottle. He sampled it, shook his head, and said to Blake, 'The man has no taste.'

Fox said, 'Okay, get on with it. I know who you are. You're Blake Johnson and you work for the White House, and you're Sean Dillon. You used to be IRA, but now you work for the Prime Minister.'

'My, you are well informed,' Blake said.

'That's because I can access anything. The trouble with computers is that all you need is the right kind of genius to break into them, and I have mine. So, you fuck with me and you'll wish you'd never been born.'

'And we'll return the favour to Don Solazzo.' Dillon shrugged. 'And by the way, no one "used to be" IRA. Once in, never out. I'm really bad news, son. You know why? Because I don't care whether I live or die.'

'Maybe I can do something about that.'

'The British Army and the SAS couldn't catch him in twenty years,' Blake said, 'so I doubt you'll have much luck. In fact, you're already running out of luck, aren't you, Jack? We know you front for the Solazzo empire. But you also have a personal sideline, a cheap liquor still in Brooklyn. Or at least you used to.'

'Hey,' Dillon said. 'Isn't that the place that got blown up last night? What a coincidence.' He smiled beautifully. 'Well, that isn't going to help the cash flow.'

Fox said, 'I don't know what you're talking about. That had nothing to do with me.'

'Oh, I believe it did,' Blake told him. 'And then there's all that family money you lost in the Asian banking collapse, money you didn't have the right to invest. Unless Don Marco knew and approved of it all? Which I doubt.'

Fox said calmly, 'What are you getting at?'

'That you're in deep shit with Don Marco unless you come up with some very considerable cash very soon.' Dillon smiled. 'And we intend to see that you don't get it.'

Fox turned to Falcone. 'Aldo, break this little bastard's right arm for me.'

Falcone moved forward, and Dillon's left foot flicked as he kicked the Sicilian under his right kneecap. At the same moment Blake took a Walther from under his jacket and laid it on the table. Falcone was down on one knee, grabbed for the table, and pulled himself up. Russo had a hand on the gun under his left shoulder.

'Is this what you want?' Blake asked. 'A gunfight at the OK Corral?'

'Not really,' Fox said. 'Let's leave it to a more appropriate time. Just go.'

'Our pleasure.' Blake stood up, and Dillon rose beside him. 'I have a line for you that I remember from some old movie I saw on television. To our next merry meeting in hell.'

'I look forward to it,' Fox told him.

They turned and went out.

Falcone said, 'They knew about the Depository.'

'So did a lot of people. It was an open secret. How many clubs did we deal with? A secret's only a secret when one person knows it.'

'You think they know about anything else?'

'No, they were just bluffing. Come on. We have to leave for London soon.' Fox drained the champagne in his glass and made a face. 'You know, that little bastard was right. This stuff is bad.'

In the bar at the Plaza, Dillon and Blake were sharing a pot of tea and Irish whiskeys when Ferguson and Hannah Bernstein appeared.

'My goodness,' Ferguson said. 'Here you two sit enjoying yourselves, when according to Captain Harry Parker somebody torched up Mr Jack Fox's illegal liquor still last night.'

'Do you tell me?' Dillon shook his head. 'Isn't that dreadful.'

'Are you coming home, Dillon?'

'Why not? I think I'm done with business here for the moment.'

'I would point out that when I saved you from the Serbs and took you on board, I offered to clear your rather terrible slate.'

'So you did.'

'But, on the other hand, you still haven't learned to behave yourself.'

'That's the Irish for you.'

Ferguson said, 'Sean, you still work for me. Use your judgement, but please keep me informed.'

'Jesus, Brigadier, I won't let you down. There's only one thing.'

'And what would that be?'

'I intend to totally destroy Jack Fox and the Solazzo family. In Ireland, London, Beirut – wherever it takes me.' Dillon turned to Blake. 'Is that okay with you?'

'It sure as hell is. I'll see the President tomorrow and retire if I have to.'

Dillon turned and smiled at Ferguson. 'There it is, Charles.'

Ferguson smiled. 'Wonderful. Absolutely delicious.' He smiled, then didn't. 'In this case I actually approve of what you're up to. You will use Superintendent Bernstein as your connection. The full facilities of the department will be available.'

He stood up, and Dillon said, 'It's the grand man you are, Brigadier!'

'Well, I *am* half Irish.'

'I'll get on with it, then.'

'All the way. Finish Fox and the family.'

'Consider it done.'

'There is one thing. It's disturbing that Fox knows so much about us. What was it he said? You can access anything with the right kind of genius?'

'That's right.'

'Well, I know such a genius in London.'

Hannah Bernstein smiled. 'Roper, sir?'

'Exactly. See that the introductions are made at the right time, will you, Superintendent?'

She nodded.

'Good. Well' – he stood up – 'time to go. We'll see you later, Superintendent?'

They left. Dillon turned to Blake. 'You didn't figure much in that. What happens now?'

'I've got to clear myself with the President.'

'Then what?'

'Let's hit the bastard in London.'

'Sounds good to me.'


Cazalet had gone down to his old family house on Nantucket. Blake couldn't wait for his return, so he ordered a helicopter on departmental authority and flew down.

The President was walking the beach with his beloved flatcoat retriever, Murchison, followed by Clancy Smith. The surf roared, the sky was grey, a little rain drifted in, and the President read for the fifth time the fax he'd received from Harry Parker. There was a roaring in the distance. Clancy had a hand to his ear and mumbled into his mouthpiece. He looked up. 'Helicopter, Mr President. It's Blake.'

'Good. Let's go back to the house.'

They were halfway there when Blake appeared.

'Give us a little space, Clancy,' the President said.

They walked along the edge of the surf, Murchison running in and out. Cazalet said, 'Idiot. I'll have to hose him down.'

'I know. Sea water isn't good for his skin.'

Cazalet waved to Clancy, who lit a Marlboro away from the wind and handed it over.

Cazalet passed the fax to Blake. 'I'm afraid I leaned on your friend Harry Parker. I asked what was happening with this whole unhappy business.'

'And he told you.' Blake smiled. 'Well, he would. After all, I placed him under Presidential warrant. So, you know everything, Mr President.'

'Yes. A bad business. But it's wonderful that Brigadier Ferguson and Superintendent Bernstein flew over to support you.'

'And Sean Dillon.'

'As always!' Cazalet smiled. 'You know, it's a remarkable coincidence, that fire destroying Fox's warehouse like that.'

'Mr President . . .'

'No, Blake, let me speak. You've been looking tired lately. I think you need a break. Let's see what a month does. You should travel. Get to London, Europe. See some sights. Hmmm? Any departmental facilities you need are yours.'

'What can I say, Mr President?'

Cazalet said, face hard, 'Nothing at all. If you and Dillon can take those bastards down, then it'll be better for all of us.' He smiled crookedly. 'However, it would seriously inconvenience me if you didn't return from your vacation in one piece.'

'Yes, Mr President. I'll see to it.'

'Good.' Cazalet flicked his cigarette into the surf. 'Now, come back to the house for lunch and then, on your way.'

At Don Marco's apartment at Trump Tower, the old man listened as Falcone related what had happened at the Four Seasons.

Don Marco nodded. 'What does my nephew intend?'

'We're going to London, landing at Heathrow.'

'He's using the Gulfstream?'

56

'Yes, Signore.' Falcone hesitated. 'You don't know this?'

'Oh, I'm sure he'll tell me when he's ready. You have my coded mobile number. Keep me informed. I wish to know what he's up to at all times.'

He held out his hand, Falcone kissed it and withdrew. Don Marco rose, went to the piano, and picked up a photo of Jack Fox, the war hero in his Marine uniform.

'What a pity,' he said softly. 'All the virtues, as well as vanity and stupidity.'

He replaced the photo on the piano and went out.

# LONDON

# 5

The following morning, Ferguson's plane landed at Farley Field, with the usual pilots, Flight Lieutenants Lacey and Parry, in the cockpit. A Flight Sergeant Madoc had also been on board, to see to the passengers' wants.

It was March weather again, the rain driving in towards the waiting Daimler. Madoc produced an umbrella as the four of them – Ferguson, Dillon, Bernstein and Johnson – went down the steps and led the way. They scrambled into the Daimler, and Ferguson leaned out to the two pilots.

'It could be a busy time ahead, so don't make plans.'

They both smiled. 'Excellent, sir,' Lacey said.

'Just one thing, Lacey. I do think you should wear correct uniform.'

Lacey was staggered. 'Brigadier?'

'Check the promotions list out today. I put you up for Squadron Leader, and for once the Ministry of Defence has acted sensibly. In addition, in view of recent hazardous pursuits at my behest, you've both been awarded the Air Force Cross.'

They stared at him. 'Good God, sir,' Parry said. 'Sincere thanks.'

'Nonsense. Go and have a drink on it.'

Ferguson closed the door, and the chauffeur drove away.

Dillon said, 'I always knew it. At heart, you're a sentimentalist.'

'Don't be stupid, Dillon, they've earned it.' Ferguson turned to Hannah. 'We'll drop these two off at Dillon's house, then carry on to my place in Cavendish Square. I suggest you contact Roper as soon as possible to arrange a meeting.'

Blake said, 'Could someone tell me about this Roper guy?'

'Well, you recall the White House Connection and Lady Helen Grant? She wanted to know how to work the computer field in a nefarious way,' Hannah told him. 'She asked the London branch of her organization for help and they sent Roper.'

'A remarkable man,' Ferguson said. 'He was a captain in the Royal Engineers, a bomb disposal expert, awarded the Military Cross and the George Cross, and then he got careless. A silly little car bomb in Belfast ended him up in a wheelchair. Computers became a whole new career for him, and he proved to have a real genius for them. As Lady Helen Grant found out.'

Blake was silent, remembering Lady Helen and the White House Connection case that had so nearly ended in disaster. So Roper had been her computer man.

'I look forward to meeting him,' Blake said.

The Daimler turned into Stable Mews, and Dillon and Blake got out. Hannah said, 'I'll contact Roper straight away.'

Blake carried the bags, and Dillon unlocked the door at the mews house and led the way in. It was small, Victorian, with Turkish carpet runners and wood block floors. The living room was delightful, sofa and chairs in black leather placed among scattered rugs, a superb painting over the fireplace.

'My God, that's fabulous,' Blake said.

'A great Victorian painter, Atkinson Grimshaw. Liam Devlin gave it to me. Remember him?'

'How could I forget? He saved our bacon. Is he still around?'

'Ninety years old and pretending to be seventy-five. Come on, I'll show you your room. Then we'll go to the King's Head on the other side of the square for what we call great pub grub in England.'

'Sean, I know what great pub grub is. It's usually the best food in London. So lead the way.'

As they were sitting in the King's Head, drinking Guinness and eating shepherd's pie, Dillon's coded mobile rang faintly.

Hannah said, 'I've contacted Roper. He lives on Regency Square, only half a mile from you.'

'Shall we go round?'

'No, he said he prefers the exercise. He operates one of those state-of-the-art electric wheelchairs. He hates being regarded as a cripple.'

'I hear what you're saying, dear girl.'

'He'll see you at Stable Mews at two-thirty.'

'We'll be there.'

'Another thing. I put out a search on the Special Branch computer. Guess who's arriving at Gatwick this evening? Jack Fox, Aldo Falcone and Giovanni Russo.'

'As Ferguson would say, quite delicious. This should prove interesting.'

He put the phone down, turned to Blake, and filled him in.

An hour later, at Stable Mews, it was Blake who happened to be at the sitting room window and looking out into the street, when he witnessed the arrival of the strange young man in the electric wheelchair. The man wore a navy blue reefer coat, a white scarf at his throat. When Blake went into the hall, Dillon already had the door open.

'Ah, Mr Dillon. I've seen your face on my computer. Roper's the name.'

He had hair to his shoulders, hollow cheeks and very blue eyes. His face was a taut mask of scar tissue, the kind you only got from burns.

'Come in,' Dillon said cheerfully.

'Only if you help me over the step. It's the one thing these gadgets can't manage.'

Dillon obliged, then pushed him along the hall into the kitchen, Blake following.

Roper said, 'What I could really do with is a nice cup of tea.' He turned to Blake. 'Lieutenant.'

Blake smiled. 'Should I say "sir"?'

'Of course. I outrank you.'

Forty-five minutes later they'd filled him in on everything they needed from him. Roper said. 'Fine. I'll go into everything. The Solazzo family, Jack Fox, the Colosseum operation, these Jago brothers. Oh, and this Brendan Murphy. I remember the name from my Irish service. A hard man, as I recall.'

'No, a fanatic, Brendan,' Dillon said. 'I had dealings with him in the old days. Hates the peace process, and now we hear he's into arms dumps – and possibly worse, this hint of an involvement with Saddam in Beirut.'

'So I'll access Army HQ at Lisburn, the RUC, the Garda in Dublin, maybe the Security Services.'

'You can do that?' Dillon asked.

'Dillon, I can even access your lot, and Ferguson probably knows that. I'm the hand of God, so leave it with me.'

'Okay,' Blake said. 'But in case you don't know, Fox turns up in London this evening, plus his two minders.'

'Falcone and Russo.' Roper smiled tranquilly. 'Mafia hard men. Ireland was my business for eleven years and terrorists were my enemy, but in a strange way you can empathize with your enemy, both IRA and Loyalists. These two wouldn't last half an hour in Derry or Belfast.'

'So, what happens now?' Blake asked.

'Well, from what I've been told, you want to see the Colosseum severely damaged.'

'Exactly.'

'Good. Then wheel me out into the street and I'll go home and organize it.'

Blake said, 'You'll be able to do it, then?'

Roper nodded. 'No problem. God wouldn't have given some people brains if He'd wanted the scum to inherit the earth.' He turned to Dillon. 'I'll see you at six at my place in Regency Square. You will then put into operation what I tell you to. Is that acceptable?'

'Bloody cheek,' said Dillon, but then he smiled. 'I'm sure it will be, so let's get on with it,' and Dillon wheeled him out.

Roper's apartment in Regency Square was on the ground floor, with a slope to the front door for his wheelchair. Everything from the bathroom to the kitchen had been designed for a handicapped person. In what would have been the sitting room was a kind of computer laboratory, with every kind of equipment on view on a workbench.

He answered the door when Dillon, Blake and Hannah Bernstein arrived. 'Ah, there you are.'

He led the way through to the sitting room. 'Here we are, then.' He tapped a keyboard and the screen started to fill. 'Colosseum Casino, Smith Street. General Manager, Angelo Mori. Minders, Francesco Camcci, Tino Rossi.' Photos appeared. After a while, he tapped again and ground plans came up.

'Lots of security,' Blake said.

'Not if you know your way in.'

'So what would be the point?' Dillon asked.

'A top casino stands on its reputation. The slightest hint of scandal, and the Gaming Act enters into it and the place can be closed down.'

There was silence. Dillon said, 'And how do we achieve that?'

'Tonight will tell you, if you do what I say and go in hard.'

'You mean go in feloniously, Captain,' Hannah said.

'That sums it up. You want this bastard, we go for the throat.'

65

Dillon said, 'That suits me, and as the Superintendent knows, I've been guaranteed the full cooperation of the Department by Brigadier Ferguson, so let's hear what you have in mind.'

'It's very simple. What's one of the oldest games of chance in the world? They loved it at the height of the Roman Empire. They still love it.'

Blake smiled. 'Craps.'

'Exactly. You simply throw the dice and pray the right number comes up. People can't resist.'

Dillon said, 'So what do you want?'

'Dice, old boy. Steal me some dice.'

'Why?' Blake asked.

'Because every casino has its own made to order. Unique. Of course, once I have them at my workbench I make a slight adjustment, put a spot of lead inside, and they become what's known in the trade as loaded dice. Now, if the house is using loaded dice, the punters are bound to lose.'

'But how do you make the house actually use the loaded dice?' Blake asked.

'That's the whole point about having house dice. You or Dillon join the crowd making a wager. When your turn comes and the dealer gives you the dice, you palm them and use the ones I've doctored. They'll have the house logo on them, so everyone will assume they're the real thing. Of course, it will be necessary to bring this unfortunate situation to the attention of the other gamblers. The results could be devastating for the casino.'

'You wicked man, you,' Dillon said.

'You or Blake, I think, should be the ones. I wouldn't dream of asking the Superintendent.' He smiled at Hannah. 'I happen to know you're Jewish Orthodox, with a rabbi for a grandfather.'

She smiled. 'My grandfather might surprise you. His poker is deadly.'

Dillon said, 'Sounds good to me. So what's the plan?'

At ten o'clock that evening, Jack Fox arrived at the Colosseum, backed by Falcone and Russo. He was stopped at the door by a large man in evening dress.

'Membership card, sir.'

'I don't need one. I own this casino.'

'Very funny.'

The bouncer put a hand on Fox's shoulder and Russo said, 'You want me to break your right arm? You just made the biggest mistake of your life.'

'Signor Fox, what a pleasure,' a voice called, and Angelo Mori, the general manager, rushed down the stairs, followed by his two minders. 'Is there a problem?'

'Hell, no,' Fox said, and smiled at the bouncer. 'What's your name?'

'Henry, sir.' He looked very worried.

'You're doing a good job, Henry.' Fox took out his wallet, extracted a fifty-pound note, and slipped it into Henry's breast pocket. 'In fact, you're doing a great job. Anyone else comes in and says they own the joint, kick them in the balls.'

There was sweat on Henry's forehead. 'Yes, sir, anything you say.'

Inside, the main room was crowded, every kind of game in progress. Fox nodded approvingly. 'Looks good. How's the cash flow?'

'Terrific.'

Fox turned to Mori's minders, Cameci and Rossi. 'You two behaving yourselves?' He used Italian.

'Absolutely,' Rossi told him. 'Don Marco is well?'

If this seemed overly familiar, it wasn't. Rossi came from the same village as the Solazzo family, close to Corleone in Sicily.

'He is very well,' Fox continued in Italian. 'And I appreciate your concern.' He turned to Mori. 'We just flew in, and I'm starving. The restaurant is still open, I trust.'

'For you, it never closes, Signore.'

'Excellent. Louis Roederer Cristal, nineteen-ninety, smoked salmon, scrambled eggs, chopped onions. I've got to watch my health.'

'But you look wonderful, Signor Fox.'

'Hell, I'm the only man in here tonight who took a bullet in the left side in the Gulf War, Angelo. I've got to be careful.'

They moved through the main room and entered the small restaurant. Mori led the way to a corner booth.

'Is this satisfactory, Signore?'

'Excellent. Put Falcone and Rossi at the next table. They'll probably stuff themselves with spaghetti bolognese, but anything they want, they get.'

'Of course.'

'Another thing. I'm expecting the Jago brothers, Tony and Harold.'

'Yes, they phoned.' Mori looked pained.

Fox laughed. 'They're terrible people, I know. Think they're the reincarnation of the Kray brothers, fell in love with their legend years ago, but the Kray brothers were special. The Jagos will never match that. Still, they're working with us. When they arrive, wheel them in.'

Mori departed. Fox took out a cigarette and Falcone gave him a light. 'Trouble with these English bastards, Signore?'

'No. They've seen too many gangster movies, but they have their uses. Nothing you and Russo can't handle. Now get me a martini.'

Half an hour later, just as he finished his scrambled eggs, the Jagos arrived. Harold, the elder, was forty, just under six feet, hair already greying, face pock-marked. Tony was thirty, smaller in every way, his right cheek disfigured by a razor scar. The one thing they had in common was the beautifully tailored Savile Row suits that both wore.

'Jack, it's good to see you.' Harold shook his hand.

'Join me,' Fox said. 'As you say in London, I may be able to put a bit of business your way.'

'Anything,' Harold said with enthusiasm. 'I mean, that security van tickle was magic.' He turned to Tony. 'I mean, it really was, wasn't it, Tony?'

Tony, a hard little bastard who was English enough not to like foreigners, said, 'If you say so, Harold.'

'Well, he does,' Fox said dryly, and snapped a couple of fingers at Falcone. 'The briefcase.'

Falcone had been carrying it all evening. He took it from under the table and passed it across. Fox gave it to Harold.

'It's all in there, page by page. I'll leave you to put the team together.'

'But what is it?' Harold demanded.

'That new development at Wapping. St Richard's Dock. The White Diamond Company.'

Harold was horrified. 'That's impossible. It's a fortress.'

'Yes, well, they forgot one thing. London's riddled with underground rivers and tunnels, some of them hundreds of years old, and one of them happens to be under St Richard's Dock. It's all in the file. Read it over and we'll talk again. If you're not interested, I'll get someone else.'

It was Tony who said, 'How much?'

'Ten million basic, maybe more. You get forty per cent.'

'Fifty,' Tony answered.

Harold said, 'Shut your mouth,' and turned back to Fox. 'I'll read the file, but I can tell you now we're in, Jack. Leave the team to me.'

'Good man.' Fox smiled. 'Now, let's have a bottle of champagne on it.'

* * *

The casino closed at two in the morning; by three all was quiet, with only a security guard in the office by the main entrance, watching TV.

Along the street beside the basement entrance was a grey British Telecom van. The rear door opened and Blake Johnson, wearing a hard hat and yellow oilskins, got out, carrying two grappling hooks, and lifted a manhole cover in the pavement. Dillon passed him an inspection lamp and a red warning light saying: Danger. Men at Work. He then passed some canvas screens and an awning against the rain. There was an army of wires and switches. Blake tried to take an interest.

Inside the van Roper, in a wheelchair, sat opposite a very simple-looking computer set-up. Dillon, in black tee-shirt and jeans, crouched beside him. Roper punched the keys.

'How's it looking?' Dillon asked.

'So far, so good. Don't worry, the great Roper is never wrong.' There was the sound of a car slowing outside and he raised a hand. 'Wait.'

Blake looked out from under the awning, the rain pitiless. The police patrol car slowed, the driver leaned out.

'What a bloody way to make a living at this time in the morning.'

'You, too,' Blake told him, putting on his best British accent.

The policeman smiled and drove away.

Dillon said, 'Let's do it.'

'Fine. As I told you, I can screw the entire security system, but only for fifteen minutes, so you'll need to be fast.'

'Hell, I've been all over those ground plans you showed me. I know where I'm going.'

'You better had. I'm starting now, so count to ten and get down to that basement door.'

Various lights flickered on the screen, reds and greens, there came a faint sound, and then Dillon was out of there, past Blake and down to the basement, pulling up his hood.

70

He had a small flashlight, but really didn't need it, for there were subdued security lights everywhere. He had no worries about cameras. As Roper had told him, they were frozen, too.

Remembering the ground plans from the computer screen, he went up the steps fast, passed through the kitchens, and emerged by the entrance to the restaurant. He could see into the glass office by the main door. The security guard was fiddling with the TV, which had gone off.

Dillon slipped through the shadows into the main gambling room and found the right table. There was a tray of dice on the table, all very neat, but he left them alone, and instead dropped to one knee by the right-hand side of the table, where the dealer stood. There was a stack of dice there. He took six, no more, and put them into his pocket, turned, and went out fast.

The security guard was still arguing with the TV. Dillon slipped through the shadow, went down the steps, and speeded into the basement, closing the door behind him. He stepped past Blake, gave him a thumbs-up, and went into the van. He took the six dice from his pocket and put them on the bench in front of Roper.

'There you go.'

'Thirteen minutes,' Roper said. 'You did well.' He tapped the keys and sat back. 'Everything normal again.'

'Now what?'

'We clear up and get out of here.'

Dillon removed his hood and went out to Blake. 'It worked. I got what he wanted, so let's get moving. I'll help you.'

'Okay,' Blake said.

Dillon collapsed the screens and awning and put them into the truck, while Blake replaced the manhole cover. A few moments later, they drove away, Dillon at the wheel.

At Roper's place in Regency Square, they sat and watched him at the bench examining the dice with an eyeglass.

'Will it be okay?' Blake asked.

71

'Of course it will, old boy. Being a perfectionist, however, I prefer solitude when engaged in sensitive work, so be good and clear off. You won't be able to use these things until tomorrow night anyway, so I've got all the time in the world.'

Dillon nodded to Blake and they stood up. 'We'll check in tomorrow, then.'

'You do that,' Roper said, ignoring them completely as he picked up a tiny electric drill of the kind used by jewellers.

The following morning at eight, Dillon's phone rang, and Ferguson said, 'As I've had no intimations of disaster, you must have pulled it off last night.'

'Absolutely. We're in Roper's hands now.'

'What are you and Blake up to?'

'We're going to the King's Head for a full English breakfast.'

'I can't wait to join you.'

Which he did half an hour later, accompanied by Hannah Bernstein. They all ordered, and Ferguson said, 'You haven't checked with Roper yet?'

'Give him a chance, sir,' Hannah said, as the waiter arrived with the breakfasts on a large tray.

Dillon said, 'Pass your bacon to me, Hannah. I wouldn't want to put your fine Jewish principles under siege.'

'You're so kind, Dillon.'

And then the door opened with a bang and Roper surged in. 'Smells great.' He turned to the waiter. 'The same for me.'

'I must say, you look astonishingly well,' Ferguson said.

'You mean for a cripple who hasn't been to bed all night?' Roper asked, and took the six dice from his pocket and rolled them on the table. They all came up ones. 'Snake eyes.' He turned to Blake. 'Isn't that what you call them in Vegas?'

'It sure as hell is.'

'Excellent. God help Jack Fox and the Colosseum this evening. I think I'll go and watch.'

'You have to be a member,' Hannah Bernstein said.

'Which, thanks to my computer, I am. In fact, you all are.' The waiter appeared with his breakfast. 'My God, this looks good.' He picked up a knife and fork and got to work. 'I assume it had occurred to you that if Dillon and Blake wanted to create mayhem in the Colosseum tonight, they also needed to be members?'

'Of course it did.' Ferguson smiled. 'And I knew you'd take care of it. It'll be an interesting night ahead of us, I think.'

'You can sure as hell say that,' Blake agreed.

# 6

Roper's expertise produced plastic membership cards for all of them, plus photos of Rossi and Cameci, the restaurant's minders, to add to those of Falcone and Russo, and that evening, at eight o'clock, they were passed through the door at the Colosseum by Henry, Roper in a light collapsible wheelchair pushed by Dillon.

The main room was already busy, waitresses in minuscule skirts moving through the crowd offering champagne. Dillon took a glass and looked up.

'Any good?' Blake asked.

'If you like sparkling wine, but champagne it's not.'

'Ah, well, Fox will be into profit margins,' Ferguson observed.

They stood in a small group by the bar, and Hannah said, 'There are a couple of villains you're interested in, sir. The Jago brothers, Harold and Tony, at the end of the bar.'

The others took a look. Ferguson said, 'Very unsavoury.'

'Yes, well, we can sort them out later,' Dillon said. 'The thing is, who's going to start the ball rolling?'

'Well, actually, I've had another of my ideas,' Ferguson said. 'We have six dice, so why not two each?'

'Brigadier, I can see why you achieved high command,' Blake told him. 'Agreed, Sean?'

'Why not?' Dillon turned to Roper. 'Here we go. Showtime.'

Roper passed the dice across and Dillon gave the others theirs. 'There you go.'

'Into action, then,' Ferguson said. 'Let's get on with it,' and turned for the dice table. 'Oh, and palm your dice smoothly, gentlemen.'

In the restaurant, Fox enjoyed his scrambled eggs and smoked salmon again and tried a little Krug champagne.

'Great stuff, this,' he said to Falcone. 'But not the vintage. It's the non-vintage that's really special. Different grapes.'

Russo appeared. 'There's a problem, Signore. You remember those two from the Four Seasons in New York, Dillon and Johnson?'

'Yes?'

'They're here now, in the main room.'

'Really?' Fox emptied his glass. 'Well, let's take a look.'

Falcone pulled back the chair, and Fox stood up and walked out into the most active part of the casino.

Russo said, 'Over there, Signore. Next to some woman and another man. In the striped suit, see?'

Fox snorted. 'That "some woman", Russo, is Detective Superintendent Hannah Bernstein of Scotland Yard's Special Branch. And that "another man" is Brigadier General Ferguson, head of a special intelligence unit for the Prime Minister. An absolutely devious old bastard. I guarantee you they're not here for a friendly game of cards.'

'So what do we do, Signore?' Falcone asked. 'Move them out?'

'Don't be stupid,' Fox said. 'This is one of the most prestigious gambling clubs in London. Scandal is the last thing we want. You expect me to expel a brigadier general and his friends? No, we wait and see what they're up to.'

The dice table was a popular one, every inch taken up by the crowd standing around. Ferguson said to Hannah, 'Would you like to have a go, Superintendent?'

'No, sir. I don't know craps. It's not one of my vices.'

'Well, it's one of mine,' Blake said. 'Let's do it.'

He had to wait ten minutes for his chance, then took the offered dice and started. Strangely enough, he did quite well for the first three throws, actually won money. Then he palmed the dice and tossed two of Roper's.

'Snake eyes.'

There was a groan from the crowd.

The dealer passed the dice to Dillon, who palmed them for the real article, and made two successful throws. Then, just when he had everything riding on the toss – 'Snake eyes!'

'Hey,' he said ruefully, 'bad luck I understand, but this is diabolical.'

Ferguson moved in. 'Let me try, old boy. Mind you, these dice do seem to have lost their edge.' He turned to the croupier. 'Let me have a new pair.'

The croupier complied. Ferguson rolled and immediately came up with snake eyes. He turned to a military-looking man with a stiff moustache next to him. 'How strange.' He laughed. 'We all keep getting the same thing.'

'Yes,' the military-looking man said slowly. The croupier's rake reached out, but the military-looking man said, 'Not so fast,' and grabbed the dice.

The croupier said, 'I hope monsieur isn't suggesting there could be something wrong?'

'Let's see.'

The man rolled the dice and threw them the length of the table: again, snake eyes. The croupier's rake reached out and the military gentleman beat him to it.

'Oh, no, you don't. That's snake eyes too many times. These dice are loaded.' There was a sudden murmur from the crowd and he turned to an ageing gentleman. 'See for yourself. Pair of ones guaranteed.'

The man threw and the result was clear. The outrage in the crowd was plain to see, and Mori hurried down the steps.

'Ladies and gentlemen, please. A misunderstanding.'

'Are you the manager?' Ferguson demanded.

'Yes,' Mori replied.

'Then oblige us by throwing those dice.'

Mori hesitated. People in the crowd shouted, 'Get on with it.' Mori threw. The dice rolled. *Snake eyes.*

The crowd roared in anger. The military-looking man said, 'That settles it. Loaded dice, and I've lost a bundle here in the last few weeks. We need the police.'

'Ladies and gentlemen, please,' Mori called.

Fox, Falcone and Russo stayed well to the rear.

Hannah Bernstein moved forward and said to Mori, 'The dice, sir, I'll have them.'

'And who the devil are you?' He was so upset he asked her in Italian.

Hannah replied with fluency in the same language. 'Detective Superintendent Bernstein, Special Branch.' She looked at the dice she picked up. 'I notice that, in accordance with the Gaming Act, these carry the club's registered mark. Do you agree?'

'Well, yes,' Mori said lamely, then added, 'Someone must have substituted false ones.'

The military-looking man said, 'Don't be stupid. What on earth would be the point of a player substituting for the real dice a pair that would make him lose?'

There was a roar from the crowd, Mori sagged across the table, and Hannah said, 'In accordance with the statutory provisions of the Gaming Act, sir, I must issue an order closing you down until such time as Westminster Magistrates Court can consider the matter. I believe you also own twelve betting shops in the City of London. Is that so?'

'Yes,' Mori told her.

'I'm afraid they must close, also. Any infringement of this order means a fine of one hundred thousand pounds with further penalties thereafter.'

'Of course.' Mori raised his voice shakily. 'Ladies and gentlemen, I'm afraid we must close by order of the police. Please leave now. Don't forget your things.'

The crowd faded, and at the rear were Ferguson, Bernstein, Dillon, Blake, and Roper in his wheelchair. At the door, Dillon turned and waved to Fox.

'Hey, there you are, old buddy. Have a good night!'

They went out. Fox turned to Falcone. 'I want to know where they go. There must be a couple of young punks available. Not Rossi or Comeci.'

Russo said, 'There's Borsalino and Salvatore in the kitchen.'

'Get them now. I know who most of them are, but not the one in the wheelchair. Then follow him to hell.'

They took Roper from his wheelchair, eased him into the Daimler, and then followed him, after folding his wheelchair.

'Now what?' Blake asked.

'We wait for Fox to react,' Dillon said.

'Shall we eat?' Ferguson asked.

'Not me, Brigadier,' Roper told him. 'I want to check out the computer again. Take me home, then you lot go and enjoy yourselves.'

But already following the Daimler was a very ordinary Ford car driven by a young man named Paolo Borsalino, with his friend, Alex Salvatore, sitting beside him. In Sicilian terms, they were *picciotti*, youngsters gaining respect, doing the odd killing, climbing up the ladder. Borsalino had acted as executioner three times, and Salvatore twice, and they were eager to do more.

The Daimler stopped in Regency Square, and Dillon got out, set up Roper's wheelchair and helped him into it. They all got out and Dillon took Roper's key and opened his door.

Ferguson said, 'We'll speak tomorrow. Excellent job, Captain.'

'We aim to please, Brigadier.'

Dillon pushed Roper up the ramp into the hall. 'You're a hell of a fella, Roper.'

'Well, considering your background, I take that as a compliment.'

Dillon closed the door and went back to the others. 'Now what?'

'Fredo's – it's round the corner from Cavendish Square. A nice Italian restaurant,' Ferguson said. 'We can have a look at what's next.'

The Daimler drove away, and Borsalino and Salvatore, parked at the end of the square, watched them go. Salvatore said, 'Now what?'

'You watch the car,' Borsalino said. 'I'll be back.'

He walked to the other side of the square and found a corner shop, the kind that stayed open until midnight. The man behind the counter was Indian. Borsalino asked for two packs of Marlboros.

'You know, I saw this guy earlier getting out of a taxi in the square in a wheelchair. I thought I knew him, but I'm not sure.'

'That would be Mr Roper,' the Indian said. 'He was a captain in the Royal Engineers. Blown up in Ireland.'

'Oh, well, I've got it wrong. Thanks, anyway.'

Borsalino returned to the Ford, called Fox on the mobile, and relayed the information, also telling him where they were.

Fox said, 'Stay there. I'll be back.'

At that point, he was still in Mori's office at the casino. He picked up the telephone and called Maud Jackson in New York. It was late afternoon there and she was enjoying a pot of tea and cookies.

Fox said, 'Maud, I'm having serious problems here in London with Ferguson and company. There's a wild card, a British Royal Engineers captain in a wheelchair, blown up in Ireland, name of Roper. I'd like to know who he is right away.'

'Where are you?'

'I'm going back to the Dorchester. We had problems at the Colosseum.'

'Sounds like a bad night. Give me an hour.'

At the Dorchester, in the Oliver Messel Suite, Fox drank Krug champagne and looked across the wonderful London view by night from the terrace. Russo was down in the suite he and Falcone were sharing, but Falcone was standing by, as usual.

'More trouble, Signore?'

'We'll see, Aldo.'

The phone rang and he answered it. Maud Jackson said, 'Boy, do I have a good one for you. This Roper was blown up by the IRA, all right, and now he's a legend – in computers. Jack, if he's into your affairs, you've got serious trouble.'

'Thanks, Maud, you're an angel.'

'Yeah, well, don't forget to send a cheque.'

Fox put down the phone and said to Falcone, 'Take him out.'

'Me personally, Signore?'

'Of course not. Get over to Regency Square. See Borsalino and Salvatore. Give them their instructions. Have them get rid of him. I smell big trouble where he's concerned.'

'At your orders, Signore,' Falcone said. 'I'll leave Russo here.'

He used Fox's Mercedes limousine, driven by Fox's Italian driver, Fabio, closed the screen, and called Don Marco on his mobile and brought him up to date.

'This isn't good,' Don Marco said. 'I'm beginning to smell trouble here myself. Keep me informed, Aldo.'

Falcone found Borsalino and Salvatore in the Ford parked in the square very close to Roper's place. They were, of course, all attention.

'Stay here for the moment. This guy in the wheelchair? You take him out, but make it look like an accident. You wait if it takes all night. You wait if it takes until tomorrow, but he's finished. *Capisce?*'

'Anything you say,' Borsalino told him.

Falcone left them, went back to the Daimler. Fabio said, 'Back to the Dorchester?'

'No, I'm hungry. Find somewhere close by where we can get something simple. You know, a bacon and egg sandwich.'

'I know just the place, Signore.'

'Good. Then we'll come back and see what the situation is.'

At the computer bank, Roper trawled all the way through from Jack Fox to Brendan Murphy, the pride of the Provisional IRA. There were some fascinating facts there. Then he tried the Jago brothers and found a litany of crime on a Dickensian level. He sat back. *Excellent.*

He checked his watch. Eleven o'clock, and he felt hungry, which was okay, because Ryan's Irish Restaurant on the far side of the square stayed open until one and knew him well.

He eased himself into a raincoat and then transferred to his electric wheelchair and made for the front door.

Rain bounced down. He raised a small telescopic umbrella as he went down the ramp and started along the pavement. Falcone, sitting in the Mercedes, saw him go.

Fabio said, 'Signore?'

'Let's leave it to the boys.'

Roper coasted along, his umbrella raised, a slightly incongruous figure. In the Ford, Borsalino and Salvatore saw him.

'Now what?' Salvatore demanded.

'We take him out,' Borsalino said. 'Come on.'

He was out of the Ford in a second, Salvatore on his heels, and ran after the wheelchair.

'Hey, Signore, you need a hand?'

Roper knew trouble when he saw it, but said, 'No, thanks, I'm fine.'

Salvatore was on one side of the chair, Borsalino the other.

Borsalino said, 'No, really, I think you need some help – like, into traffic. What do you think about that?'

'That really would be unfortunate,' Roper said.

Falcone, watching from the Mercedes, said to Fabio, 'You've been around the family for a long time. What do you think?'

'That it stinks, Signore. Where do they find these kids?'

'I agree. Just coast along and let's see what happens.'

The end of the square before the main road was dark, and at that moment deserted.

Borsalino said, 'Shit! There's no traffic here. What are we going to do?'

Salvatore said, 'Roll him down the block. We'll find it. You having a good time, my friend?'

'Depends on your point of view.' Roper's hand came out of the right-hand side pocket of his wheelchair, holding a Walther PPK with a Carswell silencer on the end. He jammed it into the back of Salvatore's left knee and pulled the trigger. There was a muted cough, and the Italian cried out and stumbled into the gutter.

Roper turned slightly in the chair, the gun raised, and Borsalino jumped back. 'You really wouldn't have got by in Belfast, old son,' Roper said. 'Not for a minute,' and as Borsalino turned to run, shot him in the back of the right thigh.

They lay together on the pavement. Roper paused and looked down. He took out a mobile phone and dialled nine, nine, nine. When the operator answered, he said, 'There are two men down on the pavement in Regency Square. Looks like a shooting.'

'Your name, sir?'

'Don't be stupid.'

He switched off his coded mobile and moved on.

In the Mercedes, Fabio said, 'My God, Signore, what do we do?'

Already, in the distance, they could hear the sound of a police siren.

'Nothing,' Falcone told him. 'We do nothing.' He watched the two men trying to get up. 'Just get out of here.'

As they left the square, a police car turned in, and as they moved up the main road, an ambulance appeared.

In Ryan's Restaurant, Roper ordered Irish stew and a pint of Guinness, phoned Ferguson on his mobile, and gave him the bad news.

'Where are you?' Ferguson asked, and Roper told him. 'All right, stay where you are. We'll come for you.'

Ferguson put down the phone at his Cavendish Square flat and turned to Hannah, Dillon and Blake. 'That was Roper. He went out for a late meal and two men of Italian persuasion had a go. Told him they'd push him into the late-night traffic.'

'What happened, sir?' Hannah asked.

'He shot them in the legs,' Ferguson said. 'Would you believe that? Left them on the pavement.'

'Frankly, I don't have the slightest difficulty in believing it,' Dillon told him. 'Jack Fox moved fast.'

'So now what?' Blake asked.

Ferguson turned to Hannah. 'Superintendent?'

'I doubt they'll talk, sir, not if they value their lives. And I doubt that this will be the last attempt that Jack Fox makes.'

'You're right,' said Ferguson. 'We'll move Roper to the Holland Park safe house. Anything he wants, you know, all his gadgets and so on, make sure he gets. I think we'll need him. Will you take care of that, Superintendent?'

'As you say, sir.' Hannah went out.

Blake turned to Dillon. 'All right, we've taken care of the casino. What do we hit next?'

Blake turned to Dillon. 'The Jago brothers? The army dump? Beirut?'

'Let's get Roper into the safe house. Once he's got his equipment in order, we'll see.'

At the Dorchester, Fox listened to Falcone's account of what had happened in Regency Square. He actually laughed.

'You mean this fuck in the wheelchair shot them both in the legs?'

'Something like that, Signore.'

Fox shook his head. 'Mind you, with what I've learned about him, I'm not surprised. You can check if he's at his house, but if he's not there, leave it. We've got other things to do.'

'Like what, Signore? I spoke to Mori. The Colosseum will remain closed, as well as the betting shops, until the police and the Director of Public Prosecutions decide what to do, which could take months.'

'We concentrate on other matters. There's the Lebanon connection that Murphy arranged.'

'Beirut, Signore?'

'No, Al Shariz to the south, I believe. Murphy is due in Beirut next week. We'll meet and agree on the goods we're supplying. Forget the casino. There's a fortune to be made there, Aldo, and he pays in gold. I'll see you in the morning.'

Falcone left, went to his room, and phoned Don Marco. The Don said, 'He's digging himself in deeper, isn't he?'

'Do you want me to do anything?'

'No. Just stay in touch.'

'Of course, Don Marco.'

The Holland Park safe house was an Edwardian townhouse in an acre of gardens surrounded by huge walls. The notice by the gate said Pine Grove Nursing Home, which it definitely wasn't.

Roper was picked up by a contingency squad Hannah had arranged, mostly ordinary-looking young men and women who were actually Special Branch, and always available to

Ferguson's demands. Two female sergeants packed Roper's clothes and three men moved equipment, according to his instructions. By one o'clock in the morning, he was in residence at Pine Grove, his various gadgets and computers plugged into sockets in what had been the sitting room.

The police departed, and a small, very pleasant woman said, 'Is everything satisfactory, Major?'

Roper was puzzled. 'Captain.'

'Oh, no, sir. Brigadier Ferguson said Major.'

'And who might you be?'

'Helen Black, sir. Royal Military Police. Sergeant Major.'

'Good God,' Roper said. 'That's an Armani suit.'

'Well, my father left me rather well off.'

'I smell Oxford here.'

'No, Cambridge. New Hall. I worked for the Fourteenth Intel undercover in Derry. You were a bit of a legend.'

'Look where it's got me. A bloody wheelchair, my bits and pieces damaged.'

'Courage never goes out of fashion, sir, in a wheelchair or not. As far as I'm concerned, you're one of the bravest men I've ever met. Now, you're probably peckish. I'll arrange for some sandwiches.'

'Tell me, Sergeant Major, are you my bodyguard? Because there are some pretty bad people out there looking for me.'

'I'm aware of that, sir.' She opened her jacket and revealed a holstered Colt automatic. 'Twenty-five millimetre, with hollow-point bullets.'

'Well, that should do it.'

She smiled and went out.

Roper phoned Ferguson, in spite of the hour, and when the Brigadier answered, said, 'What's this Major thing?'

'Well, you're still on the Army list. I thought it would give you a bit more authority to promote you. You're established at Holland Park?'

'Yes, with the redoubtable Sergeant Major Black.'

'Redoubtable is right. Inherited money, you know, so she's fairly independent-minded. Her husband's a major in the Blues and Royals. Refused a commission herself. One of the few women to hold the Military Cross. Shot two Provos in Derry. You're in good hands.'

Roper whistled. 'I'd say so. So, what's my next move?'

'I'll put Dillon on.'

There was a pause, and Dillon said, 'Billy the Kid, is that who you are now?'

'Hey, these guys didn't want to play nice, so I figured, stuff them.'

'I'm with you there.'

'So what do you want me to do? Who's next?'

'Well, we've got two choices: the Jagos and Brendan Murphy. What do you know about the Jagos?'

'Not much. They like to knock off security vans. Really old-time stuff. Sawn-off shotguns, like some British gangster movie. The thing is, finding out about the future plans of such people is difficult,' Roper went on. 'Unless Fox committed his plans to the computer, how would I know?'

'It's all a question of inside information,' Dillon said.

'And where do you get that?'

'The Jagos are gangsters, right?'

'And what does that prove?'

'Set a gangster to catch a gangster.'

'What in the hell are you talking about?'

'Harry Salter. He's a legendary name in London criminal circles. Did seven years for bank robbery in the seventies, never been inside since. He has warehouse developments, property, pleasure boats on the Thames. Still owns his first buy, a pub called the Dark Man at Wapping, by the river.'

'You sound as if you like him.'

'Well, he's saved me in the past and I've saved him. He's a dinosaur, but a very wealthy dinosaur. Even the cops have given up on him. Works with his nephew, Billy, and a couple of minders, Baxter and Hall. All the rest are accountants.'

'So, you'll go and see him?'

'That's my plan.'

'Fine. Keep me posted. Meantime, I'll check out Mr Murphy.' Roper smiled. 'I like to keep occupied.'

'See you sometime tomorrow.'

Roper sat there thinking, then the door opened and Helen Black came in with two toasted bacon sandwiches.

'Will these do?'

'Can't wait. Are you tired?'

'Not particularly.'

'Good, then would you like me to show you just how effective a computer can be if you know what you're doing?'

'What's the object of the exercise?'

'To hunt down a particularly obnoxious piece of Provisional IRA crap called Brendan Murphy.'

'Just a minute. I remember him. Derry, 'ninety-four.'

'And years before that.' Roper tried a sandwich. 'Excellent. Now, follow my instructions and I'll show you what to do.'

# 7

They all came together at Ferguson's office the following morning. When they were all settled, Ferguson said, 'Bring me up to date, Superintendent.'

'The attackers were a couple of small-time hoods employed at the kitchens at the Colosseum, named Borsalino and Salvatore. They're at Westminster Hospital under supervision. Salvatore has lost his left kneecap and Borsalino has a bullet wound in one thigh.'

'My goodness, Major Roper doesn't play patty fingers, does he?'

'Well, he wouldn't, would he, sir?' she said.

'What's their story?'

'They told the officers in charge of the case that they were attacked by two very large black muggers as they walked through the square. There was a struggle. The rest you know.'

'Nobody's safe from crime today, it seems.' Ferguson turned to Dillon. 'Now what?'

'Blake and I are going to see Harry Salter. I'll put him on to the Jagos, see if he can come up with anything. If there's a big tickle being organized, Salter will get wind of it. He owes me a favour. In fact, he owes Blake a favour. We saved his bacon on a pleasure boat called the *Lynda Jones* downriver from Wapping, when the Hooker mob were going to waste him.'

'Yes, I recall some such thing,' Ferguson said. 'Good. But meantime, what about Brendan Murphy? That's much more worrying.'

'Roper's been working on it,' Hannah said. 'But he says it'd be a lot easier if he had some more information to go on. Is there any way to find out more?'

'Well, I do have a suggestion,' Dillon said. 'While Blake and I go and see Salter, why don't you phone Liam Devlin in Kilrea?'

'Good God,' Ferguson said. 'Is he still with us?'

'He certainly is. Devlin is ageless. He liked you, Hannah, when you met. Tell him the whole story, the works. Ask him to find out what he can about Brendan Murphy. He's still the living legend of the IRA and the best source of information about anything regarding them.'

Hannah turned to Ferguson. 'Brigadier?'

'It makes sense. I have just one suggestion. Don't phone him, do it face to face. Get yourself to Dublin today.'

'If you say so, sir.'

'Yes, I do. So, people, let's get on with it.'

Hannah went back to her office, with Blake and Dillon. She picked up the phone, spoke to Farley Field, and booked the plane.

Dillon said, 'You watch yourself over there, woman. Peace process or no peace process, it's still the war zone.'

'Don't be patronizing, Dillon.'

'There are people there who'd shoot your eyes out if they could.'

She took a deep breath. 'You're right. I'm sorry.'

'Yes. Well, make sure you're carrying.'

'I will.'

'We'll leave you to it.'

He and Blake left. She took her personal notebook from her purse, found Devlin's phone number in the village of Kilrea outside Dublin. It was answered instantly.

'And who would that be disturbing my morning?'

'Hannah Bernstein.'

'Jesus, girl, and what's all this? I hear you've made Superintendent.'

'Mr Devlin, we have a big problem, and we need your assistance.'

'Where's Dillon?'

'Employed elsewhere, together with Blake Johnson.'

'Is that the FBI man Dillon and I went down to Tullamore with, to save Dermot Riley's hide? A good man. All right, give. When can I expect you?'

'I'm leaving now. I could be with you by twelve noon.'

'I'll look forward to it.'

He put the phone down, standing there in his kitchen, and smiled.

Dillon drove down Horse Guards Avenue in the green Mini Cooper.

Blake said, 'So Harry's still working the rackets.'

'Oh, sure, it's in his blood. But like I was saying, it's all smuggling – booze, diamonds, that kind of thing – no drugs. He's an old-fashioned family man, in values, anyway.'

'Aren't we all?'

They reached Wapping and pulled up outside the Dark Man. It was a typical London pub; the painted sign showed a sinister individual in a black cloak.

It was early for the drink trade, noon an hour and a half away, but it was open. They went into the main bar, which was very Victorian, the bottles ranged against mirrors, an enormous mahogany bar smelling of polish, the porcelain beer handles waiting for action.

Three men were in the corner booth, drinking tea and reading newspapers: Billy Salter, Harry's nephew, and Joe Baxter and Sam Hall.

'What's this, a thieves' kitchen?' Dillon asked.

Billy looked up, and a delighted smile appeared on his wicked face. 'Dear God, it's you, Dillon, and our American friend, Mr Johnson. We remember you.'

Baxter and Hall laughed, and Billy said, 'Well, we're not in the nick, and I suppose that's one good thing. What brings you here?' He smiled eagerly. 'Could it be trouble?'

'Why, are you getting bored, Billy?' Dillon asked. 'Let's see Harry and decide.'

'He's down at the boat.'

'The *Lynda Jones*?'

'Sure. Refurbished. His pride and joy. I'll show you. Let's take a walk.'

They went along the wharf, passing a few boats, one or two old barges sunk into the water. It started to rain as they reached the boat. Harry Salter was sitting at a table under an awning, reading *The Times*. Dora, the chief barmaid from the Dark Man, was pouring tea. He patted her ample rear.

'I've said it before, Dora, you've got a great arse.'

'Now, isn't that the poet in him?' Dillon said. 'Such a majestic choice of language.'

Salter looked up and took off his reading glasses. 'Christ, Dillon, it's you.' He glanced at Blake. 'And the bleeding Yank again. Here, what's going on?' The blue eyes hardened in the well-lined face. 'Trouble?'

'Well, let's put it this way. You owe me, and this is payback time. You'd have been dead meat when the Hooker mob had you if Blake and I hadn't stuck an oar in.'

'No problem. I always pay my debts. Anyway, I like you, Dillon. You remind me of Billy here. I mean, you don't give a stuff. Mad as a hatter.'

'Seeking death, you mean,' Dillon asked.

'That's it,' Billy said. 'You and me both, Dillon, brothers under the skin. Have we got a problem?'

91

'Well, if it is, its name is Jago.'

Billy's face turned pale. 'Harold and Tony, those two bastards.'

'You don't like them?'

Salter said, 'Dillon, we're friends, right? I'm doing well on the cigarette run from Europe. There are big profits, with the tax differential. But I've had three cargoes hijacked in two months. I know it's the Jagos, but I can't prove it. So what's your problem?'

'A guy called Jack Fox fronts for the Solazzo family.'

'The Colosseum?' Billy said. 'Hey, we know about them. The Jagos have been running with him. In-and-out jobs, security trucks.'

'Always cash,' Salter said. 'What's your interest?'

'Fox had Blake's wife murdered. She was a reporter who got close, too close, so he had her wasted.'

'Jesus,' Salter said. 'The fucking bastard.' He turned to Blake. 'Look, what can I say?'

'That you'll help us, will do.'

'Well, you can bloody well count on that. What's going on?'

'Fox needs cash flow. You won't have heard yet, but we closed the Colosseum and the betting shops down last night.'

'And how in the hell did you do that?'

Dillon said to Blake, 'Go on, tell him,' which Blake did, and Salter and his boys fell about laughing.

'Dear God,' Billy said. 'I mean, that's beautiful.'

'Yes, but the Jagos were there, and we know Fox needs a big tickle. Eyes and ears, Harry, see what you can find out.'

'We certainly will.' Salter rubbed his hands together. 'Life suddenly becomes interesting again, eh, Billy?'

Billy looked wolfish. 'It certainly does.' He turned to Dillon. 'I'm reading this paperback on philosophy. Pinched it from the hairdresser. Better than a novel. This guy Heidegger. Have you heard of him, Dillon?'

'German. A great favourite of Heinrich Himmler, I believe.'

'Never mind that. This Heidegger says that life is action and passion, and that a man fails to take part in the action and passion of his times at the peril of being judged not to have lived.'

'That's really very erudite, Billy.'

'Don't take the piss out of me, Dillon. I didn't get much schooling and I know I'm a tearaway, but I've got a brain. I like books and I know what erudite means, which is that I'm a clever bastard.'

'I never doubted it.' Dillon took out a card and scribbled numbers. 'My house, my mobile, Ferguson at his Cavendish Square flat. Do what you can, Harry.'

'Sure will, my old son.'

Dillon and Blake went to the gangplank and Dillon noticed some air bottles. 'Hey, Billy, you're still at the scuba diving?'

'Master diver now,' Billy said. 'Are you a master diver?'

'As a matter of fact, I am.'

'Oh, go and stuff yourself, Dillon. We'll be in touch,' and Billy went back to his uncle.

The Gulfstream did not carry RAF roundels, so when it landed at Dublin Airport it was simply directed to an area that handled private planes. Flight Sergeant Madoc got the door open. Like Lacey and Parry, he wore the kind of navy blue uniform used by flight crews throughout the world. He put an umbrella up against the driving rain.

'There's a limousine by the hangar,' Madoc said, and led the way towards a black Mercedes.

But there was another vehicle waiting there, a Garda police car, a uniformed officer at the wheel, a large man in a fawn Burberry trenchcoat and tweed cap sitting beside him.

He got out, smiling. 'Dan Malone, Special Branch, chief superintendent. We've never met.'

'Ah, you outrank me, sir.'

'Heard they've put you up to Super. I bet the boys at Special Branch at Scotland Yard didn't like that.'

'Malone? That's a good Irish name. We have a Detective Sergeant Terry Malone in Special Branch.'

'My nephew. English mother, born in London. Can we have words, away from the pride of the RAF here?'

They moved out of the rain into the hangar, and he took a cigarette from a crumpled pack. 'Do you use these things?'

'No.'

'Good for you. You'll live longer than me. Listen, we're all together these days, what with Europe and the peace process. And I know all about you, Superintendent, just like most of Dublin Special Branch. Your reputation precedes you. Ferguson's and Dillon's, too.'

'What are you trying to say?'

'That we're not looking the other way where the IRA is concerned. On the other hand, if Ferguson's sent you over, something's up. I'll be honest with you. I leaned on your driver, who told me he was to take you to Kilrea, and that means only one thing. You're going to see Liam Devlin, the old sod.'

'Ah, you like him, too?'

'Yes, damn you, I do. So – is there something I should know about?'

'I'm seeking information.'

'Is this a hot one?'

'It could be.' She took a chance then. 'One cop to another?'

'One cop to another.'

'Does Brendan Murphy mean anything to you?'

'That bastard? Dear God, is he in this?' He frowned. 'But he wouldn't be in this jurisdiction. He's always stayed north of the border. What is this?'

'This is just a rumour right now. Could be an arms dump in County Louth. Could be an Arab terrorist connection in Lebanon.'

'So that's why you've come to see Devlin?'

'That's right. If anyone will have heard a whisper, it'll be him.'

'No doubt about that.' Malone frowned. 'You'll keep me informed?'

'Of course. We might even need your good offices.'

'Fine. I'll hear from you, then.' He walked her back to the limousine and opened the door. 'And watch your back, peace or no peace.'

'What peace?' she asked, got in the limousine, and closed the door.

It was just after noon when she reached Devlin's Victorian cottage next to the convent in Kilrea village. She told the driver to wait, went up the path, and knocked on the door. It opened and he stood there, an ageless figure in black Armani slacks and shirt, his hair silver, his eyes very blue, a man who still held literary seminars as a visiting professor at Trinity College, but also a lifetime member of the IRA who had killed many times.

'Jesus, girl, you look wonderful.' He embraced her. 'You look grand. Come away in.'

'You're not looking too bad yourself.'

He led her to the sitting room.

He turned. 'Would you like a drink or something?'

'No, I'd like to get on with it.'

She sat down and he took the opposite chair. 'Get on with it, then.'

'Do you know a man called Brendan Murphy?'

His face hardened. 'Is that dog in this?'

'A bad one?'

'As bad as they come.' He took a cigarette from the old silver case and lit it. 'You'd better tell me.'

When she was finished, he sat there, frowning. 'Yes, that sounds like Murphy.'

95

'I was thinking. Where would Murphy get the kind of money he'd need to pay for an underground arms bunker and weaponry?'

'Drugs. Protection. This early release of prisoners the government's been doing has handed Ulster back to the Godfathers on both sides, Loyalist and Catholic.'

'Have you any information on what Murphy could be up to?'

'Only in general. The word is that he did time in Libya, not only in training but also working for various Arab outfits. He'll be the one supplying the contacts for Fox in this Lebanon business.'

'Nothing more specific?'

He shook his head, then his eyes narrowed. 'However, I might know somebody who could help. But I want your word as regards confidentiality.'

'IRA?'

'Exactly.'

She nodded. 'My hand on it.'

He reached for the phone. 'Let's see.'


In Dublin, Michael Leary was just pulling on his raincoat to go out when the phone rang.

'Leary,' he said.

'Michael, my old son, Liam Devlin.'

'Jesus, Liam, my heart's sinking already, because that can only mean you want something.'

'And don't I always? I'll meet you at the Irish Hussar for a snack, and I'll have a Special Branch superintendent with me.'

'What? The Garda I don't need.'

'No, this is the Scotland Yard variety, name of Bernstein. A woman with brains and beauty, Michael. Works with Sean Dillon.'

'My God.' Leary groaned. 'I don't want to know.'

'You'll love it, son. See you soon,' and Devlin put the phone down.

In Hannah's limousine on the way to Dublin a short while later, Devlin pulled the glass screen across and filled her in on Michael Leary.

'A nice lad. He went to Queen's University, Belfast. Read English literature. Taught for a while.'

'And then took up the glorious cause.'

'He had his reasons.'

'But an educated man taking up guns and bombs.'

'You mean all members of the IRA should be off a building site and wear hobnailed boots? Hannah, after the Second World War the Jews who fought to create Israel, the members of Irgun and the Stern gang, used guns and bombs, and many of them had been to the finest universities in Europe.'

'Point taken.'

He found a cigarette and opened his window to let the smoke blow away. 'I might also mention, with my usual modesty, that I was educated by Jesuits myself and took a first-class honours degree at Trinity.'

'All right, I surrender. I can't talk. I've killed people myself. It is just that I don't like bombs.'

'And neither do I.'

'So, more about Leary.'

'Michael was on the active list for years. We worked together, except that he liked the bombs more than you or I do. He was running one in a truck over the border to Ulster, and it went off. Killed the two men with him and took off half of his left leg. The good news was he was still in the Republic, so he didn't end up in the Maze prison.'

'So his active career was over?'

'Oh, he ran the Dublin intelligence section for the chief of staff, but once the peace process started he'd had enough. He knows Dillon well, from Derry in the old days, when they were facing soldiers.'

'And now what?'

97

'He writes thrillers. The kind you see on the stalls at airports, and doing well.'

'Good God.' She frowned. 'Will he help?'

'Let's put it this way: he's like a lot of people these days. Big for peace. We'll see.'

Devlin directed the driver to a quay on the River Liffey, where they parked outside the Irish Hussar.

'It's a favourite with good Republicans and Sinn Fein supporters, and the food is excellent,' Devlin told her.

The bar was very old-fashioned with mahogany and mirrors, bottles offering every kind of drink. It was busy, people sampling good simple pub food. Leary sat in a booth in the far corner. He had a pint of Guinness at his right hand, a plate of Irish stew in front of him.

'Don't get up,' Devlin told him. 'This is my friend Hannah, so let's start with that.'

Leary looked at her, a good-looking man of forty-five, black hair streaked with silver. He hesitated, then held out his hand. Hannah also hesitated, then took it.

'Sit down.'

'The stew looks good,' she said, as a waitress appeared. 'I think I'd like to sample that.'

'And you, Professor Devlin?' the waitress asked.

'Ah, now you're stroking me.' He turned to Hannah. 'Eileen's a student at Trinity. For her sins, she comes to my occasional seminars.'

'Nonsense, you're the best, everyone knows that,' Eileen said.

'Which gets you an A for your next essay. An all-day breakfast for me. A grand old playwright and novelist called Somerset Maugham once said that to dine well in England you should eat breakfast three times a day. Bushmills Whiskey for me, my love.'

'A mineral water would do fine for me,' Hannah said.

'Still writing through the night, Michael?'

'The leg, Liam. Hurts like hell at night, so I can't sleep and I refuse to take the morphine.'

'I'd stick to the Bushmills if I were you.'

Eileen brought the drinks and departed. Leary went back to his stew. 'So, what's it about?'

'Brendan Murphy. Friend of yours?'

'Nobody's friend, that one. As far as I'm concerned, he's a gangster. A disgrace to the movement.'

'Would the chief of staff share your view?'

'Certainly. All the old hands want peace to work, Liam, except for people like Murphy . . .'

'Who have a vested interest in keeping things going,' Hannah said.

'Exactly. Splinter groups like the Continuity IRA, the Real IRA, they all have other agendas.'

The breakfast and the Irish stew arrived and they started to eat.

'And where would Murphy be now?' Hannah asked.

'God knows, Superintendent.' Leary pulled up short. 'As you must know better than most, these days in the Republic, Ulster, and the UK, they're letting them out, not locking them up. Murphy can come and go as he pleases. He's only in trouble if he crosses the line with the Provisional IRA.'

'Would he be dealt with?'

'Certainly. No question. We're an army, Hannah, with rules and regulations. Now what's all this about and why should I help?'

'Because fifteen years ago I saved your life in County Down after you were shot. Got you over the border.'

'Liam, I paid off on that one when you, Dillon and that Yank were after Dermot Riley, and I told you he was back and probably at the farm at Tullamore, and down you went.'

'And you told the chief of staff, who sent Bell and Barry down. Two walking ape men. They tortured Bridget Riley, with cigarette burns on the face.'

99

'And Dillon killed Bell and you shot Barry in the back. We got it all from Dermot.'

'Yes, disgraceful in a man of my age.' Devlin nodded. 'All right, tell him, Hannah.'

Which she did. The underground bunker in County Louth, Fox, the Lebanese connection. Everything.

Leary sat there frowning, then said, 'Let me make one thing clear, and I'm speaking for Provos in general here. We won't give up our arms. History has shown that to be an unwise thing to do.'

'So, you're happy to think that this bunker might exist and Murphy's in charge.'

'No, I'm damn well not, and the chief of staff won't be pleased.'

'You'll tell him?' Hannah asked.

'I have no choice.'

'Ah, well, for once, you've got something in common, you two,' Devlin said. 'So what can you do, Michael?'

'We can trawl County Louth, but it's a hell of a lot of county and Murphy has a lot of hard-line friends there, so I'm not hopeful.' He frowned suddenly. 'I've just thought of something. Sean Regan. Remember him, Liam?'

'From Derry,' Devlin said. 'Shot a military policeman and cleared off to America. As I recall, the peeler recovered.'

'That was two years ago. Regan came back and was working with Murphy in Europe. Apparently, he was on a plane from Paris to Dublin three weeks ago that was diverted to Heathrow because of fog. His name came up on the computer security check and he was lifted.'

'I wonder why I don't know about this.' Hannah frowned.

'Well, according to my information, the Secret Intelligence Service picked him up at Heathrow on one of their special warrants and spirited him away. I'd have thought you'd have known that. Don't your departments share information?'

100

'Only some of the time.'

Devlin turned to Hannah. 'What do you think?'

'If Regan's been working for Murphy, he might well know something. Frankly, it's our best lead.'

'I can't see that there's anything else I can do,' Devlin said. 'Michael here will spill the beans to the chief of staff, and if I do get any crumbs from the table, I'll let you know.'

They got up and walked to the door. Outside, Leary shook Hannah's hand. 'Superintendent, it was a sincere pleasure, but don't let's make a habit of it,' and he walked away.

Devlin smiled. 'A decent enough stick. Anyway, back to the airport in that grand limousine of yours. I'll drop you off and the driver can take me back home.'

Leary sat in the parlour of the chief of staff's suburban home, and the great man listened while his wife served tea and scones.

'Did I do right?' Leary asked.

'Of course you did. Murphy's a poisonous animal. I've no time for him and neither has the Army Council.'

'So what do we do?'

'I'll have our people check out things in Louth, although I don't expect much from that.'

'So?'

The chief of staff smiled. 'If Ferguson's on this case with Sean Dillon . . .' He smiled. 'Well, for once we're on the same side. Sean can do our dirty work for us.'

At the airport, Hannah's limousine drove into the hangar where Lacey and Parry waited. The Gulfstream was outside in the rain. As Hannah and Devlin got out, the Garda police car returned and Malone emerged.

'Liam, you old sod,' he said.

'And stuff you, too,' Devlin said genially, and they shook hands.

Malone said, 'Anything come up?'

Hannah looked uncertain, and Devlin said, 'Go on, he's on your side.'

She told him about the meeting with Leary.

Malone said, 'So anything Murphy's involved with certainly isn't official with the IRA.'

'What about this thing with Sean Regan?' she asked.

'Not a word, and I'd have known.'

'So somebody's playing silly buggers,' Devlin said.

Hannah nodded. 'I'll have to sort that out when I get back.' She held out a hand. 'Liam, you're a treasure.'

'Hell, you can do better than that, girl.' He kissed her. 'Take care, and tell Sean to watch his back.'

'That's something he's good at. Goodbye, Superintendent.'

Lacey and Parry were already inside, and Flight Sergeant Madoc gave her a hand up the steps. The door closed, the engines turned over, the Gulfstream moved away.

'A hell of a woman,' Malone said.

'You can say that again.' Devlin smiled. 'Now you can dismiss your car, join me in my luxurious limousine that the good Superintendent has loaned me, and we'll return to the Irish Hussar, where you can buy me a very large Bushmills.'

'Me, in that hotbed of Republican gunmen?'

'I seem to recall that your younger brother, Fergus, was one.'

'We don't talk about that.'

'As I said, the Irish Hussar.' Devlin smiled. 'It will do my reputation no end of good being seen in the company of the police. A great comfort to me.'

The Gulfstream climbed steadily out over the Irish Sea, and Hannah called Ferguson on her Codex Four.

'Ah, there you are. How did it go?'

She brought him up to date, Regan included. 'So there you are, sir. We should have been told. There is supposed to be interdepartmental cooperation.'

'Not with the Secret Intelligence Service, as long as Simon Carter is Deputy Director. Leave it with me.'

He sat there at his desk, thinking about it, then picked up the phone and spoke to Dillon, who was in the outer office with Blake.

'Get in here. I've had the Superintendent on the line and we could have a problem.'

# 8

Dillon and Blake listened as Ferguson related Hannah Bernstein's adventures. When he was finished, Blake said, 'This is surely unacceptable, one major intelligence department hugging secrets to itself that could be of possible crucial importance to others.'

'Yes, well, Carter's always been good at doing his own thing, and to hell with anyone else.'

'Seems to me it's time to remind Carter,' Ferguson said, 'that the particular circumstances of my position as head of the Prime Minister's personal security service give me extraordinary powers. Including over him.'

'That I'd love to see,' Dillon told him.

Ferguson smiled, picked up his phone, and dialled a number. 'Ah, that you, Carter? Look, something's come up and I need to see you. I want your input on something before I speak to the Prime Minister . . . Yes? Good. I'll see you at the Grenadier in St James's in thirty minutes.'

'Nothing like being decisive,' Blake said.

'Well, as you Yanks say, you ain't seen nothing yet. Order the car, Dillon, I'll find a warrant or two, and we'll be on our way.'

* * *

The Grenadier was a pleasant traditional London pub, with old-fashioned dark oak booths. Carter was already there in a corner, sipping a glass of sherry. A small, pale-faced man with white hair, he reacted angrily at the sight of Dillon.

'Really, Ferguson, I've told you before. I object to this murderous swine's presence.'

'Well, take it up with the Prime Minister. He employs him.'

'God save your honour,' Dillon said cheerfully. 'It's a blessing, the grand man like yourself allows me in the same room.'

'Oh, go to hell.'

Ferguson said, 'You'll remember Blake Johnson.'

'Yes, the American.' Carter offered a reluctant hand and turned to Ferguson. 'So what is this?'

'An IRA renegade named Brendan Murphy's up to no good, and I need to know what it is.'

'Nonsense, that's old hat, Ferguson. Murphy isn't a problem any longer, not since the peace process overwhelmed the land.'

'It's the great liar you are,' Dillon told him, and turned to Blake. 'This is the Deputy Director of the Security Services, a faceless man who never worked in the field himself.'

'Damn you, you Irish swine.' Carter was furious.

'Now, that's a racist remark,' Dillon said. 'I could take you to the tribunal.'

'Exactly,' Ferguson agreed. 'And as my sainted mother was Irish, then as a half-Irishman I take it very personally.'

'I'd say you've just insulted his mother's memory,' Blake put in.

'Could we get on with it?' Dillon asked. 'You lifted a man named Sean Regan at Heathrow three weeks ago, when his plane to Dublin was diverted because of fog. Why?'

'Don't be stupid, Dillon. He shot a military policeman in Londonderry a couple of years ago and fled. The policeman nearly died.'

'So you're going to stand Regan up on trial at the Old Bailey?' Ferguson asked.

'We might.'

'But you won't, because of the peace process. We're letting them out of prison now, not banging them up.'

Carter was strangely confused. 'Come on, Ferguson, we're in the hands of our political masters.'

'Not as far as I'm concerned. We're in the hands of the law. The truth is, you're holding Regan to squeeze anything you can out of him in case it may be of future use.'

'So what?'

'Not any more. Where are you holding him?'

'Wandsworth.' Carter answered as a reflex.

'Not any longer.' Ferguson produced a paper from his inside pocket. 'That's a warrant from me as head of the PM's security squad, authorizing me to, as quaint legal language has it, take possession of one Sean Regan.'

Carter was outraged. 'Now, look here, Ferguson.'

'No, you look here. The difference is that I *did* serve in the field. I was an eighteen-year-old second lieutenant in the Hook in Korea in 'fifty-two, and I've seen more villains here than you've had break-fasts. So don't argue. Just countersign the order. Here's my pen.'

He offered it and Carter took it, hand shaking, and signed the document. 'My turn will come, Ferguson.'

'I don't think so.' Ferguson blew on the ink. 'Now go away.'

Carter suddenly looked helpless, got up, and stumbled out. Blake said, 'Why is it I don't feel sorry for him?'

'Because he isn't worth it,' Ferguson said. 'So, gentlemen, Wandsworth Prison next stop.'


Ferguson, Dillon and Blake waited in the interview room at Wandsworth until the door was opened, and the kind of prison officer who looked as if he'd been a sergeant in a Guards regiment pushed Regan in.

Dillon said, 'Good man yourself, Sean.' He turned to the others. 'Always gave us a problem, the two of us being Sean.'

Regan said, 'Jesus, is that you, Dillon?'

'As ever was. Come to take you away from your cell and the stench of the lavatory buckets. This is Brigadier Charles Ferguson, your new boss. The other fella is a Yank, and FBI, so watch it.'

'What in the hell is going on?'

Ferguson turned to the prison officer. 'Give us a moment.'

'Certainly, sir.'

The man went out, and Dillon said, 'Brendan Murphy. We know you've been part of his outfit.'

Regan was thrown, but tried to brazen it out. 'I haven't seen Brendan in years.'

'So Carter didn't manage to wheedle anything out of you?'

'I've said I don't know what you're talking about.'

'Don't waste my time,' Ferguson told him. 'You shot a military policeman in Derry two years ago and fled to the States. Since then, you've worked for Murphy in Europe.'

'It's a lie.'

Dillon said, 'Don't be stupid. You shot a peeler. All right, he didn't die, but at the Old Bailey you'll pull ten years for attempted murder. Imagine Wandsworth or maybe Parkhurst, year after year. You'd be afraid to take a shower.'

'No.' Regan was shaken. 'Mr Carter said if I cooperated I wouldn't do time.'

'Yes, well, unfortunately, I'm in charge now,' Ferguson told him. 'Now make your mind up. A comfortable safe house where you'll fill us in on Brendan Murphy's doings, or a very unpleasant future.'

Regan, in despair, said, 'Brendan would cut me to pieces. He's a sadist.'

'Which is why we'll have to take good care of you.'

He nodded to Dillon, who knocked on the door, which opened and the prison officer appeared. Ferguson took his warrant out.

'Take this prisoner to his cell, allow him to collect his belongings, then present this document to the Governor, authorizing his release into my custody.'

'Certainly, Brigadier.'

Regan was pushed out, and Ferguson turned to Dillon and Blake. 'So, we take him to Holland Park, where you, Dillon, will squeeze out the last drop of juice.'

'My pleasure, Brigadier,' Dillon said.

They delivered Regan to Holland Park and drove in through the electronic gates. The security guards wore neat navy blue blazers and flannel slacks.

'Nursing home? What is this?' Regan asked.

'It's a fortress,' Ferguson told him. 'And the gentlemen in blazers are all military police. There's no way out of here, as you'll find for yourself.' He turned to Dillon. 'Let Helen settle him in and feed him. You and Blake stay. I'll be back.'

His Daimler drove away. They took Regan up the steps between them, his wrists still manacled. The door opened and a very large man appeared.

'Mr Dillon, sir.'

'Another one for you, Sergeant Miller, one Sean Regan. He shot a Royal Military Policeman in Derry two years ago.'

'That would be Fred Dalton.' Miller's face was like stone. 'He survived, but had to take a medical discharge. Oh, I'll take good care of you, Mr Regan.'

He reached for Regan's left shoulder with a hand the size of a meat plate, and Helen Black came down the hall stairs.

'Is this the prisoner, Sergeant Miller?'

Miller got his feet together. 'Yes, ma'am.'

'Good. Room ten, unpack him, then we'll have sandwiches and tea in the parlour.'

'As you say, ma'am.'

Regan turned. 'What is this? Who's she?'

'Sergeant Major Black, and don't be a male chauvinist, Regan,' Dillon said. 'She shot two Provos in Derry and holds the Military Cross.'

'Fuck you, Dillon.'

'That's bad language in front of a lady. We can't have that, can we, Sergeant?' he asked Miller.

'We certainly can't, sir.' Miller squeezed Regan's left arm very hard. 'Up we go, there's a good gentleman.'

Blake said, 'Now what?'

'Oh, they have a canteen, a kitchen. We won't starve.' Dillon smiled. 'We'll sort Regan out later.'

Upstairs, Regan was astounded. He had a decent bedroom, a bathroom, a view of the garden, even if it was through barred windows. He even had a fresh shirt, blazer and slacks, like the guards'. Miller took him downstairs to a small sitting room, a gas fire flickering in the hearth. There was soup, ham sandwiches and a glass of dry white wine. Miller stood by the wall, enigmatic.

Regan, slightly euphoric at the difference from Wandsworth, said, 'Could I have another glass of wine?'

'Of course, sir.'

Miller poured the glass of Chablis, and behind the mirror Ferguson, Dillon, Hannah – who had just arrived – and Helen Black watched.

Ferguson said, 'You all know the story by now. This is a bad business, so we make sure he talks. I'd like you to go in, Sergeant Major, and you, Dillon. Facts, that's what I need.'

'Certainly, sir.' Helen Black nodded to Sean. 'Good guy, bad guy, suit you, Sean?'

'Nothing better. Takes me back to my days at the National Theatre.'

'Yes, you *have* told us that one before. Let's do it.' She led the way out. 'But follow my lead.'

'Shall I leave, ma'am?' Miller asked, as they stepped into the room.

'No, I might need you, Sergeant.' Her voice was different and very hard. 'This is a Provisional IRA gunman. He crippled Fred Dalton. Do you think Fred was his first?'

'I doubt it, ma'am,' Miller said coldly.

'Right, but I'd like you to manacle him, Sergeant. Once a killer, always a killer.'

'Certainly, ma'am.'

'Now, look here,' Regan protested.

'Just hold out your wrists and be a good boy.'

Regan was sweating and very, very worried. He'd had three weeks in Wandsworth, with the lavatory bucket, the twice-a-week showers, the unwelcome attentions of certain wild-eyed prisoners, and others: basic English criminals who didn't like the IRA. The contrast of his treatment at the safe house spoke for itself. In a way, he'd thought he was going to be all right, but now he had this woman who looked like his elder sister, acting like the Gestapo.

She unbuttoned her jacket, revealing the holstered Colt. 'Now then, let's get started.'

Roper had joined the group on the other side of the mirror. 'She's really very good.'

'Outstanding,' Blake agreed.

'And still won't take a commission,' Ferguson said.

'You can't buy her, sir,' Hannah put in.

'I know,' Ferguson sighed. 'Very depressing.'

And then, Helen Black started to work.

The change was astonishing. This pleasant, decent Englishwoman seemed to take on a new persona.

'I've been fighting people like you for years. The bomb and the bullet, women and kids – you couldn't care less. I shot dead two of your bastards in Derry. They were parking a van with fifty pounds of Semtex on board outside a nurses' hostel. Well, we couldn't have that, could we? I took a bullet in the left thigh, got the bastard who did it, then sat up and got his friend in the back as he ran away.'

Regan was terrified. 'For Christ's sake, what kind of woman are you?'

She grabbed his jaw and shook his head painfully from side to side. 'The Apache Indians used to give their prisoners to their women to go to work on. I'm *that* kind of woman.'

'Excellent,' Ferguson said. 'She should be at the National Theatre herself.'

'You crippled a comrade of mine. Fred Dalton.' She took out her Colt and touched him between the eyes. 'These are hollowpoints, you scum. I pull this trigger and your brains are on the wall.'

'For God's sake, no,' Regan cried.

Dillon caught her wrist and turned the gun. 'No. Sergeant Major, this isn't the way.'

She turned, as if in fury. 'I'll be back.' She walked out.

Regan was shaking. Dillon said to Miller, 'Uncuff him, Sergeant, he isn't going anywhere.'

'As you say, sir.' Miller got out a key and unlocked the manacles. Dillon opened his old silver cigarette case, took out two cigarettes, lit them, and gave Regan one.

'There you go, just like in *Now Voyager*.'

Regan was shaking. 'What in the hell are you talking about?'

'Never mind, Sean, I've a weakness for old movies. Now listen. Me, I got smart. I could have faced a Serb firing squad, but Ferguson is an extraordinarily powerful man. He saved my life, and in return I dropped working for the glorious cause and work for him instead. Which means I'm alive.' Regan was trembling, and Dillon turned to Miller. 'A large brandy, Sergeant.'

'Certainly, sir.'

Miller opened a cupboard and returned with a glass, which Regan emptied at one throw. He looked up at Dillon. 'What do you want?'

'What's best for you. Look, Ferguson's in charge now, and you did shoot that fella, Dalton. Peace process or not, he'll make you stand up in court if he wants to.'

On the other side of the mirror, Ferguson said, 'In you go, Sergeant Major.'

Helen Black went back into the sitting room, a document in one hand. 'All right, I've had enough. It's back to Wandsworth for you, you bastard.'

Regan simply fell apart. 'For God's sake, tell me what you want, just tell me.'

'Excellent,' Roper said. 'Pure Gestapo. They used physical abuse much less than people realized. Didn't need to. They just messed with their heads.'

Ferguson said to Hannah, 'We won't overwhelm him.' He turned to Roper. 'You and Blake stay here. You come in with me and do your Scotland Yard bit, Superintendent.'

Ferguson walked in with Hannah and said to Miller, 'Give him another brandy, Sergeant.'

'Sir.' Miller did as he was told, and Regan took the glass with shaking hands and drained it.

'Do I have a deal?'

'That depends on what you have for me.'

Regan looked at Dillon, who said, 'The Brigadier's a hard man, Sean, but a moralist. If he says it, he means it.'

Hannah said, 'Mr Regan, I'm Detective Superintendent Bernstein of Special Branch. I'd be interested to know if you can assist us in our inquiries regarding the activities of one Brendan Murphy.'

Regan said, 'What do you want to know?'

'I understand there's an underground concrete bunker somewhere in County Louth.'

'Semtex, machine guns, mortars,' Dillon said. 'Enough to start a civil war. Where is it, Sean?'

Regan said, 'Close to Kilbeg.'

'Jesus, son, there are Kilbegs all over Ireland.'

112

'Well, this one is in Louth, like the Superintendent says, just south of the border in the Republic and south of Dundalk Bay. Near Dunany Point. Very remote.'

'I know that area,' Dillon said.

'You wouldn't last long, Dillon. They're a funny lot. Strangers stand out like a sore thumb.'

Ferguson said, 'Let's be specific.'

'When I fled to the States, I was helped by a wealthy Irish American group who were a bit radical. Didn't approve of peace. I brokered a big financial deal for Brendan. The idea was to prepare for the future, the next war.'

'Which explains the bunker,' Ferguson said.

'But where did the arms come from?' Dillon asked.

Behind the mirror, Roper was making notes.

'Oh, that was a Mafia connection. Brendan had worked with them in Europe. A fella called Jack Fox.'

'Fronting for the Solazzo family?' Hannah said.

'Well, I always figured he was fronting for himself. He supplied the arms.'

'Anything else?' Hannah asked. 'Lebanon, for example?'

'Christ, is there nothing you don't know?'

'Get on with it,' Dillon said.

'Murphy was trained in Libya years ago, has strong Arab contacts, can even get by with the language, enough to order a meal, anyway.'

'So?' Ferguson asked.

'Well, Fox controls the Solazzos' drug operations in Russia, so he has big contacts. Murphy has the Arab link.'

'Which Arab link?'

Regan hesitated. 'Saddam. Iraq.'

'That's nice,' Dillon said. 'What's intended?'

'There's a freighter down from the Black Sea next week. Called the *Fortuna*. If it's on time, it's due at a place called Al Shariz, south of Beirut, next Tuesday.'

Dillon took over. 'Russian crew?'

'No, Arab. All Army of God.'

'And the cargo?' Regan hesitated. 'Come on, what's the bloody cargo?'

'Hammerheads.'

There was a pause, and Hannah turned to Ferguson. 'Hammerheads, sir?'

The door opened and Blake entered. 'Sorry, Brigadier, but I know all about those. They're short-range missiles mounted on a tripod that only take two minutes to erect. Their range is three hundred miles. Nuclear-tipped. They wouldn't take out Israel or Jordan completely, but Tel Aviv wouldn't look too good.'

Ferguson turned to Regan. 'Have you told me the truth, told me everything?'

Regan hesitated again. 'When the boat gets in, the *Fortuna*, Brendan will be on board. Fox meets them, gets paid in gold. Five million.'

'Dollars or pounds?' Dillon asked.

'How the fuck would I know? Paid on the boat is what I heard, because they want to arrange another consignment a month later.'

'And all this is true?' Ferguson asked.

'Yes, damn you.'

Ferguson turned to Helen Black and Miller. 'Send him back to his room.'

They took Regan out between them, and Roper came in after they left.

'I've had a thought,' he said. 'I've got details of Fox's Gulfstream. It's parked at Heathrow, as I recall. Let me check its movements.'

They followed him to his ground-floor suite, where all his equipment had been set up. Roper started on the computer, fingers deft on the keys.

He grunted. 'Fox has a slot booked out of Heathrow for Monday morning, destination Beirut.'

'Wonderful,' Dillon said. 'Regan was telling the truth.'

'So what now, sir?' Hannah asked.

Ferguson said, 'We can't send in the SAS, and we do have other business with Fox. Something more subtle is needed.'

Hannah said, 'The Israelis wouldn't like this, Brigadier.'

'Exactly what I was thinking.' Ferguson turned to Dillon. 'You went to Beirut the other year with the Superintendent here. Stayed at the Al Bustan.'

'How could I forget it? It overlooks some excellent Roman ruins.'

'You remember my man there, Walid Khasan?'

'Very well. Lebanese Christian. He and the Superintendent got on rather well. Which is not surprising, considering that he was actually Major Gideon Cohen of Mossad.'

'Lieutenant colonel, now.'

'Had a nice sister, Anya, I remember. A lieutenant.'

'Captain, now.'

'And there was another one – what was his name? Captain Moshe Levy?'

'Major. Everything goes up in the world, Dillon. Yes, I think Colonel Cohen might be interested. I'll give him a call.'

Lieutenant Colonel Gideon Cohen wore uniform only on occasion. Sitting in his office now at the top of a secluded building in Tel Aviv, he was wearing a white shirt and linen slacks, all very unmilitary for a Mossad colonel. Forty-nine years of age, he had olive skin, and hair that was still black and down to his shoulders.

His sister, Captain Anya Shamir, sat at a corner desk, working a computer. She'd been a widow since her husband's death on the Golan Heights.

In the other corner, Major Moshe Levy sat at a second computer. He was in uniform because he'd had a report to make at Army headquarters, and wore khaki shirt and slacks, paratroopers' wings and decorations. The phone on Gideon Cohen's desk rang.

A voice said, 'This is Ferguson. Are you coded? I am.'

'My dear Charles, of course I am.' Cohen waved to Anya and Moshe. 'Ferguson from London.'

He pressed the audio button on his telephone. 'Charles, old boy.'

'Don't call me old boy just because you went to Sandhurst. I'm glad to say I still outrank you.'

'Something special, Charles?'

'Something rotten in the state of Lebanon.'

'Tell me.'

Which Ferguson did.

When he was finished, Cohen said, 'Hammerheads. We can't have that.'

'Jerusalem wouldn't look too good after one of those.'

'Exactly. Charles, I need to consider this.'

'What you mean is, you need to talk to the general, your uncle.'

'I'm afraid so.'

'That's no problem. But this is a black one, Gideon. Keep it close.'

In his penthouse office, General Arnold Cohen, head of Mossad's Section One, the group with special responsibility for activities in Arab areas, listened gravely.

When his nephew was finished, he said, 'Hammerheads. This is very serious.'

'So what do we do? Call an air strike on this boat, the *Fortuna*?'

'In Lebanese waters? Come on, Gideon, we're supposed to be nice at the moment while our British and American cousins castigate Saddam.'

'And he's going to send Hammerhead strikes up our backside.'

His sister, Anya, standing with Levy by the window, said, 'Can I make a point, Uncle?'

'Of course you can. You've gotten away with murder with me ever since you learned to speak, so why should this time be different?'

'Why don't we use Dillon, Uncle? He's hell on wheels, that one – remember that job with him in Beirut the other year? He was incredible.'

'She's right,' Levy put in. 'What's important here is disposing of this *Fortuna* boat and its cargo with a minimum of fuss, right?'

'So?'

'So we make it a small-scale operation. With Dillon to call on, the three of us – Anya, Moshe, me – can handle it in Al Shariz. The right equipment, and we can blow the damn boat to hell.'

'He's right,' Gideon Cohen said. 'No adverse publicity. No air strikes.'

'I like it,' the general said. 'Get on with it.'

Ferguson said, 'Fine, Gideon. I'll send over Dillon. Also an American colleague, Blake Johnson, who works directly for the President. You'll find him most useful. I'll put Dillon on.'

A moment later, Dillon said in bad Hebrew, 'How are you, you lying dog?'

'Dillon, we seem to have business together.'

They switched into English. 'I'm not sure how we'll do this,' Dillon said. 'If we're to blow this *Fortuna* out of the water, we'll need mines, Semtex, some scuba equipment.'

'We'll take care of it. We'll keep it low-key. Myself, Levy, my sister. With you and this American, that's five. We don't want to draw attention, although things have changed since you operated in Beirut, my friend. It's not quite the war zone it used to be. People are trying to build up the infrastructure again, tourism and so on.'

'Where would Fox stay? Beirut?'

'No, there's an old Moorish palace in Al Shariz which has been refurbished as a hotel. I'd say he'll be there. It's called the Golden House.'

'No good for us, then.'

'No problem. We'll come up on a motor yacht, like tourists. You and your friends can stay on board.'

'We can't exactly sit in the bar at the Golden House, though. We don't want Fox to know it's us. It'd be much better if he thought it was an Israeli job.'

'Do you recall my sister Anya?'

'How could I forget? She played a lady of the night better than a lady of the night.'

'Enough to ensnare this Fox.'

Dillon laughed. 'Enough to ensnare friend Fox.'

'You and Johnson, Levy and myself, we'll stay on our boat, the *Pamir*, well out of the way. Anya can squeeze what she can out of the guy. We'll send the *Fortuna* down when we're ready.'

'You Israelis are such morally committed people,' Dillon said. 'But you'll sink that boat, crew and all, without a flicker.'

'Not even half a flicker,' Cohen said. 'See you soon.'

Dillon hung up, and Ferguson said, 'So, here we go again.'

Hannah Bernstein said, 'What about me, sir?'

'Not this one, Superintendent. Dillon and Blake, plus our friends from Mossad, are enough. What I'd like you to do is get a little more basic with friend Regan as regards the bunker in County Louth.' He turned to Roper. 'I'm sure the Major here will be more than willing to help.'

'A pleasure, sir,' Roper said.

'Sorry, Hannah, I'll have to love you and leave you.' Dillon turned to Blake and smiled, a strange excitement there. 'Here we go, old buddy, back to the war zone again.'

# LEBANON
# AL SHARIZ

# 9

Brendan Murphy leaned over the rail of the small coastal freighter, the *Fortuna*, and watched the distant lights of Syria. The ship was Italian-registered and had definitely seen better days, but under its battered exterior the essential bits, the engines, were in excellent condition. They'd left the Black Sea two days earlier and had made good time.

The man who approached him, wearing a seaman's reefer coat, held a cup of coffee in one hand, which he passed to him. His name was Dermot Kelly and he had unfashionably Irish blond hair and a hard, pocked face. He lit a cigarette.

'Jesus, Brendan, they're all fugging Arabs, this crew. If I light up in the saloon, they glare at me. Lucky I brought a bottle on board.'

'Fundamentalists,' Murphy said. 'Army of God, this lot. They're just waiting for death in the service of Allah, so they can go to Paradise and have eternal pleasure and all those women.'

'They must be crazy.'

'Why? You mean we're Catholics and we're right, and they're Muslims and they're wrong? Come off it, Dermot.'

An Arab, in a reefer coat the same as Kelly's, came down a ladder from the bridge. He was the captain and his name was Abdul Sawar.

'How's it going?' Brendan demanded.

'Excellent. We'll be on time.'

'Well, that's good.'

Sawar said, 'Any problems?'

'Well, I miss bacon and eggs for breakfast,' Kelly told him.

'We do our best, Mr Kelly, but some things are not possible.'

'Well, you'd probably have a problem in reverse in Dublin,' Kelly told him.

'Exactly.'

Sawar went back up the ladder, and Murphy said, 'Don't stir the pot, Dermot. You can't expect good Irish bacon on an Italian boat crewed by Arabic fundamentalists off the coast of Syria.'

'All right, so I'll just think of the money.'

'The gold, Dermot, the gold. Speaking of which, we'll check it out.'

He led the way to the stern of the ship, and went down a companionway to a rear saloon. There were two cargo boxes wrapped in sacking.

Dermot lit a cigarette. 'They look like shite to me.'

'Five million in gold, Brendan.'

'How do we know?'

'Because Saddam wants another cargo next month, so he won't screw around with this one.'

'Do you think it's all going to work?'

'Like a Swiss watch. Fox will be on a plane. We'll offload the gold, and take it to the airport at Beirut, where the right officials have been bribed. The plane is routed to Dublin, but it puts down at an old air force base in Louth on the way. We unload our half and Fox carries on, announcing a mid-air change of destination.'

'Where will he go?'

'Supposedly Heathrow, but on the way there, when the plane is in uncontrolled air space, he'll put down on this estate nearby in Cornwall, called Hellsmouth. There's an RAF aerodrome there from the Second World War. The runway's a bit rough, but it can take a plane like the Gulfstream.'

'Sounds good to me, Brendan.'

'And me, Dermot.'

The other man smiled, took a half bottle of Paddy whiskey from his pocket, unscrewed the top, and drank deeply. He passed it across.

'Well, here's to Irish bacon and eggs, soda bread and rain.' He smiled. 'I miss the rain, Brendan. The good Irish rain.'

Gideon Cohen, his sister and Moshe Levy had left a yachting marina on the coast near Haifa in a forty-foot boat of a kind regularly rented by tourists interested in diving. There were stocks of air bottles in the stern, bunks for seven people below, a good kitchen galley, every convenience.

Cohen's passport was British, in the name of Julian Grant; his sister and Levy had become a Mr and Mrs Frobisher, also British. Their background being impeccable, and Lebanon desperate for tourist money, they'd had no trouble getting the necessary visas, and pushed towards Al Shariz through the late afternoon.

Cohen was at the wheel, Levy lounging beside him, Anya looking out of the half-open window.

'So, let's go over it,' her brother said. 'You and Moshe book into the Golden Palace, and do remember, Moshe, this is my sister you're sharing a suite with.'

'How could I forget, Colonel?'

'Fox is booked in with these two hoods, Falcone and Russo. You make yourself available in the bar, Anya, just in case there's information available.'

'Oh, dear,' she said. 'Here I go again. Stage Six at MGM, playing the whore.'

Her brother smiled, and hugged her with his spare arm as he steered. 'No, the good-looking whore.' He shook his head. 'This is a bad one, little sister. We can't make a mistake.'

'Well, at least we have Dillon.'

He laughed out loud. 'My God, yes, the poor old *Fortuna* doesn't know what's going to hit it.'

On the plane on the way to Beirut, Dillon said to Blake, 'So, we're interested in establishing an electronics factory, a joint Anglo-American project, jobs for all. Three days in and out.'

'No problems?' Blake asked.

'Certainly not. They're still trying to build up the country again, while surrounded by people who want to cut each other's balls off.'

'So, we join Cohen's boat, look like recreational scuba divers.'

'And send the *Fortuna* to the bottom. Hammerheads, the lot,' Dillon said.

'And the crew?'

'Murdering fanatics. If they didn't want the risk, they shouldn't have joined.'

'But, Dillon, there's five million pounds in gold on board.'

'Yes, isn't that, as Ferguson would say, delicious? It also goes to the bottom. A fabulous expression of conspicuous consumption.' He waved to Flight Sergeant Madoc. 'Bring me another Bushmills, I'm celebrating imagining how Jack Fox will feel.'

Fox booked into the Golden House, with Falcone and Russo. He had a nice suite on the first floor – marble, scattered rugs, all very Moorish. He felt good. The Colosseum was a bad memory, and his lawyers seemed to think they might be able to fix things. Whether they did or not, the gold from the *Fortuna* was a certainty. Added to that, the cash Murphy owed him in Ireland from Irish-American arms orders would take the pressure right off.

'Everything okay, Signore?' Falcone asked.

'Couldn't be better. Tonight's the night, Aldo. Gold, there's nothing like it. It's still the one commodity you can rely on. You've checked with the harbourmaster?'

'Yes, Signore, the *Fortuna* is due in at ten. A crew of twelve, all Arab. It left the Black Sea the day before yesterday.'

'Where will they anchor, on the pier?'

'No, it's full. A few hundred yards out in the entrance to the bay.'

'Excellent. I'll have a shower, then dinner. I'll see you later.'

Their plane landed in early evening. Dillon and Johnson booked in as Russel and Gaunt and took a taxi to Al Shariz. On the way, Dillon called Cohen on his mobile.

'Lafayette, we are here. I'm saying that on behalf of Blake.'

'Well, we're here, too. Lower yacht basin. *Pamir*, Pier Three.'

'See you soon.' Dillon switched off his phone and relayed the information to the driver.

On the *Pamir*, Cohen looked through a pair of Nightstalker glasses and watched the *Fortuna* drop anchor. He said to Anya, 'Off you go. All I want to know is what he's up to. It could give us a clue to his movements.'

'Sure,' she said.

'Another thing.' He was strangely awkward. 'Duty is duty, but you're my beloved sister. Don't get close to this one. He's bad news.'

She kissed his cheek. 'Hey, little brother, don't worry.'

She booked into the hotel, changed, then went down to the bar, resplendent in a black mini dress, her dark hair to her shoulders, and looking terrific. She sat at the bar, and Fox, over by the window, Falcone and Russo at the next table, saw her at once. He nodded to Falcone, got up, went to the bar, and sat next to her.

'Hi, there.'

'An American!' She smiled. 'What are you doing here?'

'Investigating tourist prospects,' he said glibly. 'What about you?'

'Oh, I'm over from London with my husband, on the same errand.'

'Your husband?' Fox was disappointed.

'Yes, well, he's been called to Tel Aviv. Left me on my own for three days.'

Fox put his hand on hers. 'That's terrible, a nice-looking lady like you all on her own. But you've got me now. Have you eaten?'

'No.'

'Well, join me.'

Which she did, for a sumptuous meal, part Arab, part European, and lots of Cristal champagne. She endured his questing hand on her thigh and waited. Finally, Falcone, who had stood by the window, answered a mobile, came over and whispered.

Fox squeezed her thigh. 'Listen, I've got to go.'

'What a pity.'

It was ten o'clock. He said, 'I'll be a couple of hours. Will you still be here?'

'Of course. I'll see you.'

He went out with Falcone. She followed, and stood in the shadows of a palm tree and shrubbery while they talked on the terrace.

'The *Fortuna* is in, Signore.'

'Good. We offload the gold in two hours.'

'There's just one thing I don't understand,' Falcone said. 'These Hammerheads are short range?'

'Absolutely.'

'So if we're talking Iraq, I'm puzzled. I mean, we're off the coast of Syria, so they can't be fired from Iraq.'

'Aldo, you don't get the point. They're very easy to set up and fire. The *Fortuna* is going to be a gun platform. The entire crew, as you know, is Army of God. All they want to do is take out Tel Aviv. Jerusalem, they're funny about. After all, it's the second most important Muslim city.'

'My God, they're animals, these people.'

126

'Depends on your point of view. Now let's get moving.'

Anya called her brother on her mobile and relayed the information. Gideon said, 'Right, get out of there now. I'll expect you within the next half hour.'

On the *Pamir*, Dillon, Blake, Cohen and Levy were sitting under the stern awning having a look at the harbour chart when Anya arrived. She paid off the taxi and stepped over the rail.

'Jesus, woman,' Dillon told her. 'You look like page sixty-four in *Vogue* magazine. You should be a young Jewish mother having babies and making your husband's life miserable. Instead, you're still going around shooting bad guys.'

'It's my nature, Dillon. Who's your friend?'

'Blake Johnson. Former FBI and works for the President now, so let's have some respect here.'

She shook hands with Blake. 'Nice to meet you,' she said and turned to her brother. 'As I told you, I overheard Fox talking to one of his men on the terrace. The gold is definitely on board, as well as the Hammerheads. The worrying thing is that the boat is to be used as a gun platform, with Tel Aviv a possible target.'

'Not if we blow that thing out of the water.'

'I couldn't put it better myself,' Dillon told him.

'And sooner rather than later,' Blake put in. 'The boat's here, and Fox will want it offloaded as soon as possible. We know from Roper that he has a return slot booked for seven o'clock tomorrow.'

'Right, then let's get on with it.' Cohen turned to Dillon. 'How do we do this?'

'Well, you remember in 'ninety-four in Beirut, when we blew up the *Alexandrene* with all that plutonium on board?'

'You mean, *you* blew up the *Alexandrene*,' Anya said.

'And how did you do that?' Blake asked.

127

'Took a shallow dive, went up the anchor chain, created a little mayhem, dropped a block of Semtex in the engine room, and that was that.'

Cohen said, 'Sounds good to me.'

'A one-man show?' Blake said. 'I don't like it.'

'Blake, Vietnam was a long time ago.'

'Stuff that kind of talk, Sean. We go in together.'

Dillon sighed. 'All right, it's your funeral.' He looked out as orange flickered on the horizon, and in the distance the security lights gleamed on the *Fortuna*. 'Let's get on with it. Time to save the free world again.'

Falcone, Russo and Fox went out to the *Fortuna* in a water taxi and pulled up to a steel stairway at the side of the ship. Fox told the boatman to wait and led the way up to where Brendan Murphy, Dermot Kelly and Captain Sawar waited. Fox and Brendan embraced.

'You're looking good,' Murphy said.

'And you, old buddy, and you'll have an even broader smile when you know what's on shore and on its way to my plane.'

'Come and have a look.'

Murphy led the way down to the stern saloon, where the two cargo boxes waited.

'Five million, Jack,' he said. 'It makes me feel God is on my side.'

'That's because you're Irish, you daft bastard,' Fox said. 'Let's go and have a drink and then we'll offload this lot. I've got a water taxi waiting.'

Beside the *Pamir*, an inflatable waited, Dillon and Blake aboard in black dive suits with a single air bottle each, weight belts around their waists. Each had a dive bag with a Browning Hi-Power with a Carswell silencer inside. Dillon also carried two three-pound blocks of Semtex, with three-minute timer pencils.

Gideon Cohen said to his sister and Levy, 'I'll take them out. You wait here and be ready for sea.'

Anya hesitated, then picked up an Uzi submachine gun and stepped in beside Dillon and Blake.

'Not this time. You might need back-up and Moshe is better with the boat than I am.'

Cohen sighed. 'You're a great trial to me. Okay, take the Nightstalker and monitor what happens.'

They moved out into the harbour and floated to a halt a hundred yards from the *Fortuna*.

Dillon said, 'Here we go,' and pulled down his diving mask and reached for his mouthpiece.

At only ten feet, there was enough illumination from the security lights to give the water a kind of glow. He paused beside the steel stairway, released his jacket and air tank, and took the Browning from his dive bag and cocked it. His face half-covered by his diving hood, he surfaced, Blake beside him, and an Arab seaman appeared at the top of the stairway. Dillon shot him instantly, the Browning near noiseless, tumbling him into the water, and started up. Blake, somewhere behind him, had another problem.

The Arab who crewed the water taxi had been shocked to see Dillon surface and kill the seaman. He tossed his cigarette into the water, stood up, and Blake, with no options, had to shoot him.

On deck, it was quiet only for a moment, then voices called. On the bridge, Captain Sawar moved out on to the flying bridge, a machine gun in his hands.

'Selim, are you there? What is it?'

Dillon called in Arabic, 'It's Mossad, you dog. We've come for you.'

Sawar fired his machine gun blindly down into the darkness of the deck, and Blake, scrambling up beside Dillon, fired back, shattering a window up there. Fox and Falcone and Russo, who were on the bridge, ducked down.

Fox said, 'What the hell gives?'

'Israelis. Someone down there said Mossad.'

'Cover me,' Dillon said to Blake, and ran crouching through the dark to the engine room hatch, pulled it back, took out the two blocks of Semtex from his dive bag, activated the timing pencils, then dropped them down and closed the hatch.

As Dillon ran back to rejoin Blake, who was firing up at the bridge, Sawar made a bad mistake. He switched on more security lights. Dillon and Blake ducked behind a lifeboat, as Sawar fired his machine gun again, and there were cries from members of his crew as they surged on to the aft deck from below, all armed.

Sawar fired repeatedly, Falcone and Russo joining in, and Anya, crouched in the inflatable, sprayed the deck and bridge with fire from her Uzi. Sawar took a bullet in the head and went down. Fox and his two men crouched, Falcone with blood on his face from a glass splinter.

'Now get out of it, Blake,' Dillon said. 'They're three-minute timers, remember. Take the port side. There's another lifeboat there that will give us some protection.'

Anya looked through the Nightstalker. 'I can see them. They're sliding to the port rail,' she said to Moshe Levy.

'Well, they would. Dillon will have planted the Semtex. There's maybe two minutes left.'

'Then get moving.'

He pushed the engine up to top speed, and went round the prow, Anya still firing up on the side deck and bridge, and Dillon and Blake jumped. Fox, peering out of a side window, saw them go, saw the inflatable surge on. Anya tossed a line, Dillon and Blake grabbed it, and the inflatable vanished into the darkness.

'They've jumped ship, Signore,' Falcone said. 'They didn't stay long.'

And Fox, his senses sharpened by years of hard living, jumped to an immediate conclusion.

'That's because they accomplished what they came here to do. Let's get out of here now!'

He scrambled down the ladder and they followed, running into Murphy and Kelly on the side deck.

'What the hell is going on?' Murphy demanded.

'Mossad. They've planted explosives. Move it!'

'Christ.'

They went down the steel stairway fast and crowded into the water taxi. Fox started the engine, Falcone and Russo threw the dead Arab into the water, and Fox took the boat away fast.

They were perhaps a hundred yards away when the explosion took place. The deck lifted, the bridge buckled, flames shot up into the night. Two or three men jumped from the stern, then the *Fortuna* seemed to break in half and went down very fast indeed. There was burning oil, faint screams.

'Shall we go back, Signore?' Falcone asked.

'What for? All I want to do is get back to the airport and get out of this fucking place. Take over.'

He lit a cigarette as they moved towards the pier. Murphy said, 'It's all gone, not just the missiles but the gold.'

'I know. Isn't life hell?' Fox had an insane desire to laugh.

'But how did they know?'

'This is the Middle East, Brendan. The Israelis have had considerable experience at giving the Arabs a hard time. You think they can't find out what Saddam is up to? You think their friends everywhere from London to Washington can't find out?' He tossed his cigarette into the water. 'On top of that, the bastards can fight.'

'All that gold. I can't believe it.'

'Well, better get used to it.'

'Back to Heathrow now?'

'No point sticking around here. Do you and Kelly want a lift?'

'No, we're going to Paris, then Dublin.'

They crashed on to the pier. Fox had left a limousine with an Arab driver waiting. He said, 'I'm going back to the Golden House to pack and move on. Do you want a lift there, at least?'

'No, we'll get a taxi and go right to the airport.'

'No luggage – you lost it all on the boat. They'll think that's funny.'

'I know this place. There's a late-night bazaar. We'll pick up some stuff. No problem.'

'Good.'

They moved away from the others to the end of the pier. Murphy said, 'Christ, I needed that gold.'

'So did I,' Fox said.

'So what will you do?'

'I've something laid on in London that should take care of things.'

'Jesus, do you need a hand?'

'Not this time. What about you?'

'Back to Kilbeg to reflect. I'm not broke.'

'You still owe me on a lot of that equipment in the bunker. I know you've got at least a million on hold there.'

'I know, I know. A few bank raids will take care of the expenses, and the war will start again soon anyway.'

Fox held out his hand. 'Good luck. Stay in touch.'

'I will.'

They went back to the limousine, Fox, Falcone and Russo got in, and it drove away.

Murphy smelled the warm air, the aroma of spices. 'Disgusting, this place, Dermot. Let's go home to some civilization.'

Blake had a bullet crease on his right shoulder. Anya gave him first aid. On the *Pamir*, there was a certain jubilation.

Dillon and he changed, then went into the saloon. Moshe Levy was pouring wine into glasses, and Anya came in from a shower in a towelling robe, drying her hair.

'Where's Gideon?' Dillon asked.

'Making a phone call.'

Gideon was talking to his uncle at his apartment in Tel Aviv. General Cohen listened and slapped his thigh. 'Marvellous. What a coup.'

'Dillon and Blake Johnson are returning to London soon.'

'Well, tell them they go with my blessing. And Anya, she is well?'

'She should get a medal. She was wonderful.'

'Mossad doesn't give medals, you know that. But I *will* give you all a nice dinner.'

In Beirut, Fox, Falcone and Russo boarded their plane, discreetly observed by Lacey and Parry, who had been supplied with photos. The plane rose steadily to fifty thousand feet and turned into the Mediterranean. Russo sat at the back and a woman flight attendant offered drinks and a menu. Fox waved her away.

Falcone sat opposite him. 'Now what, Signore?'

'I don't know, Aldo. I've just lost a fortune. Murphy's lost a lot, and he owes me God knows how much for those arms in that bunker in County Louth. The Colosseum is closed down.' He took a deep breath. 'We've only got the Jagos left and that White Diamond Company job. Ten million. Four to them leaves me with six.'

The attendant handed Falcone a vodka martini. He savoured it and said, 'Why not the full ten, Signore? Why not all the proceeds? Russo and I could handle it. It'd go a long way to making up what you just lost.'

Fox tasted his glass of champagne. 'You really are a very bad man, Aldo. But I like it.'

Falcone smiled, recalling his conversation in the washroom at the airport with Don Marco on his mobile. He'd recounted the whole sorry affair.

Don Marco had said, 'It just gets worse. If I didn't know better, I'd say it was Dillon and Johnson again. But you say it was the Israelis?'

'No doubt about it. They identified themselves.'

'It's like he was snakebit. All right, Aldo, watch out for him, okay?'

Remembering, Falcone said, 'The Jagos. They're *animali*, Signore. As I say, let Russo and me take care of them.'

'It's certainly an interesting thought.' Fox smiled. 'We'll see.'

In London, Ferguson listened to Dillon on his Codex and nodded. 'What an absolutely marvellous result. Our friends at Mossad have performed magnificently, but you and Blake haven't done too badly, either.'

'Why, Brigadier, praise from you is praise indeed.'

'Don't let it go to your head, Dillon. We'll see you soon.'

He sat there by the fire in his flat, thinking about it, then called for his Daimler, got a coat on, and told his driver to take him to Pine Grove, where he knew Hannah Bernstein was working on Sean Regan. Helen Black greeted him and took him to Roper's suite, where the Major sat at one of his screens, Regan on one side, Hannah on the other.

'Well, children, you'll be delighted to know that Al Shariz has resounded to a most satisfactory explosion. The SS *Fortuna*, crewed by Army of God fanatics, is no more. Not only the Hammerheads, but the five million in gold, which was supposed to have been split between Murphy and Fox, has gone down, thanks to Czechoslovakia's gift to the world, Semtex, in one hundred fathoms of water.'

'Holy Mary,' Regan said.

'A moment, Brigadier.' Roper punched at the keys and checked his screen. 'Two hundred fathoms, actually. There's a trench in that harbour. Be a little difficult to retrieve, anyway.'

'What next, sir?' Hannah asked. 'Kilbeg?'

'How far have we got?'

'Oh, Sean's being very cooperative. I'm assembling a ground plan,' Roper said. 'Would you like to see?'

'No, let's wait for Dillon and Blake.' He turned to Hannah. 'Any word from Salter?'

'No, sir.'

'I think I'll go and see him.'

'Do you want me to come, sir?'

Ferguson shook his head. 'No, you continue here with Regan and the Major.' He turned to Helen Black. 'How would you fancy an excursion into the London underworld, Sergeant Major?'

'Why, I can't think of anything I'd like more, Brigadier.'

'Good, let's be on our way, then,' and Ferguson led the way out.

# LONDON

# 10

Salter and Billy were in the Blind Beggar, one of London's most famous pubs, in its heyday the haunt of gangsters such as the Kray brothers, the Richardsons and others. It was crowded and busy at that time in the evening, although a lot of the crowd were tourists, for organized trips were very much a part of the scene.

Salter waved to a small man, an albino in a black tee-shirt and suit. 'One of the best lock and safe men in the business, Billy. Manchester Charlie Ford. The big black guy with him is Amber Frazer. Very good with his hands, though, mind you, he's got a brain. They're an item.'

'What do you mean, an item?' Billy asked.

'You know, gay. Homosexual.'

Billy shook his head. 'Well, all I can say is they're missing out on a damn good thing.'

'Takes all sorts, Billy. We'll have him over.'

He beckoned, and Ford approached, with Frazer by his side. 'Charlie, my old son, and Amber.' Salter shook hands. 'My nephew, Billy. Watch yourselves. He's a right villain.'

'Aren't we all?' Ford said.

'Join us for a drink. I might be able to put a bit of business your way.'

He'd already heard that Ford and his friends were booked up, but was testing the water.

'What are you suggesting, Harry?' Ford asked.

'Well, I'm organizing something big. I won't say what, but I'd need a top man with your skills, and let's face it, Charlie, you *are* the top man.'

'When are we talking about?'

'Next couple of weeks.'

'No way, Harry, I mean, next month could be all right, but I'm booked right now.'

'Well, good for you. It's a nice one, I hope.'

'Very nice, Harry, very special.'

'Say no more. What I don't know, I can't talk about.' He kept the façade going. 'What about Phil Shapiro?'

'Got turned over last week. They're holding him at West End Central. You could try Hughie Belov. Mind you, he claims to be retired, but he taught me a lot. Depends on what you're offering.'

'Thanks for the idea,' Salter told him.

At that moment, the Jago brothers walked in and stood at the end of the bar. Ford said, 'Got to go, old son. See you around.'

'Take care,' Salter told him.

Ford and Frazer joined the Jagos. Billy said, 'That settles it, I'd say.'

'Yeah. But we still need to know exactly what they're up to.'

'How do we do that?'

'The old-fashioned way. Follow them to see where it leads. Come on.'

Baxter and Hall waited in the Range Rover parked up the street. Salter said, 'Don't bother with me, I'll get a taxi. You wait with Billy. The Jagos are inside, with Manchester Charlie Ford. When they come out, follow them. You've got those night glasses in the glove compartment, Joe, the Russian things.'

140

'Sure have, Harry.'

'Get on with it, then,' and Salter walked away.

It was half an hour later that the Jagos emerged, with Ford and Frazer. They went up the street to a Ford station wagon, got inside, and drove away. To Billy's surprise, they were aiming for home territory, Wapping. There was plenty of late evening traffic and Baxter stayed well back. The station wagon finally turned into a narrow road between old warehouses, mostly refurbished.

'St Richard's Dock,' Baxter said. 'They turned all the old warehouses into offices and such last year.'

'Any housing, apartments?' Billy asked.

'No.'

'Then what the hell are they up to? Pull in at the end of the street and give me those glasses.'

Baxter parked in the shadow of a wall and they got out. Billy focused the glasses, as the Jagos and the other two got out and went down stone steps to the shingle beach beside the river. They started to walk, and Billy watched, for they were clearly seen in the strange green glow of the glasses.

'The tide's out,' Hall said. 'Otherwise, they'd be swimming.'

'They've disappeared,' Billy said. 'We'll wait.'

It was ten minutes later that the Jagos and the others reappeared and walked back along the beach. They climbed the steps, got in the station wagon, and drove away.

'Okay,' Billy said. 'Get the torch from the Range Rover, Joe, and we'll take a look.'

He found what he was looking for with no trouble, an arched entrance to a tunnel, dark and wet, lichen growing over the ancient stoneware. There was a damp river smell to everything. He led the way, probing the darkness with the torchlight, and came to a huge rusting iron grille gate. There was a lock, everything corroded tight.

'So what are they up to?' Baxter asked.

141

'God knows, but we'll find out. Back to Harry,' and he turned and led the way out.

In his personal booth at the end of the bar at the Dark Man, Harry Salter sipped beer and listened. 'St Richard's Dock. I've got a piece of that, Billy.' He called to Dora and she came round the bar. He put an arm round her waist. 'Have a look in the file in my office, love, St Richard's Dock.'

'Anything for you, Harry.'

'Yes, I know that, only just get me the bleeding file.'

She was back in a couple of minutes. He opened the file, took out a plan and checked it. 'Two merchant banks, estate agent, property developers, two restaurants, the White Diamond Company.' He sat back. 'Jesus Christ, no, they couldn't. I mean, a place like that these days. It's state-of-the-art security. The bleeding works. I can't believe this.'

Strangely, it was Billy who said, 'Just take it slowly, Harry. Let's consider what they were doing on the beach in that tunnel.'

'You're right, Billy, you're learning.' He turned to Hall. 'Have a look in the saloon bar. See if that old geezer Handy Green's in. He usually is. Used to be a barge captain. There's nothing he doesn't know about the river – more than me, and that's saying something.'

Hall went off, and returned a moment later with an ancient and wizened man, all shrivelled up inside a reefer coat and jeans.

Salter said, 'Handy, my old son. Come and join us for a drink. I think you might be able to help me.'

'Anything, Harry, anything I can do, you know that.'

'The thing is, Handy, I've got a problem. You know St Richard's Dock?'

''Course I do, Harry.'

'They've redeveloped all the warehouses, offices, all that.'

'Finished it last year. I used to work the boats, the old sailing barges from there when I was a kid.'

142

'There's an interesting thing,' Harry said. 'Billy happened to be on the beach there and noticed the entrance to a tunnel.'

'Well, he would, if the tide was out. If the tide's in, the entrance is covered. It's called St Richard's Force.'

'What the hell is that supposed to mean?' He took the large brandy Dora brought and gave it to the old man.

'Oh, it's a medieval thing. Force meaning pressure, and when the tide goes up, the water goes in that tunnel like you wouldn't believe.' Handy swallowed his brandy greedily. 'The thing is, Harry, it's an interest of mine, London under the ground. There's tunnels from Roman times, Norman times, Tudor sewers, then the Victorians covered everything up. I mean, all these modern multi-storey buildings and office blocks haven't the slightest idea of how many tunnels and sewers go through their foundations.'

'And you do?'

'Always been an interest of mine.'

'And St Richard's Dock?'

'Riddled, Harry, it's like a honeycomb down there.'

'Are you sure?'

'Harry, I've got old books with maps, Victorian.'

'Really?' Salter turned to Billy. 'Do me a favour, Billy, take Handy round to his place and get these books. I'll phone Ferguson, tell him what we've got.' Which he did, and Ferguson, alerted on his mobile, returned to Pine Grove.

An hour later at Pine Grove, Handy Green sat with Roper and showed him some very interesting plans in some very old books. Roper checked the information, then got to work. Ferguson and Salter watched with Billy. Baxter and Hall were in the canteen. The screen came alive with ground plans.

'Extraordinary,' Roper said.

'What is it?' Ferguson asked.

'A network of Victorian tunnels and sewers adjacent to the St Richard's Dock infrastructure. There are places where

143

you'd only need a sledgehammer to smash through Victorian brick into the St Richard's basement.'

'So what's that bleeding mean?' Salter demanded.

Roper said, 'Let me check the St Richard's specifications.' His fingers moved on. Finally, he nodded. 'Interesting. State-of-the-art security, but it's all external. If you come up like a mole, you're home free.'

'That's it, it must be,' Salter said.

'I'd say.' Roper turned to Ferguson. 'Brigadier?'

'Looks like it, but when are they going to do it, that's the thing.' He turned to Salter and his nephew. 'Will you stay on the case? We know the place, but we need to know the time.'

'Well, I don't think it's on Tuesday, if you follow me. Not from what Manchester Charlie Ford indicated. It'll be a week to two weeks.'

'Well, do what you can.'

'A pleasure, Brigadier. It makes a change being on the right side for once. Come on, Billy, we'll leave and take Handy with us. Tell you what, we'll keep an eye on the beach.'

They left, and Ferguson said to Roper, 'Do you have anything for me on County Louth?'

'I've extracted everything I can from Regan. From what I've surmised, I've done a breakdown on the Kilbeg place. Do you want a quick look?'

'If you like.'

When Roper was finished, Ferguson sat there thinking about it. 'A tricky one.'

'Very.'

'But I think it should be done sooner rather than later, in view of what's happened.'

'I'd be inclined to agree.'

'Let's have something in the canteen and wait for Dillon and Blake.'

'Just one thing, Brigadier.'

'Feel free.'

'I'm an old Irish hand, and I tell you now, there's no way you can drive into that coastal area of County Louth and pretend to be tourists.'

'Yes, I can see that. You're suggesting a sea approach?'

'It's the only way.'

'Show me County Down, Louth, the Scottish coast.'

Roper tapped it up obediently. 'There you go.'

Ferguson said, 'What would you say about Oban on the west coast there? Would that be a suitable point of departure?'

'Perfect, Brigadier.'

'Excellent.' Ferguson took out his mobile and called Hannah Bernstein at the office. 'Dillon not in yet?'

'Just landed at Farley Field, sir.'

'Good. I want him down here, Blake, too. Things are moving, Superintendent. We're going to make an Irish expedition. Speak to transportation. A motor cruiser, that kind of thing.'

'Certainly, sir. Home port?'

'Oban. Any equipment Dillon needs, we'll call him when he arrives. Make the meeting here and come yourself. I'm sorry, but I may have to put you in harm's way again.'

'It's what I'm paid for, sir.'

Dillon and Blake wolfed bacon and eggs and listened to Ferguson and Roper.

Hannah said, 'I think it might be useful if Dillon and Sergeant Major Black had another chat with Regan, sir, just to make sure he's being honest.'

'A sensible idea,' Ferguson said. 'Let's do it.'

They went up to Roper's suite first and he showed them the situation at Kilbeg on the screen. 'It's very remote, a village on the coast, population a hundred or so. Scattered farms, hard-line Catholic Republicans. You couldn't move an inch without the whole countryside knowing.'

'So it's got to be by sea,' Ferguson continued.

Dillon nodded. 'That's right. We'll go under cover of darkness. Do a frogman job, if necessary.'

'Transport's already arranged a suitable boat from Oban,' Hannah said, 'called the *Highlander*. They'll need to know what equipment you want as soon as you can.'

'No problem. I'll draw up a list. Are you coming, Blake?'

'I sure as hell am.'

'Also the Superintendent,' Ferguson said. 'I want an official police presence.'

Dillon sighed. 'At it again, Hannah, trying to get your head blown off. What is it, guilt?'

'Get stuffed, Dillon.'

'Hey, for a nice Jewish girl with a Cambridge degree, that really is elegant.'

She laughed in spite of herself. 'Now what?'

'Oh, let's look at the map again.'

Roper went over it. 'There's this old abbey which is the entrance and cover, but the interesting thing is this rural farmhouse to the east. That's an emergency exit. Regan says they only keep a couple of guys in the bunker as caretakers. Murphy turns up occasionally. He's the local hero.'

'Fine,' Blake said. 'We go in and blow it to hell.'

Ferguson nodded. 'Let's have Regan in for interrogation. You, Sergeant Major Black, Dillon. The same variety hall act, just in case there's something he forgot.'

When Sergeant Miller brought in Regan, Dillon was sitting by the fire. 'Ah, there you are, Sean. They tell me you've been very helpful.'

'I've done all I've been asked.'

Behind the mirror, Ferguson, Blake, Hannah and Roper watched. Suddenly, Roper said, 'He's lying, the bastard's lying.'

'How do you know?'

'Body language, instinct. I don't know, but there's something he hasn't told us.'

'Right, Sergeant Major,' Ferguson told her. 'Put the boot in.'

She burst through the door a moment later, boiling over with rage. 'I'm sick of lies, Dillon. This little sod's lying through his teeth. There are still things he hasn't told us.'

She took out her silenced Colt, and Miller, playing his part, caught her wrist. 'No, ma'am, that's not the way.'

The Colt discharged into the ceiling and Regan cried out in terror.

'All right, anything – anything you want.'

Dillon shoved him down into a chair.

'Okay, we've got Kilbeg, the bunker, the village, even the old granite quarry pier below the cliff. But what did you leave out?'

Regan hesitated, and Helen Black said, 'Oh, this is a waste of time. Let's send him back to Wandsworth.'

'No, for God's sake.'

'There's something. What is it?' Dillon demanded.

'It's the money. Brendan has one of those safes in the floor of the bunker office. He's supposed to have a million pounds in there, proceeds of bank raids, exploitation, that kind of thing.'

'So?' Helen Black demanded.

'He owes that to Fox for arms supplies.'

'Really,' Dillon said.

'Only he's lying. He keeps fobbing Fox off. He's got nearly three million in there.'

Dillon almost fell about laughing. 'Jesus, you mean you're telling me that if we blow the place up, we'll not only be stiffing Murphy, but also Fox? That's beautiful.' He turned to the mirror. 'Isn't that a joy, Brigadier? Come on in.'

Ferguson came in, with Hannah and Blake. 'Very naughty, Regan. Still playing stupid games.'

'Yes, he's an untrustworthy sod,' Dillon said. 'In the circum-stances, I think I'd like to take him along.'

'Really?'

'Just in case of problems. What if there's more he hasn't told us?'

Ferguson nodded. 'Yes, I take your point. Would you agree, Superintendent?'

'Well, she'll need to, as she'll have to take care of the bastard.'

'What are you getting at?' Hannah asked.

'There's no sense in wasting time. If you get the quarter-master to fill my order and have the boat ready, Blake and I will fly up later this afternoon. There is an RAF base near Oban. We'll get things shipshape. They'll fly back and pick you up in the morning and do the return journey. We'll do the trip tomorrow afternoon and hit Kilbeg tomorrow night.'

'You're not wasting time, are you?' Ferguson said.

'Can't see much point, Brigadier.'

'Fine by me.'

'There's just one thing,' Dillon said. 'Blake took a bullet at Al Shariz.'

'Hell, it's a crease only. Anya fixed it.' Blake was indignant.

'Blake, if we do have to go in underwater, it isn't on.'

'So what you're saying is you want another diver?' Ferguson said. 'It's a bit short notice, but if I phone Marine Headquarters they could possibly find someone from the Special Boat Squadron.'

'No good. They cut their hair, those boys, they'd never pass for locals. Now, SAS at Hereford have plenty of lads who haven't seen a barber in months. That's so they can go undercover in Belfast at a moment's notice and look like they're off a building site.' Dillon smiled.

'That makes sense,' Blake said. 'When you put me in there undercover the other year, I recall it was dicey as hell.'

'So,' Dillon said. 'I've got another diver in mind.'

'Who?' Ferguson demanded.

Dillon told him.

The Brigadier laughed helplessly. 'Oh, I like it. I really do. Do you mind if I come with you and hear him turn you down?'

'No problem, Brigadier, it'll be the best pub grub in London. Meanwhile, though, I want Blake's shoulder checked out by Daz at Rosedene.'

'Rosedene?' Blake asked.

'A private clinic we use near Pine Grove. We have a very nice man, a professor of surgery at London University, who, shall we say, helps us out.'

Ferguson said to Regan, 'Fancy a sea trip to Ireland, do you?'

'I don't have much choice, do I?' But already, his mind was racing.

Ferguson turned to Helen Black and Miller. 'Take him away. The Superintendent will pick him up tomorrow.'

'Fine, sir.' Miller took Regan by the arm and she followed them out.

Ferguson said, 'All right, Dillon, take Blake to Rosedene. The Superintendent will phone ahead and make sure Daz is there. We'll go back to the office. I'll meet you for lunch.' He laughed. 'I can't wait to get his reaction. Hope he's a patriot.'

'People like him usually are, Brigadier.'


Rosedene was an exclusive townhouse in its own grounds. The receptionist greeted Dillon like an old friend, spoke on the phone, and a pleasant, middle-aged woman in matron's blue came out of her office. She had the accent of Ulster, like Dillon, and kissed him on the cheek.

'Have you been in the wars again, Sean?'

'No, Martha, but he has,' and he introduced Blake.

'Well, let's get on with it. Mr Daz is waiting.'

'Mister?' Blake was puzzled.

'In England, ordinary physicians are "doctor", but surgeons are "mister".' Dillon smiled. 'And only the English could explain that to you. In his case, he's also "professor".'

She took them along a corridor and opened the door into a well-equipped operating theatre. Daz, in a white coat, was sitting at a desk reading some papers, a tall, cadaverous Indian with a ready smile.

He got up and took Dillon's hand. 'Sean, it's not you this time. What a change.'

'No, it's my friend, Blake Johnson.'

'Mr Johnson, a pleasure. And what is the problem?'

'A superficial gunshot wound. I mean, it's nothing.'

'It never is, my friend.' Daz turned to the matron. 'Under the circumstances, Martha, I'd rather not have one of the girls in. Would you be kind enough to assist?'

'Of course, Professor. I'll get ready.'

Daz said, 'Stay if you want, Sean.'

Blake, stripped to his waist, stood while Daz and Martha, suitably robed, got to work.

'My goodness, you *have* been to the wars.' Daz probed under the left ribs. 'Bullet scars are always distinctive.'

'Another here,' Martha said. 'Under the left shoulder.'

'Vietnam,' Blake said. 'A long time ago.'

'But not this, I think,' Daz said, as Martha cut away the pad on the right shoulder. He made a face. 'Nasty.'

'Hell, it's nothing,' Blake told him.

Daz ignored him. 'Yes, well, *nothing* requires some very careful stitching. How many would you say, Martha? Fifteen? Perhaps twenty. In the circumstances, I don't think a local anaesthetic will do. We'll need a general. Get Doctor Hamed for me. I know he's here. He can assist.'

'Now, look here, I don't want to be on my back,' Blake said. 'I've got things to do.'

'Not if you have a crippled shoulder for the rest of your life.'

Martha said, 'Do as you're told, Mr Johnson. You're not a stupid man.' She turned to Dillon. 'Leave him to it. Check in this afternoon.'

'For God's sake, Sean,' Blake said.

'No problem. If you're not fit, you can come up to Oban tomorrow with Hannah and Regan.'

At that moment, Billy Salter drove up to St Richard's Dock in the Range Rover and parked. He got out and walked along the embankment to where an old Ford van was parked, opened the door, and got in beside Joe Baxter, who was looking down at the shingle beach through a pair of old binoculars. He lowered them.

'What is it?' Billy asked.

'Well, having nothing to do, we checked out that café where Manchester Charlie Ford has breakfast. The thing is, he wasn't only with the big beast.'

'Go on, surprise me.'

'Connie Briggs.'

'Well, that's good. He's about the best on any kind of electronic security system in London.'

'I know, he's a genius.'

'Who else?'

'Val French.'

'Jesus. The big expert with the thermal lance. Cut up those security boxes on that Gatwick gold bullion job like sardine cans. We all know that.'

'So do Scotland Yard, but they couldn't prove it.'

'So why are we here?'

'They all came down in a Toyota van. We followed. They got out carrying a couple of canvas bags, went along the beach, the tide being out, and went along to the tunnel entrance. Sam's down there now, tucked behind that old wreck.'

Billy took the binoculars, focused them, and at that moment Manchester Charlie Ford and the others came out of the tunnel and went back to the steps up to the dock.

They all got in the Toyota and drove away. 'Give me the torch and let's take a look.'

'Let them go,' Billy said.

The tunnel was damp from the receding early morning tide, the brickwork green, as Billy switched on the torch. The rusting iron grille was there as before. The only difference was that the huge old lock had gone and the gate responded to a strong heave.

'Well, well,' Billy said. 'Let's take a look.'

They followed the tunnel, sloshing through two or three inches of water. It seemed to go on for ever and there were side tunnels.

'All right,' Billy said. 'Enough is enough. We're under the dock and there's nothing important. Let's go back.'

They arrived back at the Dark Man at noon and found Salter in his usual booth. He listened and nodded.

'Okay, it's on, and it's got to be the White Diamond Company. I'll check with Ferguson.'

At that moment, Ferguson and Dillon walked in.

'I can't believe it,' Billy said. 'We were just talking about you and here you are.'

'Magic, Billy,' Dillon said. 'It's with me being from County Down.'

'What are you after, Brigadier?' Salter asked.

'Cottage pie for lunch and an indifferent red wine would do, for a start.'

'Yes, well we've got news for you,' Billy said, and told him.

Ferguson took out his mobile and called Roper at Pine Grove and relayed the information. 'I'm concerned with timing here. It's just occurred to me. If you could access the White Diamond Company, we might find something is going on.'

'Leave it with me, Brigadier.'

Ferguson put his phone down. 'So, we could be in business, gentlemen. It's an OBE for you, Harry, for services to the country.'

'Fuck off, Brigadier.'

Dora appeared. 'Cottage pie, love, and a bottle of that Krug champagne, as Dillon's here.'

She walked away and Dillon said, 'It's the great man you are, Harry.'

'What are you trying to do, you little Irish git, butter me up?'

'Actually, yes. I need a favour.'

'What favour?'

'I need a master diver, and the only one I know on short notice is Billy.'

Salter was totally shocked. 'You've got to be kidding.'

'No. My American friend Blake took a bullet in the shoulder and won't be too fit. I'm taking a boat into a remote part of the Irish coast, where there's an underground bunker full of the wrong kind of weapons waiting to be used in the next round of the Irish troubles. I intend to blow it to hell, and as friend Fox has a financial interest, I'll get extra pleasure.' He turned to Billy. 'Listen, you young dog, it'll be a good deed in a naughty world. Are you with me?'

Billy had an unholy light in his eyes. 'By God, I am, Dillon. These fucks come over and blow up London. Let's go and blow them up.'

'Billy?' his uncle said.

Ferguson's phone rang. He listened, then said, 'Fine. I'll talk later.' He drank a little champagne. 'That was Major Roper. He's accessed the White Diamond Company's computer. They're receiving a consignment of top-grade diamonds on Thursday. Ten million pounds' worth.'

Dillon said, 'So we know where we are.' He turned. 'Harry?'

Salter said, 'What the hell, we're with you.'

153

'Excellent.' Dillon smiled. 'It's Scotland for you, Billy, and a nice sea voyage.'

'Christ,' Billy said. 'I get seasick.'

'We'll stop at a pharmacist and get you some pills on the way to Farley Field. That'll be three hours from now, after which you'll be winging your way north.'

'I've never been to Scotland,' Billy said.

'Well, we'll take care of that.' Dillon smiled as Dora brought plates of food to the table.

'Cottage pie and Krug champagne, and God help Brendan Murphy.'

# SCOTLAND
# IRELAND

# 11

Blake was flat out when Dillon called at Rosedene to check on his condition. Hannah was with him. Daz was at the university, but Martha was there.

'He'll be fine, but not particularly fit for a while,' she said, and frowned. 'He's not going to get up to any nonsense, I hope, Mr Dillon? I know what your lot are like, and he honestly isn't up to it.'

'I know, Martha. I know. We'll take it as it comes. I'm flying off to Scotland, so keep the Superintendent here informed.'

'Trouble again?' she asked.

'Always is.' He kissed her cheek.

'Oh, well,' she said, and gave him the ancient toast. 'May you die in Ireland.'

'Oh, thanks very much.' Dillon laughed. 'See you soon.'

He and Hannah left.

On the way to the Dark Man, she said, 'It could be a hard one, Sean.'

'I know, and Blake won't be up to it. Frankly, in his condition, he'd be a liability.'

'What do you want me to do?'

'Try and lose him. With luck, you won't have to do much.

Maybe Martha could give him a pill.'

'Always the practical one, aren't you.'

'He's a good man, Hannah, I'm the bad one. I don't care about that, but I do care about him.'

'I'll never understand you.'

'I don't understand me. Join the club. I'm just passing through, Hannah, I'd have thought you'd have realized that by now.'

Dillon phoned ahead, and Billy was waiting outside the Dark Man with his uncle, Baxter and Hall.

Harry said, 'I actually care for this young bastard, so bring him back in one piece, Dillon. Notice I didn't say *try*, so don't let me down, because if you come back alone . . .'

'I get the picture,' Dillon said. 'In you get, Billy.'

The driver put the case in the boot and Billy sat in front, nervous and excited. 'Christ, Dillon, what have you got me into?'

'High adventure, Billy. You'll come back and join the Marines.'

'Like hell I will. Independent spirit, me.'


At Farley Field, the department's quartermaster, a retired sergeant major, waited with his list.

'All loaded, Mr Dillon. Walthers with Carswell silencers, three Uzi machine pistols with silencers. Stun grenades, and half a dozen of the fragmentation variety, in case you have trouble, plus the Semtex and timers.'

'What about diving equipment?'

'Standard suits and fins as issued to the Special Boat Service. Our local agent in Oban will put six air bottles in the stern rack. That should suffice.'

'Excellent.' Lacey was already in the Gulfstream with Parry; Madoc waited at the bottom of the steps.

Dillon kissed Hannah on the cheek. 'We who are about to die salute you.'

'Don't be stupid. I'll see you tomorrow.'

'I know, and watch Regan. He's a devious little sod.'

158

'I thought that was you.'

It was such a stupid remark, and instantly regretted, but Dillon smiled. 'Ah, the hard woman you are.'

He pushed Billy up the steps in front of him, Madoc followed and closed the door, and the Gulfstream moved away.

'Why?' Hannah whispered. 'Why do I say things like that?' And yet she knew that, for her, his past condemned him. All those years as the Provisional IRA's most feared enforcer, all the killing.

She looked up as the Gulfstream lifted. 'Damn you, Dillon,' she said. 'Damn you.'

In his suite at Pine Grove, Roper trawled the computer and came up with results. He checked again, then phoned Ferguson.

'Fox and his two goons are booked into the Dorchester for a week.'

'Anything else?'

'Murphy and Dermot Kelly are booked on an Air France flight from Paris, arriving in Dublin around what the Irish call tea time.'

'Any idea of the onward destination?'

'Come on, Brigadier, it must be Kilbeg. They think he's Robin Hood up there. If you want to check, why don't you call in a favour from that Chief Superintendent Malone at the Garda Special Branch?'

'What an excellent idea,' Ferguson said.

He thought about it, then rang through to Malone in Dublin. 'Charles Ferguson, Daniel.'

Malone groaned. 'What in the hell do you want, Charles?'

'A favour.'

At Dublin Airport, Murphy and Kelly landed at four-thirty, proceeded through customs with light luggage, went out of the concourse and approached an old Ford saloon car. The driver was named John Conolly, the man beside him Joseph Tomelty; both were hard-line Republicans and had been members of Murphy's group for many years, all boyhood friends. They shook hands with Murphy and Kelly.

'Good to see you, Brendan,' Conolly said. 'Did it go well?'

'A total fuck-up,' Murphy said. 'Couldn't have been worse. Let's get out of it. Make for home and I'll tell you.'

They all got in and drove away, and Malone, sitting in an unmarked car with a driver, said, 'Jesus. Conolly, Tomelty, plus Brendan and Dermot Kelly. The old Kilbeg Mafia. There's no doubt where they're going, but follow at a discreet distance and let's make sure they're taking the right road north.'

Twenty minutes later and well outside Dublin, he tapped the driver on the arm. 'Turn back. It's got to be Kilbeg.'

A few minutes later, as the car returned to Dublin, he called Ferguson on his mobile and told him what had happened.

'So it's Kilbeg?' Ferguson said.

'I'd say definitely. Are you going to give us trouble here, Charles?'

'Don't be silly, Daniel, we're doing ourselves a favour and you a favour. Leave it alone and I'll keep you informed.'

'One more question. Since you're running this, it means Dillon's involved.'

'Obviously.'

'Then God help Brendan Murphy.'

Ferguson put down his phone and turned to Hannah, who had been listening. 'You heard? Murphy and company are on their way to Kilbeg.'

'I'll let Dillon know, sir, in case it affects his plans.'

'It won't make much difference. You know what he's like. He'll go in tomorrow night anyway, Murphy or no Murphy. Just like a bad war movie.'

'I know, sir. He has a kind of death wish.'

'Why?'

'God knows.'

'You really have it in for him, Superintendent.'

'You couldn't be more wrong, sir. Actually, I like him too much. He reminds me of Liam Devlin, that combination of scholar, actor, poet and absolutely cold-blooded killer.'

'Just like Sir Walter Raleigh,' Ferguson said. 'Very bewildering, life, on occasion.'

Dillon and Billy were delivered by an unmarked RAF car driven by two uniformed RAF sergeants named Smith and Brian.

'Checked it out earlier,' Sergeant Brian said. 'That's the *Highlander* two hundred yards out.'

'Well, it doesn't look much to me,' Billy told him.

'Don't go by appearances. It's got twin screws, depth sounder, radar, automatic steering. Does twenty-five knots at full stretch.'

'Good. Let's get cracking,' Dillon said.

'Right, sir, we've got a whaleboat to take your gear out.'

Forty minutes later, the gear was stowed, everything shipshape. Brian said, 'You've got the inflatable, with a good outboard motor. We'll get back now.'

'Thanks for a good job,' Dillon told him.

The sergeants departed in the whaleboat, and Dillon's mobile rang. It was Hannah Bernstein, bringing him up to date on the Kilbeg situation.

'Murphy being there, will it give you a problem?'

'Only if I can't shoot the bastard. How's Blake?'

'Still on his back.'

'Good, let's keep it that way. We'll see you tomorrow.'

Oban was enveloped in mist, and a fine rain was driving across the water, pushed by a light wind. Above on the land, low clouds draped across mountain tops, but beyond Kerrera the waters of the Firth of Lorn looked troubled.

'This is Scotland?' Billy said. 'What a bloody awful place. Why would anybody come here for a holiday?'

161

'Don't tell the tourist board, Billy, they'd lynch you. Now, we've things to do. We can go ashore and eat later.'

He laid out the diving equipment in the stern cabin. 'I don't need to explain this to you, you're an expert, but let's check over the arms.'

They laid the Walthers, the Semtex, the Uzis and stun grenades on the main saloon table. 'Let's give you a quick course on the Uzi, Billy. The Walther is simple enough.'

They spent half an hour going over things, then Dillon took one of the Walthers and led the way up to the wheelhouse. There was a flap to one side of the instrument board. He found a button, pressed, and inside was a fuse board. He cocked the Walther, slipped it inside, and closed the flap.

'Ready for action with ten rounds, Billy. Remember it's there. It's what is called an ace in the hole.'

'You think of everything, don't you?'

'That's why I'm still here. Let's go ashore and eat.'

He switched on the deck lights before they left and they coasted to the front at Oban on the inflatable and tied up. There was a pub close by that offered food. They went in, had a look at the menu, and opted for fish pie.

Dillon ordered a Bushmills, but Billy shook his head. 'Not me. I never liked the booze, Dillon. There must be something wrong with me.'

'Well, most things in life are in the Bible, and what the good book says is: wine is a mocker, strong drink raging.' He smiled. 'Having said that, I'll finish this and have another.'

Later, back on the *Highlander*, it started to rain harder. They sat on the stern deck under the awning, and Dillon went through everything from Katherine Johnson's death in New York to Al Shariz.

Billy said, 'These Mafia guys are fucks, Dillon, and Murphy's no better.'

'That about sums it up.'

'So we take them out?'

'I hope so.'

The rain drummed on the canvas awning and Dillon poured another whisky.

Billy said, 'Listen, Dillon, I know a little bit about you, the IRA hard man who switched sides. But every time I ask my uncle how it all happened, he clams up. What's the story?'

Maybe it was the rain, and maybe it was the whisky, but instead of giving him a hard look and telling him to mind his business, Dillon felt himself talking, the words coming slowly but steadily.

'I was born in Ulster, my mother died giving birth to me – a heavy load to bear. My father took me to London. He was a good man. A small builder. Got me into St Paul's School.'

'I thought that was for toffs?'

'No, Billy, it's for brains. Anyway, I liked the acting. Went to the Royal Academy. Only did a year and joined the National Theatre. I was still only nineteen. My father went home to Belfast and got caught in a firefight between IRA and Brit paratroopers.'

'Jesus, that was a bastard.'

Dillon poured another whisky, looking back into the past. 'Billy, I was a damn good actor, but I went back to Belfast and joined the IRA.'

'Well, you would. I mean, they killed your old man.'

'And I was nineteen, but they were nineteen, Billy, mostly a lot like you. Anyway, the IRA had access to camps in Libya. I was sent for training. Three months, and there wasn't a weapon I didn't know inside out. You wanted a bomb, I could make it, any bomb.' He hesitated. 'Only that side I never liked. Passers-by, women, kids – that isn't war.'

'That's how you saw it, war?'

'For a long time, yes, then I moved on. I was a professional soldier, so I sold my services. ETA in Spain, Arabs,

163

Palestinians, also the Israelis. Funny, Billy, the job I've just done in Lebanon, blowing up a ship with arms for Saddam. Back in 'ninety-one, I worked for them.'

'You what?'

'Gulf War. I did the mortar attack on Downing Street in the snow. You wouldn't remember that.'

'I bleeding well do. I've read articles. They used a Ford Transit, then a guy on a motorbike picked up the bomber.'

'That was me, Billy.'

'Dillon, you bastard. You nearly got the Prime Minister and the entire Cabinet.'

'Yes, almost, but not quite. I made a great deal of money out of it. I'm still rich, if you like. Later, I got into trouble in Bosnia. I was due to face a Serb firing squad, only Ferguson turned up, saved my miserable skin, and in return I had to work for him. You see, Billy, he wanted someone who was worse than the bad guys, and that was me.'

There was a kind of infinite sadness, and Billy surprised himself by saying quietly, 'What the hell, sometimes life just rolls up on you.'

'You could say that. The kid who was an actor at nineteen carried on acting just like in a bad movie, only he became the living legend of the IRA. You know those Westerns where they say Wyatt Earp killed twenty-one men? Billy, I couldn't tell you what my score is, except that it's a lot more.' He smiled gently. 'Do you ever get tired? I mean, really tired?'

Billy Salter summoned up all his resources. 'Listen, Dillon, you need to go to bed.'

'True. It's not much good when you don't sleep very well, but there's no harm in trying.'

'You do that.'

Dillon got up, rock steady. 'The trouble is, I don't really care whether I live or die any more, and when you're into the business of going into harm's way, that's not good.'

'Yes, well, this time you've got me. Just go to bed.'

Dillon went down the companionway. Billy sat there thinking about it, the rain beating down relentlessly, dripping off the awning. He'd never liked anyone as much as he liked Dillon, never admired anyone as much, outside of his uncle, anyway. He lit a cigarette and thought about it and suddenly saw a parallel. His uncle was a gangster, a right villain as they said in London, but there were things he wouldn't do, and Billy saw now that Dillon was the same.

He looked at the bottle of Bushmills morosely. 'Screw you,' he said, then picked it up, and the glass, and tossed them over the rail.

He sat there, the rain falling, feeling curiously relaxed, then remembered the paperback on philosophy, took it out of his pocket, and opened it at random. There were some pages about a man called Oliver Wendell Holmes, a famous American judge who'd also been an infantry officer in their Civil War: *Between two groups of men that want to make inconsistent kinds of worlds, I see no remedy except force . . . It seems to me that every society rests on the death of men.*

Billy was transfixed. 'Jesus,' he said softly, 'maybe that explains Dillon,' and he read on.

He awoke in the morning in the aft cabin, and was lying there, adjusting, when he was aware of a loud cry. He threw aside his blankets and went up the companionway in his shorts. It was still raining relentlessly and mist draped the whole of Oban harbour. As he looked over the rail, Dillon surfaced a few yards away.

'Come on, the water's wonderful.'

'You must be bloody mad,' and then Billy cried out. 'Behind you, for Christ's sake.'

Dillon turned to look. 'Those are seals, Billy. No problem. They're intelligent and curious. You get them a lot around here.'

He struck out for the ladder and climbed it, his shorts clinging to him. There was a towel on the table under the awning and he picked it up.

'What a bleeding place.' Billy looked out across the harbour. 'Does it always rain like this?'

'Six days out of seven. Never mind. Get dressed and we'll take the inflatable and go back to that pub. We'll get an all-day breakfast, just like in London.'

'Well, I'm with you there.'

Hannah Bernstein called in at Rosedene around nine-thirty and found Martha in reception.

'How is he?'

'Not wonderful. The bullet gouged deep. We thought twenty stitches and ended up with thirty. Look, I don't know what's going on, but he isn't fit to go anywhere. The professor is checking him out now. I'll go and see how he's doing.'

Hannah helped herself to coffee from the machine and was sipping it when Daz appeared.

'Listen, tell me the truth,' he said. 'He's as woozy as hell, yet he keeps trying to tell me he's got important things to do, and I presume by that he means the usual kinds of things you, Dillon and the Brigadier get up to.'

'Absolutely, only this time it's something so dangerous that there's no way he can be involved in his condition. Dillon will handle it.'

'Yes, well, he would, wouldn't he? What do you want from me?'

'I know it sounds unethical, but couldn't you sedate him?'

'Hmm. That might be the best solution.' He turned to Martha. 'He really needs a sound sleep. You know what to do.' He smiled at Hannah. 'If you want to see him, better do it now.'

Blake was propped up, his right shoulder and arm bandaged, and looked awful, his face haggard. Hannah leaned over and kissed his cheek.

'How are you, Blake?'

'Terrible. I just need a rest. A couple of hours, and I'll be fine. When are we leaving?'

'Later this afternoon, but take it easy for now.'

'Christ, it hurts.'

Martha, lurking in the background, came forward with a glass of water and a couple of pills in a plastic cup. 'Here you go,' she said to Blake.

'What are these?'

'Painkillers. You'll feel a lot better soon.'

Hannah held his hand for a while, and slowly it relaxed and slipped away, as he stared blankly at her.

'There he goes,' Martha whispered. 'He'll be asleep for hours.'

They went out and found Daz at reception signing a few letters. He looked up. 'All right?'

'On his way to dreamland,' Martha told him.

'Good. I must go. I've got an operation scheduled at Guy's Hospital.' He smiled at Hannah. 'You'll monitor the situation?'

'The Brigadier will. I'm needed elsewhere.' She nodded to Martha and went out with him to where the Daimler waited. 'Can I give you a lift?'

'I was going to get a taxi, but, yes, a lift would help.'

'Ministry of Defence first, then you belong to Professor Daz,' she told the driver, and they drove away. 'I hate March weather,' she said. 'Bloody rain.'

'Oh, dear, it's like that, is it?' Daz smiled. 'As may not have escaped your attention, I'm a Hindu, Hannah. Personal vibrations are important to me, and I sense you're up to your neck in trouble again, the Dillon kind of trouble.'

'Something like that.'

'When will you learn?'

'I know. I'm a nice Jewish girl, unmarried, with no kids, but very good at shooting people.'

He took her hand. 'Hannah.'

'No, don't say a thing. Dillon and I will go off and save the world again, only increasingly, I wonder what for.'

In Ferguson's office, she said, 'So what's the situation? Dillon and Billy Salter are fine. They're both master divers and Dillon is an expert boat handler. That leaves me and Sean Regan.'

'And without Blake, you're one short.'

'Exactly, sir.'

Ferguson got up, went to the window, and looked out. He turned. 'This kind of black operation works best without official special forces intervention. That's why I haven't given the Kilbeg bunker to the SAS. It has to be the kind of job that never happened.'

'Yes, I see that, sir. On the other hand, we could do with another gun, just to be on the boat when Dillon and Billy are doing their thing on shore.'

'It's a difficult one. Do you have any thoughts?'

'Yes, I do actually. An excellent gun.'

'And who would that be?'

She told him.

Dillon and Billy were sitting in the window seat at a pub in Oban, just finishing a superb Scottish breakfast of kippers, poached eggs and bacon, washed down with hot steaming tea, when Dillon's mobile rang.

Hannah said, 'Blake isn't good. They've sedated him. He'll be out for hours.'

'So you'll be on your way with Regan?'

'Yes, but Sean, we've got a problem. With you and Billy on land, and me with Regan on the boat, we need another gun. No big deal, just somebody reliable who really knows what he's doing.'

'And who would that be?'

She told him what she'd suggested to Ferguson, and Dillon laughed. 'Why not? There's nothing like a professional soldier. When will you leave?'

'Two o'clock. Be with you about four-thirty.'

'I look forward to it.' Dillon closed his phone and smiled. 'There you go, Billy, you'll have to mind your manners.'

'What do you mean?'

So Dillon explained.

Ferguson accompanied Hannah to Pine Grove when she went to pick up Regan. He was in Roper's suite again, going over a few points, and Helen Black stood by, with Miller.

Roper said, 'Well, I think the bastard's told the truth, or his version of it, anyway.'

'I damn well have,' Regan said.

'You'd better.' Ferguson smiled coldly. 'If not, I'll see you stand in the dock, Regan. Fifteen years.' He nodded to Miller. 'Take him and prepare him to move out. Put the manacles on.'

Miller complied, and Ferguson said, 'Get on with it, Superintendent.'

Hannah said, 'We've got a problem, Sergeant Major. You are aware of most of the facts, but let me summarize. We're sailing to County Louth from Oban late this afternoon. There'll be Dillon and Billy Salter, and me to guard Regan. Blake Johnson is unwell after the treatment for his gunshot wound. We're short a gun.'

'I see.' Helen Black smiled. 'How long have I got to pack?'

'Half an hour.'

'Then I'd better get moving.' She was out of the door instantly.

Later, at the main entrance, Hannah led Regan down the steps and eased him into the Daimler on to one of the extra seats. The driver had put the luggage in the boot and Ferguson stood at the top of the steps with Helen Black, who wore a khaki jumpsuit. They were alone for a moment.

'I'm grateful, Helen.'

'Tony's in Bosnia at the moment,' she said, referring to her husband. 'The Household Cavalry has two troops there.'

'I know, my love.'

'There's no need to worry him, but you'll obviously see to things if anything goes wrong.'

'My dear Helen.' He kissed her cheek. 'Just believe in Sean Dillon. He is a bastard of the first order, but my God, he's good.'

'You didn't need to tell me, not with the years I spent in Ulster. See you, Charles, and thanks for asking me to the party.'

At Farley Field, the Gulfstream was ready. Madoc loaded the luggage, then took them in. As Parry and Lacey came on board, Hannah made the introductions.

Lacey said, 'There's a bit of a headwind. It'll be an hour and forty-five minutes, but could run to two.'

He joined Parry in the cockpit, the engines started, and they moved away, taking off very quickly and climbing steeply.

Regan held out his manacled wrists. 'Can I have these off? I'm not going anywhere.'

Helen Black laughed. 'That's true.' She took out a key and unlocked him.

Madoc appeared from the galley. 'Tea, ladies.'

'An excellent idea,' Hannah said.

'Personally, I'd like an Irish whiskey,' Regan told him.

Madoc looked at Hannah, who nodded. 'Give him what he wants, Sergeant.'

Helen Black turned to her. 'Well, here I go, into the war zone again.'

As they returned to the *Highlander*, Billy said, 'Jesus, Dillon, not only two women, but both coppers.'

'Yes, Scotland Yard Special Branch variety and Royal Military Police. But remember one thing, Billy: they've both killed more than once in the course of duty. They both know what they're doing.'

'What have I got myself into?'

'Well, as Heidegger said, and you quoted him to me, life is action and passion . . .'

Billy cut in. 'Okay, so it's going to be bleeding active and terribly exciting.'

'You'll love it, Billy,' Dillon said, as they coasted in and he reached for the *Highlander*'s ladder.

# 12

The rain continued relentlessly. Billy was coiling a rope under the awning when a voice called, '*Highlander*, ahoy.'

Hannah, Helen Black and Regan were standing on the jetty beside a Range Rover, the driver in plain clothes but obviously RAF.

Billy called down the companionway, 'They're here, Dillon.'

Dillon came up on deck and looked across. 'Fine. I'll go and get them.'

The inflatable coasted in at the bottom of the steps and Hannah called, 'Everything okay?'

'Absolutely. Let's have the luggage.'

There were only three bags and the driver brought them down. Regan followed, hands manacled again. He held up his wrists to Dillon. 'I might as well be on a Georgia chain gang.'

'You deserve to be, you shite.' Dillon shoved him into the boat. 'Go on, get in there.' He turned to greet the women. 'Sergeant Major, Superintendent. A fast boat and a passage by night. Action, passion, we've got it all here.'

'How riveting,' Helen Black said. 'I can't wait,' and she stepped into the inflatable.

Dillon handed the luggage up to Billy, and Helen climbed in, followed by Hannah. Hannah looked around the *Highlander*. 'My God, I must say it looks pretty basic.'

'Underneath its lack of a good paint job, it's superb, so don't worry,' Dillon said. 'Just get settled in, stick Sean in the saloon, and let's get on with it.' He turned to Regan. 'Just remember one thing, we're back with the old movies again: one false move and you're dead.'

'Come on, Dillon, you're going to kill me anyway.'

'Not if you're good.'

They put Regan in the saloon, the two women settled into the aft cabin, and Dillon made ready for sea. He took Billy, Hannah and Helen into the wheelhouse and went over the controls, then showed the women the Walther in the fuse box beside the wheel.

'Just in case.'

The sea was starting to flood in through the entrance to the harbour, and the *Highlander* was rocking from side to side.

Billy said, 'Jesus, I feel terrible,' and he turned, went out on deck, and vomited over the side.

Dillon followed, took a plastic pill bottle from a pocket of his reefer jacket, shook the pills out, and offered them. 'Get them down, Billy. They'll make a difference.'

Hannah said, 'Kindness and consideration from the great Sean Dillon?'

Dillon smiled. 'Sticks and stones, Hannah, not that it matters. We've got to leave if we're to make tonight's schedule, so I've other things to worry about. We'll discuss the plan of attack later. The wind's force five to six at the moment, but it should ease later.'

They left at three, and ploughed out into the turbulent waters, the sea running heavily. Dillon stood at the wheel alone. After a while, Helen Black came in with a mug.

'Tea,' she said. 'I believe that's your preference.'

'It's the grand woman you are.'

'I'm part Irish, too, Dillon, from my father's mother's side. In spite of thirty years of war, it seems we're somehow inextricably mixed.'

'Eight million Irish in the UK, Sergeant Major, and the population of the Republic only three and a half million. It's a puzzle.'

'You and the Superintendent, that's a puzzle, too.'

'She's a hard woman, Hannah, a moralist. She finds it difficult to forgive my wicked past. You, on the other hand, understand perfectly. We've both been down the same road on different sides.'

'Yes. That's the problem, isn't it?' And she left.

Billy turned up an hour later with another mug of tea. 'Are you okay, Dillon?'

'I'm fine, but what about you?'

'The pills worked. It's Regan who's in trouble. You'd better give me some more of those pills.'

Dillon handed him the bottle. 'Take care of it, Billy. Let me know how he is.'

Perhaps half an hour later, Billy came back. 'He's lying down, but I think they're doing the job.'

'Good.'

Billy said, 'Dillon, on the White Diamond job. I've been thinking.'

'Go on.' Dillon turned to automatic pilot and lit a cigarette.

'So they've sliced through the grille entrance and we know those tunnels go right into the St Richard's Dock basement. Then all you need is a sledgehammer to break through those old brick walls.'

'So?'

'But the vaults. I still don't see how they get past the electronic security.'

'Neither do I. But there must be a sophisticated explanation. It's like computers, Billy. They're state of the art, too, but if you can get in, if you can access the files, then all is revealed.' Dillon smiled. 'Don't worry. Harry's on the case, and so is Roper. They'll come up with our answer. All I'm concerned with now is Kilbeg, and taking you back to the Dark Man in one piece, because if I don't Harry will want an explanation.'

'Hey, stuff that, Dillon. I'll do my thing.'

'Okay, time for truth, Billy. Since Blake isn't here, it's the women I'm leaving behind. I'll need you to go on shore with me. How do you feel about that?'

'Great.' Billy smiled. 'Never better. I'm with you, Dillon, all the way.' And he went out.

It was into early evening when the wheelhouse door opened and there was the smell of fried bacon sandwiches.

'And tea,' Hannah said.

'Now what's a nice Jewish girl doing, giving me bacon?'

She ignored him. 'Where are we?'

'Islay to the east. Rain's a bit squally.'

'Can I take over?'

'No need. I'll go on automatic pilot.'

Dillon checked the course, then locked on. He attacked the sandwiches. 'Fabulous. Any word from London?'

'No.'

He finished the sandwiches and drank the tea. 'There you go. Thanks, love.'

'I really think you should go and lie down for a couple of hours, and let me take over.'

'Hell, what do women know about boats?'

The wheelhouse door swung open and Helen Black came in. 'Don't be a chauvinist pig, Mr Dillon. I don't know if the Superintendent knows boats, but I do. My husband and I race them as a hobby, so do shut up and go and rest. You're going to have a very hard night.'

175

Dillon raised his hands. 'I give in to this monstrous regiment of women. I'll leave you to it, ladies,' and he went below.

Hannah, too, went, and Helen Black took the wheel, enjoying it as she always had, increasing speed as heavy weather threatened from the east. She thought about her husband, Tony, serving in the hell of Bosnia with the Household Cavalry. It was a source of hurt that just because the Households were the Queen's personal bodyguard and rode round London in breastplates and helmets on horseback there were those who thought they were chocolate soldiers. In fact, they'd served in the Falklands, in the Gulf War, in Ireland, and in most of the rotten little wars in between.

Her trouble was that she was a woman and she was a soldier and she loved the army. Of course, Dillon had been a soldier too, to be fair. She rather liked him, although he'd been the worst of the enemy.

Against the early darkness she could see the outline of one of the Irish ferries, red and green navigation lights visible. She altered course a couple of points, then increased speed, racing the heavy weather that threatened from the east, and the waves grew rougher.

By now it really was dark, only a slight phosphorescent shining from the sea, and then the door opened and Dillon appeared.

'How are things?'

'A bit rough.'

He tapped the radio, got the weather channel, listened, and added, 'That's okay. The wind's going to drop soon. Why don't you go and get some coffee? I'll hang on, then I'll put her on automatic pilot and we can discuss what's going to happen. An hour, an hour and a half, we'll hit the Louth coast.'

'Fine.' She nodded and went out.

Half an hour later, Brendan Murphy, Dermot Kelly, Conolly and Tomelty arrived at Kilbeg and pulled up outside the Patriot public house. Murphy led the way in, running through torrential rain.

It was a typical Irish pub for either side of the border, with a bar, beer pumps, and a log fire in the hearth. There were only three old men at the fire and the landlord behind the bar, one Fergus Sullivan.

'Jesus, Brendan, and it's grand to see you.'

They shook hands. Brendan said, 'You're dying the death tonight.'

'Well, it's Monday night. What can I do for you?'

'Beds for me and Dermot. We've business elsewhere at the moment. We'll have a drink now and see you later.'

Sullivan poured four Irish whiskeys and a fifth for himself.

'Up the IRA.'

'And confusion to the English,' Murphy said.

A short while later, inside the grounds of the ruins of Kilbeg Abbey, they entered an ancient hall and approached a dark old oaken door at one end banded with iron that looked as if it had been there for centuries. In fact it was a modern replica backed by steel plate of the finest quality. Murphy took a transceiver from his pocket and pressed the button. There was the murmur of a voice.

'Murphy,' he said. 'Open sesame.'

A moment later, one half of the door opened electronically. He and Kelly passed through into a short tunnel and went down a flight of concrete steps. There was electric light, another door opened, and in moments they were into a concrete corridor, painted white, very functional, and then into the main part of the bunker.

Two men stood waiting: Liam Brosnan, tall, heavily built, with hair to his shoulders, and Martin O'Neill, the direct opposite, small and red-haired. The only thing they had in common were the AK47 assault rifles they carried.

'Well, at least you're on your toes,' Murphy said. 'Any problems?'

177

'Only one, Brendan,' Brosnan told him. 'Down at the entrance where the tunnel slopes to the steps, there's about a foot of water.'

'Show me.'

They led the way, and Murphy and Kelly followed. It was dark down there and, unlike the rest of the bunker, cold.

'Why is there no heat on, no light?' Murphy demanded.

'Well, that's the point, Brendan. The rest of the bunker's okay, but this part under the old farmhouse is on a separate system and the flooding must have screwed it up.'

'It's the rain,' O'Neill said. 'It's been terrible during the past two weeks.'

'I can tell it's the bloody rain, you eejit,' Murphy said. 'But if the electricity isn't working, that cocks up the entrance. There aren't any bars. They weren't necessary when it was electronic.'

'I've chained the handles and padlocked them,' Brosnan told him. 'I was waiting for you, Brendan. I know you would want someone reliable.'

'Exactly. Don't worry, there's that fella Patterson in Dundalk that builds the fancy houses. He knows which side his bread's buttered on.'

'I know who you mean.'

'You call him and tell him I'll see him at the Patriot for breakfast at eight-thirty tomorrow. Explain the flooding and tell him I expect miracles. He'll attend to it or he'll get a bullet in his left knee, and that's only for starters.'

They walked back through the storage areas. Mortars stacked neatly, the kind of missiles and heavy machine guns that could shoot down a helicopter, AK47s and Armalites still greased and brand new from the factory. Cases of Semtex.

Murphy lit a cigarette and said to Kelly, 'Look at it, Dermot. Just waiting to be used, and those old women in London talk peace.'

'You're right, Brendan.'

'Our day will come. I'll just check the office.'

It was at the end of the tunnel, small, functional, with filing cabinets, a computer system and a desk. He said to Brosnan and O'Neill, 'Wait outside.'

Kelly closed the door. Murphy knelt behind the desk and lifted a section of carpet. Underneath, set into the concrete floor, was an old-fashioned safe with a simple keyhole. He felt under the desk, found a key on a magnetic block, and opened the flap.

Inside were packets of currency, sterling and dollars, all wrapped in transparent plastic bags. He handled a few.

'You think this is cash, Dermot? It's not, it's power. With money you can do anything, and there's almost three million here.'

'What about Fox, Brendan? You know what I mean? What you owe him?'

'Hey, stuff Fox. Look what happened at Al Shariz. It was a total fuck-up, and all because of Fox. It must have been. I mean, how were the Israelis on to us? I know it wasn't me.'

'So you aren't going to pay him what you owe him?'

'Am I hell.' Murphy locked the safe and put the carpet back.

'What if he makes trouble, Brendan?'

Murphy laughed. 'Make trouble for me, the Mafia? Dermot, this is Ireland, the one place in the world where they're powerless. We're the ones with power, Dermot, you and me, so let's get on with it and go and crack a bottle and have a decent supper at the Patriot.'

They all sat round the saloon in the *Highlander*, a large-scale map laid across the table.

'Kilbeg village,' Dillon said. 'The abbey is quarter of a mile to the east. The bunker is underneath.' He tapped the map. 'There, where the site of a ruined farmhouse is indicated, is, according to Sean here, the exit to the bunker.' He looked at Regan, who sat on one of the bench seats, wrists manacled. 'Isn't that so, Sean?'

'To hell with you,' Regan said.

'So how do you intend to play this?' Helen Black asked.

'Well, according to Regan, there are only two caretakers in the bunker. I intend to act very quickly, very economically. Blow the exit door, go in, dispose of them, and leave a hundred-pound block of Semtex to take the place out. They're storing Semtex there as well as arms. It'll be like Bonfire Night.'

'Which, if I'm not mistaken, celebrates Guy Fawkes *failing* to blow up Parliament,' Hannah Bernstein said.

'Well, I won't fail.'

'What about me?' Billy asked.

'You can watch my back,' Dillon said. 'Guard the exit door after I go in.'

'Oh, great. So I'm standing around like a ponce.'

'Don't be a silly boy, Billy. I'll need you watching out for me.'

'So how do you intend to do it?' Helen asked.

'Right, there's the pier that used to serve the old granite quarry. Yachtsmen call in here occasionally and usually anchor in the bay, according to Roper's information. What we'll do is this. We'll take the boat in to the pier, you in charge, Sergeant Major. Billy and I will wear diving suits. We'll offload diving equipment on to the pier, in case we have to come back the hard way. You will take *Highlander* a hundred yards out into the bay, and anchor.'

'Fine,' Helen said.

'Billy and I will have transceivers, and so will you, so we'll be in touch. The farmhouse is what, a quarter of a mile away? This will be the ultimate in-and-out job. With luck, it'll be so clean that I'll call and bring you into the pier to pick us up.' He smiled and turned to Billy. 'No need to get your feet wet.'

'Well, that's nice. It's bleeding cold out there.'

Dillon turned to Sean Regan, sitting there, sullen, on the bench, manacled hands on his knees.

'Now we come to your part, son. Is there anything you haven't told me?'

'I've told you everything I know.'

'I hope so, for your sake, because if you haven't you're dead in the water. And that's not just a figure of speech.' He turned to the others. 'Right, people, that's the way it is, so let's get it done.'

It was nine o'clock and pitch dark when they drifted in, the engines a muted throbbing. Dillon left it to Helen Black. She steered one-handed, holding a pair of Nightstalkers to her eyes, and hardly touched the pier. In a second, Dillon was over with a line and ran it round a bollard.

'Right, Billy, pass the gear up.'

Billy wrestled with air bottles and other things and Dillon stacked them on the pier.

'All right, son, let's have you.'

Billy joined him. 'First time in Ireland, and what a bloody place.'

'The hob of hell, Billy.' Dillon called to Helen Black. 'On your way.'

The *Highlander* moved out and Dillon checked his transceiver. 'Hey, you still love me, Superintendent?'

'Don't be silly,' she replied, and then added. 'For God's sake, Dillon . . .'

'I know, take care. Well, here we go to save the British way of life. An Irish gunman and a well-known London gangster. Why is it that people like us have to do it?'

He switched off, checked his Uzi, and slung it across his chest. Billy did the same. Dillon checked his Walther, and, again, Billy did the same. Having heard Dillon talking on the transceiver, he said, 'Do you know the answer? Why *is* it people like us have to do it?'

'Billy, a great English writer once said – it's ironic that when it comes down to it – that it's men of a rough persuasion who

181

have to do all the hard things that the general population are incapable of doing, and then the general population disowns them. It's called being a soldier.'

'But I'm not a bleeding soldier.'

'You're a gangster, Billy. It's the same thing, so shut up and follow me.'

On board the *Highlander*, Hannah obeyed Helen Black's orders and dropped the anchor. Below, Sean Regan sat on the bench, manacled, and thought about things. He was a practical man, and had survived for many years in the Irish struggle by being so.

However, try as he could, Dillon's reputation wouldn't go away and it was that of the ultimate hard man. The Brits used him on situations they didn't want to go to court. If he was on your case, you were dead.

With the best will in the world, Regan couldn't imagine a fate other than being tossed over the side into the Irish Sea, a convenient corpse, and there was no way he could risk that. A desperate plan came to him, and before he could hesitate, he acted. He knocked a tray bearing a teapot and cups off the table and fell on his knees.

A moment later, Hannah appeared. 'What is it?'

'My gut's killing me. I think it must be those seasickness pills.'

She crouched and checked him out. 'That bad?'

'I need the necessary. For God's sake, I might mess myself.'

She pulled him up and took him out to the lavatory. He held out his hands. 'Come on, you can't move in there. I couldn't get my trousers down with these things on.'

She hesitated, then took out her key, uncuffed him, and pushed him inside. She stood against the wall and waited.

Regan sat down, breathed deeply, then stood up, shoved the door open hard, catching Hannah and knocking her against the wall. He went up the companionway fast, ran out on deck, past Helen Black as she emerged from the wheelhouse, and vaulted over the rail. The cold March Irish Sea took his breath away, but he struck out for the shore with all his strength and vanished into the dark.

Hannah appeared on deck. 'Goddammit, he conned me. I was such a fool.'

'Happens to us all.' Helen Black tried her transceiver. 'Dillon, are you there?'

But in the valley area up from the cliffs the signal was poor, and there was no reply.

Sean Regan hit the shore, colder than he'd ever been in his life, and immediately started to run, making his way up the cliff path and turning for Kilbeg. He burst into the Patriot fifteen minutes later. There were three drinkers at the bar, Conolly and Tomelty two of them.

He fell across the bar in front of Sullivan, and Tomelty raised his head by his hair. Regan said, 'Thank God you're here. We've got trouble.'

'Well, tell the man here.'

Regan turned and saw Murphy get up from the bench before the fire.

'Why, Sean, I thought the Brits had you in Wandsworth. How in the hell did you get here?'

Suddenly, Regan realized he was in deep trouble here, too, and tried to recover. 'Never mind that, Brendan. Dillon's here, Sean Dillon. He's here to destroy the bunker.'

'Really?' Murphy said. 'But how would he know? Have you been shooting your gob off?'

'Please, Brendan. They took me out of Wandsworth. Beat the shite out of me.'

'Well, I must say you don't look too bad,' Tomelty said.

'We came over on a boat. Anchored off the old pier. I managed to get away. There are a couple of women on board, one Special Branch, that Bernstein bitch, the other is military police.'

'And Dillon?'

'He's gone to take out the bunker with another guy. He's going in by way of the exit at the farmhouse.'

Murphy shook his head. 'And how would he know about all that?'

'Jesus, Brendan.'

'No, you, Sean.'

At that moment, there was a rumble in the distance. Kelly ran out of the pub entrance, then came back in. 'It's the abbey. Some sort of explosion. Shall we get up there?'

Murphy cursed. 'No. It's a waste of bloody time now.' Murphy pushed Regan to the door. 'Let's get out of here, down to the pier.'

A few moments earlier, as Dillon and Billy had reached the exit door in the old farmhouse, Helen Black managed to get through.

'Dillon, for God's sake.'

'What?'

'We've got a crisis. Regan escaped. Jumped in the bay and swam for it.'

'Well, that's damn unfortunate.'

'Will you abort?'

'Like hell. We're at the exit now. We'll go in hard and get out quick.' He switched off.

Helen said to Hannah, 'He's still going in. I'll take the inflatable to the pier. Time could be crucial here.'

'Maybe I should go,' Hannah said.

'Not this time. Now I've got to get moving.'

At the exit door, Dillon stopped, took a magnetized block from his bag, and slammed it over the lock. 'Stay here and wait for me, Billy.'

He stepped back, the lock blew, and the doors folded inwards. Dillon ran in, took a smoke grenade from the bag, and rolled it down the corridor. The water considerably reduced its efficiency, but he ran on, pulling out a stun grenade, but again, swallowed by the floor, it wasn't very effective.

Behind him, Billy muttered, 'What the hell,' raised his Uzi, and went after Dillon.

Brosnan and O'Neill were having a late supper in the office when they heard the noise, grabbed their Uzis, and ran out. A certain amount of smoke remained from the grenade and they crouched from the half-shock of the stun grenade. A moment later, Dillon ran out of the fog headlong, and Brosnan rose to meet him, but Dillon was faster, his Uzi battering Brosnan back against the wall.

Dillon stumbled to one knee and O'Neill stood up in the murk. 'I've got you now, you bastard.'

He raised his AK and Billy came in on the run, firing his Uzi, and shot him to pieces. Billy dropped on his knees, breathing deeply, and Dillon stood up.

'Don't fall down on me now, Billy. This is the good bit.'

He kicked open the office door, produced five blocks of Semtex from the jump bag, took timers from the bag, and inserted them. He left one on the office floor and pushed Billy.

'Out you go. Three minutes.' He dropped the blocks one by one, as they ran through the bunker, splashed through the water, and made it out of the exit. As they went down the slope to the cliffs, the explosion rumbled underground.

Murphy was into the car, with Regan, Kelly, Conolly and Tomelty, and roaring out of the village within seconds of the explosion. When they reached the top of the road, he said to Tomelty, who was driving, 'Switch off the engine.'

They coasted down the hill and braked to a halt. Helen Black, sitting in the inflatable, heard nothing.

Murphy said, 'Not a sound. You go along the strip of beach, Tomelty. You and I will take the pier, Conolly, and be very, very quiet.' He turned to Regan. 'And you be especially quiet.'

They moved out. Helen Black sat there in the inflatable. There was a footfall on the beach. She turned and took out her Walther, and a flashlight was switched on from the pier.

'Well, I know you're not Bernstein, I'd recognize her, so I suppose you must be the sergeant major.' Murphy frowned. 'You wouldn't be Black, would you? The one from Derry?'

'My God, you've got a brain.'

'Down you go, Tomelty,' Murphy said. 'Get her gun.' He turned to Kelly. 'You and Conolly take her out to the boat. If the Bernstein bitch argues, tell her you'll shoot this one.' He turned to Tomelty. 'You and I stay here for Dillon.'

The inflatable moved away. Tomelty said, 'What about Regan?'

Murphy said, 'Silly me. I was forgetting.' He turned to Regan and took a Browning from his pocket. 'You sold us out, you shite. You're lucky I don't have time to make it longer.'

The silenced Browning coughed and Regan went off the pier into the water.

On the *Highlander*, Hannah looked through the Nightstalker as the inflatable coasted in. 'Are you all right?' she called.

Kelly said, 'We've got your sergeant major here and I've got a gun to her head. If you're not sensible, I'll kill her stone dead.'

Helen Black called, 'Don't listen, Hannah, do what you have to do. You heard the explosion. We've achieved our object. To hell with these people.'

Conolly hit her across the side of her head with his pistol. She cried out. Kelly said, 'I mean it.'

'All right.' Hannah stood back, her Walther in her left hand.

A moment later, Kelly boarded, followed by Helen Black and Conolly, who took the Walther from Hannah's grasp.

'There's a good girl.'

Black was wearing paratroop boots with her jumpsuit. Stuffed into the right one was the Colt .25 hollowpoint. At that moment, she could have pulled it out in the darkness of the deck and shot both men. But what would that mean for Dillon and Billy? She decided to wait.

Dillon tried to get her on the transceiver and got no reply. On the *Highlander*, Kelly started the engines and moved in to the pier, and Conolly tied up. Dillon and Billy came down the hill on the run, and in the slight light of a quarter moon, the rain having stopped, saw the boat move in.

'They've come for us,' Billy said, gasping for breath.

'So it would appear.'

They hit the end of the pier, looked down at the deck with the light on, and saw Kelly push Hannah and Helen out, he and Conolly both holding guns to the women's backs.

Murphy came out of the shadows with Tomelty. 'They mean it, you bastard. You want them dead?'

'Certainly not,' Dillon said. 'Do as he says, Billy, guns on the floor.'

Billy complied, and Murphy lit a cigarette. 'Damn you, Dillon, I always admired you, but this time you've cost me money.'

'Not you, Brendan, Jack Fox.'

Murphy laughed incredulously. 'My God, is that what this is about, a personal feud?'

'You shouldn't have joined, Brendan.'

'Neither should you, Dillon. Now you and your friend get on board so we can move to where the water's deeper, because that's where you're going.'

Dillon and Billy went down the steps to the deck and joined Helen Black and Hannah; Murphy followed with Tomelty. Kelly was at the wheel, Conolly joined the others.

'You know what?' Murphy said. 'It's a waste of good women, but I'm going to kill the lot of you.'

He was looking at Hannah when he said that. Helen Black, close to the wheelhouse, pulled the Colt out of her boot and shot Kelly in the back of the head. The boat swerved, and everyone fell over. As Conolly tried to get up, she pushed herself upright, shot him dead, then ducked and dived over the rail as Murphy tried to shoot her.

At the same moment, Dillon grabbed Billy by the arm. 'Over!' he cried, and pushed him over the rail after Helen Black. As he tried to follow, Tomelty, still on the deck, grabbed his ankles, and Dillon went down.

'You bastard.' Murphy kicked him in the side. 'You're finally dead meat, Dillon, and you, bitch. Those two in the water aren't going anywhere. Fifteen minutes at this season of the year and it's hypothermia time. You two will get it quick, at least.'

Billy, close to Helen on the port side, said, 'I'm going to try for that gun in the wheelhouse.'

He didn't wait for a reply, simply jackknifed and went under the *Highlander* from port to starboard, scraping his back under the keel, surfaced, and reached up for the rail. As he pulled himself on board and slithered for the wheelhouse, he heard the exchange between Dillon and Murphy, unaware that, looking beyond Murphy and Tomelty, Dillon had seen him arrive.

'Come on, Brendan, why all the dialogue? In Derry in the old days, we didn't talk about it, we did it.'

On his knees in the wheelhouse, Billy dropped the flap and got his hand to the Walther, which Dillon had left cocked. He turned and shot Tomelty twice in the back, shattering his spine.

Murphy started to turn, shocked as Tomelty went down; Hannah kicked sideways at his left leg and he stumbled,

188

which was Dillon's moment. He grabbed at the gun hand and came breast-to-breast.

'Now then, you dog.'

He pushed hard, Murphy staggered back, and they went over the stern rail.

And the sea was Dillon's, the master diver's element, not Murphy's. They went down perhaps ten feet. Dillon got an arm around Murphy's throat and then the anchor on its chain scraped his back. He grabbed it with his right hand and held on fast. Murphy kicked and struggled and Dillon held his breath until he was bursting, and then Murphy stopped struggling. Dillon let him go and surfaced.

He managed the ladder and hung there and Hannah looked over. 'All right, Dillon? What happened to Murphy?'

He hauled himself up. 'What do you think happened? As the Sicilians have it, Brendan Murphy is asleep with the fishes.'

He sat on the deck, his back to the wheelhouse. Billy was there, and Helen Black.

'You okay, Sergeant Major?'

'I'm fine, Mr Dillon.'

'And you, Billy?'

'What the fuck did you get me into, Dillon?'

'Billy, you saved the pass, to use an old-fashioned phrase. You were fantastic. The SAS couldn't have done better. On top of that, you've given Superintendent Bernstein a severe problem. Try not to get arrested, because she'll feel terribly guilty if *she* has to arrest you.'

Billy grinned and turned to Hannah. 'What do I have to do? Take up good works?'

'Just don't give me a problem, Billy.'

'Trouble is, I've been giving people a problem all my life.'

Dillon said, 'Let's get the bodies over the side. And do me a favour, Sergeant Major – take us out. I'll do a quick change and I'll be up to relieve you.'

'Leave it to me.'

'Come on, you two,' he said to Hannah and Billy. 'Let's get into dry clothes,' and he led the way below.

An hour later, Charles Ferguson was in his Cavendish Square flat, enjoying a nightcap, when his phone rang. Dillon was at the wheel alone, the others below. Pushing out into the Irish Sea, he had switched to automatic pilot and lit a cigarette as he spoke.

'Is it yourself, Brigadier?'

'Dillon! Where are you?'

'On our way back to Oban.' Dillon was using his Codex Four mobile. 'We can talk.'

'What's happened?'

'Well, the Kilbeg bunker is no more, and the sergeant major's proved a treasure. Killed two of Murphy's gang. Billy saved our bacon by killing another at the right time.'

'Good God! Is everyone all right?'

'Oh, right as rain, Brigadier. We're a tough lot.'

'Well, thank God for that. And Murphy?'

'Oh, I saw to him myself.'

'Well, you would, wouldn't you? So what now?'

'I'd say, six hours to Oban. The weather's not too good. If you could alert Lacey and Parry for a flight back to London around breakfast time?'

'Consider it done.'

'How's Blake?'

'A post-operational infection. Daz and Martha have it in hand.'

'That's good. Fox is really going to be mortified over this lot.'

'I like that, Dillon, a good choice of words. I'll see you tomorrow.'

Dillon sat there at the wheel, and then the door opened, there was a bacon smell, and Billy appeared, a plate of sandwiches in one hand and a mug of tea.

'There you go, Sean.'

Billy turned to leave, and Dillon said, 'Billy, you were great. Harry will be proud of you.'

'Yes, but he won't know, will he? What I mean is, nobody knows unless they've done it, been there, bought the tee shirt, isn't that what they say? Jesus, Dillon, this wasn't some punch-up in an East End pub. I killed two men tonight.'

'They shouldn't have joined, Billy, if they didn't want the risk. Remember that.'

'Okay, I suppose so. So – now it's the Jagos and Fox?'

'Yes. I suppose it is.' Dillon finished the last sandwich. 'Go on, Billy. Get some sleep. You've earned it.'

Billy left, and Dillon turned from automatic pilot to manual and took the *Highlander* onwards over an increasingly turbulent sea.

# LONDON

# 13

Jack Fox had gone down to the Grill Restaurant at the Dorchester to enjoy an English breakfast. He was reading *The Times* and just finishing poached eggs, sausage, ham and toast, when Falcone appeared.

'We've got a problem, Signore.'

'What now?' Fox asked.

'I've just seen Sky Television's news programme. I think you should see for yourself.'

'That bad?' Fox asked.

'I'm afraid so, Signore.'

In the suite, Fox watched the next news update with horror. The story of a large explosion at Kilbeg in County Louth led the hour. There were pictures of the Irish police on site, and reports of some kind of IRA connection, although the IRA and Sinn Fein had denied it. One thing was certain – four bodies had drifted on to the beach, three dead from gunshot wounds. The fourth was Brendan Murphy, a well-known dissident who had left the Provisional IRA and formed his own group. The suggestion was that the PIRA had taken his men out. It was thought that the explosion had involved an underground arms bunker, and this was being investigated.

There was a ring at the door. Russo answered and returned with a waiter carrying a tray with fresh coffee. He was dismissed and Russo poured.

Falcone said, 'Murphy owed you money, Signore.'

'Well, we can kiss that goodbye,' Fox said.

Falcone said, 'Please forgive me if I overstep the bounds, Signore, but I've been loyal to you for so many years that I feel I can ask this question: How bad are things?'

Fox looked at him. 'Pretty bad, Aldo. But we still have one ace in the hole left. The White Diamond Company heist on Tuesday.'

'You said ten million sterling.'

'With four to the Jagos.' Fox smiled. 'And you disagreed.'

'I sure did, Signore. I say we take the lot.'

'I'm beginning to agree, Aldo, but afterwards. Let these bastards do the hard work.'

Falcone smiled broadly. 'Excellent, Signore.'

'Okay, get in touch with the Jagos. I want a meet at lunch-time. Pick a quiet pub.'

'I'll arrange it, Signore.'

Falcone left to make the arrangements, but first he phoned Don Marco who, because of the time difference, was still in bed, but then, Falcone's instructions had been to call at any time of the day or night. The Don listened patiently.

Finally he said, 'Fucked again, my nephew. Fucked at the Colosseum, then at Al Shariz, and now in Ireland. You know what they say, Aldo? Once is okay, twice is coincidence, and three times is enemy action.'

'So what do we do, Don Marco?'

'Nothing. This is Jack's problem. He succeeds or fails on his own. But if he fails . . . Understand me, Aldo. I'll never let any physical harm come to him. He's my nephew. But the family needs a leader in whom it can be confident. This diamond heist is his last chance. If something happens to that, too . . . Jack's out. *Capisce?*'

'*Capisco*, Don Marco.'

In the back bar of the Horse Guards pub not far from St Richard's Dock, Harold and Tony Jago waited. It was misty on the river and a little rain drummed against the window.

Harold looked out. 'I like it like this, Tony, it's the way the Thames should be. England for the English, eh? Who needs Europe? A bunch of frogs and krauts.'

'You're right, Harold. Mind you, we're stuck with the fucking Mafia right now.'

'They don't worry me. We can handle them.' At that minute, Manchester Charlie Ford came in through the far door, Amber Frazer with him.

'Jesus, here they come,' Harold said. 'What a pair. I mean, if they want their own thing instead of a woman, that's all right, but I don't like blacks. They're nothing but trouble.'

Ford had the file under his arm and passed it across. 'Everything's taken care of, Harold.'

'Good. Let's wait for Fox. What do you want to drink?'

At Rosedene, Blake was feeling a lot better and greeted Dillon and Helen Black with enthusiasm when they turned up.

'Miller filled me in. We watched Sky Television. You really took them apart.'

'Which just leaves the White Diamond Company.'

'Hey, don't leave me out this time, Sean. I want to be part of that.'

'You can't be, because I won't be part of it, and neither will Bernstein or Ferguson. We've given it to Harry Salter. We're not involved, Blake.'

'Okay, but I can't just sit around here. I need to be with you.'

'Fine. If Daz will release you, that's okay by me.'

Daz agreed he could go, as long as Blake did not take part in any physical activity, so just before noon they repaired to Ferguson's office at the Ministry of Defence, Blake wearing a sling for his right arm. Hannah stood beside Ferguson at his desk.

The Brigadier said, 'I hardly need to say well done. However, we're left with the final nail in Jack Fox's coffin, the White Diamond Company job. What happens now, Superintendent?'

'Frankly, sir, the Salters won't talk to me. It's up to Dillon.'

'Well, according to Roper, tomorrow's the day because that's when the big diamond consignment comes in.'

'What we do know is that they've cut open the old grille gate in the tunnel,' Hannah said. 'The thing we still don't know is, once they've smashed into the basement, how do they bypass the security to get into the vault?'

'That's what I'm going to see Harry Salter about,' Dillon said. 'I'll take Blake. You stay out of it, Hannah. I know you don't like our using a villain like Salter, and I don't want to offend your fine police morality.'

At the Horse Guards, Harold sat reading the file, then passed it to Tony. 'It's not only good, it's bloody good.' At that moment, Fox, Falcone and Russo came in. Harold got up. 'Good to see you. We're just finishing things.' They sat, but Falcone and Russo as usual stood at the wall.

'So, where are we?' Fox demanded.

'Hey, your file was sweetness and light,' Harold said, 'but Charlie here has put in some extras that will truly delight you.'

'Tell me.'

Afterwards, Fox nodded. 'Excellent. There's only one change. I've just had more recent information that the take will be more like twelve million than ten. More for everyone, Jago. So keep our eye on the ball, people.'

'We sure will, Jack,' Harold said.

Fox got up. 'I'm in your hands. You're the experts, we'll keep out of it. Stay in touch.'

He went out, followed by Falcone and Russo. Tony Jago said, 'So we do all the fucking work.'

'Never mind,' Harold told him. 'For a payday like that, I'm glad to do the work.'

Ferguson went into the Dark Man with Dillon and Blake. Salter and Billy were in the end booth and Dora was giving them shepherd's pie.

'Smells good,' Ferguson said. 'Takes me back to Eton. We'll have the same. Blake needs building up.'

'Blake looks bloody awful,' Salter observed.

'Have you seen Sky Television, Billy?' Dillon asked. 'A terrible business in Ireland. An underground bunker blown up, bodies drifting in on the beach, one of them a hard man named Brendan Murphy. Everyone believes the Provos in Dublin were behind it. He wouldn't do as he was told.'

'Yes, I did see that,' Billy said. 'Terrible what goes on over there.'

Dora brought their food, and Dillon laughed. 'He did well, your boy, Harry. Saved my life by killing one bastard in the bunker and saved all of us, killing another on the boat.'

Salter was shocked. He turned to Billy. 'You never told me.'

'Yeah, well, you never believe anything I say.'

'My God, you are a chip off the old block, after all.'

'I'd say he's a chip off his own block,' Ferguson said and started to eat. 'Roper definitely thinks tomorrow. The big consignment arrives at the White Diamond Company from South Africa. And I'm told the stakes are higher. Twelve million, not ten.'

'Really?' Salter said. 'Then I'm sorry for them.'

'Why?'

'It's too big, Brigadier. I'm not an educated man, I go by experience, and nobody knows more about the London underworld and thieving than I do. What screwed up the Great Train Robbery was the size. Biggest criminal haul ever. There was no way society and the law could tolerate that, so they turned on the big guns.'

'That makes considerable sense,' Ferguson agreed.

Blake said, 'Yes, but Jack Fox is desperate. He has to be. He needs a big one.'

'Oh, sure, and Manchester Charlie Ford and his team are greedy and stupid and will all be back on landing D at Wandsworth before they know it,' Salter said.

Dillon finished his food and accepted the glass of bar champagne that Dora put at his elbow. 'Let's go over this again, Harry. They've got Manchester Charlie Ford, one of the best lock and safe men in the business; Amber Frazer, a heavy; and Connie Briggs, a hotshot on security and electronics.'

Salter told him, 'Did you know he went to London University? From a well-known family of villains. His mother was real proud, him doing that. Got this degree. What they call first-class honours.'

'My, that is good,' Ferguson said.

'They threw a big party. I was there. He gets a research job for British Telecom, but it's not worth enough money, so what does he do? Starts putting himself about.'

Billy said, 'He really is a genius where the electronics caper is concerned, Dillon.'

'I'm beginning to believe you. And Val French?'

'Well, he's a top man with a thermal lance, cutting, all that. I'd say he'd have sorted out the gate and organized smashing through the tunnel wall into the basement.'

They'd all finished their food and Dora cleared the table. Blake was sweating, his forehead damp; he didn't look good.

Salter said, 'Bring him a brandy, Dora. You don't look well, my old son.'

'I've been worse,' Blake said. 'But thanks anyway.' He hesitated. 'I suppose someone should bring this up, for form's sake, and it might as well be me. Shouldn't someone be notifying the White Diamond Company that they might be in trouble, Brigadier?'

200

'I take your point, Blake. But we're not into ethics here.'

'We're into finishing off Jack Fox.' Dillon's voice was hard. 'As long as we ruin things for him, that's okay.'

'All right, all right,' Blake said. 'Just thought I'd ask. And while we're at it, how *do* we think they're going to get into that vault?'

'Well, it isn't the thermal lance man,' Dillon said. 'He'd be there all night trying to get into the kind of strong room they'll have in here. I'd say it's the electronics whiz kid.'

'I agree,' Harry said. 'But that doesn't get us any further.'

There was a pause, and it was Billy who said, 'What we need is more information, and the only way to get that is to pick up one of the team and squeeze him dry.'

Harry laughed out loud. 'My God, you really are learning. Who would you suggest? The one who's least important, the one whose absence wouldn't be a burden.'

'The heavy, Amber Frazer,' Dillon said.

'I'd say so.'

'Brilliant.' Harry Salter turned to Ferguson. 'We lift this guy tonight. Leave it to us. We'll deliver him to your safe house at Holland Park, then we'll review the situation.'

'This is illegal, of course,' Ferguson said. 'He hasn't done anything.'

'Not yet,' Dillon said. 'But I'm sure you could think of something. After all, isn't this why we didn't bring the Superintendent?'

'You're right, of course. It's in your hands, Harry. I may call you Harry?'

'You can call me any bleeding thing you like.'

'Excellent, then if your Dora can come up with an indifferent glass of red wine, I'll drink your health and leave you to it,' Ferguson told him.

It was ten o'clock that night when Amber Frazer and Manchester Charlie Ford emerged from a small Italian restaurant in Notting Hill. Harry and Billy had been waiting for some time, sitting in their car. Ford hailed a cab, patted Amber's face, and got in.

'Brilliant,' Billy said as Amber turned and walked away.

They trailed him and Billy pulled in at the pavement a little further along. Harry Salter got out. 'Amber, my old son, I thought it was you.'

'My God, Harry, what are you doing here?'

'Looking for you, so get in the car.'

Amber, alarmed, tried to turn away, and Salter pushed the muzzle of a gun he was carrying in his right-hand pocket against Amber's back.

'Is that a gun, Harry?'

'Well, it's not my finger. Yes, it's a gun, and it's silenced, so I could blow away your spine, leave you on the pavement and drive away and no one would hear a thing. Get in the car.'

Amber did as he was told and Harry got in behind him and took out the gun. 'Listen, Amber, I know you like to think you're some kind of Mike Tyson, and you've got big muscles, but not with a bullet in your stomach. So do as you're told.'

Billy said, 'Evening, Amber,' and drove away.

At the safe house, Amber sat wondering what the hell was going on, Miller at the door. After a while, it opened, and Dillon and Helen Black came in, followed by Harry Salter.

'Look, what's this about?' Amber stood up.

Dillon kicked him very hard in the right ankle. 'Sit down.'

Helen Black said, 'Is this the man, Mr Salter?'

'Definitely. He's involved with a gang of known criminals: Charles Ford, Val French, Connie Briggs. I understand their intention is to rob the White Diamond Company tomorrow night of a very large consignment from South Africa. I also understand there's a Mafia connection, a man named Jack Fox.'

Amber panicked. 'Here, what is this? I don't know what you're talking about.'

Dillon said to Helen Black, 'Dear me, if this little caper goes through, he'll still be legally a part of it, am I right?'

'Absolutely.'

'What kind of sentence would he pull?'

'Minimum of ten years.'

Amber was sweating now. 'Look, for God's sake.'

'No, for your sake,' Salter said.

There was a pause, and then Helen Black said, 'If you help us in the matter, you'll be released within the next few days and put on a plane back to Barbados.'

'And if you don't, it's back to the shower at Wandsworth,' Dillon said.

Frazer had done a particularly nasty stretch at Wandsworth a couple of years earlier, and he had no desire to repeat it. He loved Charlie, but . . . Charlie could take care of himself.

'Okay.' Amber took out a handkerchief and wiped his face. 'Give me a drink.' Helen Black nodded to Miller, who went to the sideboard and poured a large Scotch. Amber swallowed it down. 'Okay, what do you want to know?'

On the other side of the mirror, Ferguson stood with Hannah, Blake and Billy. 'A good start,' he said.

'Depends on your point of view, sir,' Hannah said.

'Well, my point is getting a result. I'm like a lot of people these days, Superintendent, sick of the bad guys getting away with it, as our American cousins would say. War is war, and this is a kind of war. If you're not happy, go back to the office.'

'There's no need for that, sir.'

'I hope not.'

In the interview room, Salter said, 'All right, Amber. Manchester Charlie Ford, you, Connie and Val are going to hit the White Diamond Company for Jack Fox. We know you've already cut open the grille gate in the tunnel from the river.'

Amber was shocked. 'How do you know that?'

'We know everything, old son.'

Dillon leaned against the wall and lit a cigarette. Helen took up the story. 'The gate is open, you go up the tunnel, smash a hole through an old Victorian brick wall and you're into the basement of the White Diamond Company.'

'Only what we can't understand, old son, is how you're supposed to do the job,' Salter said. 'I mean, all that security, all those alarms.'

Amber didn't reply, and Dillon said, 'It's a waste of time, Sergeant Major. Ship him up to Wandsworth and charge him with conspiracy.'

'As you say, sir,' Helen Black said.

Amber said, 'No, for God's sake, I'll tell you. Give me another drink,' which Miller did. Amber swallowed it down just like the other. 'Okay, what do you want to know?'

'First of all, the security man?'

'No problem. He takes over at six o'clock from the other guy. Always gets coffee and a big box of sandwiches from the takeaway at the end of the street. There's a girl there who Charlie knows. She's going to put a couple of pills in the coffee. They take a while to act, but when they do, he's out for three or four hours.'

'But the security system?' Helen Black said.

'That's Connie Briggs. He's a genius at electronics. He's got hold of this thing called a Howler. When you switch it on, it screws up all electronic systems in a given area. TV video security, gate locks, vaults, the lot.'

'My God,' Helen Black said. 'I can't believe it.'

'Of course!' Dillon said. 'Oh, what an ass I am! I've seen those things. They work, believe me.' He turned to Amber. 'So it *is* tomorrow night?'

Amber nodded. 'Seven o'clock. It's got to be early because of the tide.'

'Will Fox be there?' Dillon asked.

'No way. It's all down to us and the Jagos.'

The door opened and Ferguson came in, trailed by Billy, Hannah and Blake Johnson. 'Thank you, Sergeant Major,' the Brigadier said. 'Take him out and keep him secure.'

Black and Miller took Amber Frazer between them, and Blake said, 'Well, now we know.'

'The only trouble is, Fox isn't taking part,' Hannah said.

'Well, he wouldn't,' Dillon told her. 'He's too careful to get directly involved in a caper like this. We have to settle for foiling the robbery and banging up the lot of them, including the Jagos. The end result will still be that Fox loses his hope of a big killing with those diamonds.'

'His last hope,' Blake said.

'Exactly.' Dillon nodded. 'So how do we handle it?'

Harry Salter said, 'I've been thinking. My Joe, Joe Baxter, when he was doing a five stretch at Armley Prison in Leeds, did a learning programme. Did welding, all that stuff. You know, oxyacetylene.'

'So what are you suggesting?' Ferguson asked.

'Well, it would run something like this, Brigadier,' and Harry Salter told him.

They all listened, and Ferguson burst into laughter. 'My God, that's the best thing I've heard in years.'

# 14

The following day, Fox was having a light lunch in the Piano Bar at the Dorchester, tagliatelle alla panna, noodles in a cream and ham sauce, just the way he liked it. The waiter poured him a glass of Krug, and Falcone came down the stairs.

'I've been to the Colosseum, Signore. Mori has laid off most of the staff. He's kept on Rossi and Cameci.'

'I know. That damn Ferguson. Any word from Ford?'

'No, Signore.'

'Today's the day, Aldo. Make or break time.'

More than you know, Falcone thought.

Manchester Charlie Ford had expected Amber for lunch, and when he failed to turn up he tried Amber's mobile. When it rang at Holland Park, Helen Black nodded, Miller stood behind and Amber answered.

'Hey, where are you?' Charlie demanded.

'Sorry, Charlie,' Amber mumbled. 'I've got a terrible toothache. I've only just managed to find a dentist who could give me an appointment.'

'You poor sod. Okay, I'll see you this evening.'

'I don't know, Charlie. This thing could knock me out of commission.'

There was a brief silence. 'Well, I suppose we can manage if we have to. Me, Tony and Harold. But be here if you can, okay, Amber?'

'I'll do my best, Charlie.'

'Well, you do that, darling. Stay well.'

Amber switched off the phone and looked at Helen Black. 'Was that okay?'

'You should be on stage, Amber.'

For some strange reason, he perked up. 'You really think so?'

'Absolutely. Much better than prison. Maybe you shouldn't go back to Barbados. Maybe you should get an education grant and try the London Theatre School.'


There was a final meeting at Fox's suite at the Dorchester: the Jagos, Ford, Briggs and French. Falcone and Russo stood by, and Fox nodded to Russo, who got a bottle of champagne from the basket and thumbed off the cork. He filled glasses all around.

Fox raised his and toasted the others. 'To the big one. They'll all have to sit up and take notice.' He turned to Ford. 'Everything okay?'

'Amber isn't up to snuff. He's got some sort of tooth infection. He rang me up from the dentist.'

'We don't need the black,' Tony Jago said. 'We can manage. Enough of us as it is.'

'You know best.' Fox nodded.

Tony said, 'So you're sure you're not joining us?'

'Don't be silly. That tunnel would be rather crowded.'

'But you don't mind joining us to share out the loot.'

Falcone, leaning against the wall, straightened, but Harold took charge. 'You shut your mouth,' he said to his brother, 'or I'll give you a slapping.' He turned to Fox. 'Look, I'm sorry. He's young.'

'Well, we all were once,' Jack told him and smiled. 'Come on, another glass of bubbly, and then, as I believe the Irish say, "God bless the good work."'

It was six o'clock that evening when Hannah answered her doorbell and found Dillon on the step.

'Ferguson expects us at his place to wait out what's happening. I've got the Daimler.'

'I'll get my coat.'

She was out in a few minutes, he opened the rear door for her, and she climbed in behind the driver. Dillon leaned in through the open window and tapped the driver on the shoulder.

'Take the Superintendent to Brigadier Ferguson.' He smiled at Hannah. 'I'll see you later. I've got things to do.'

Hannah opened her mouth in surprise, but the Daimler moved away before she could reply.

Outside the Jagos' house in Wapping, a large white truck bearing the sign ELITE CONSTRUCTION drew up.

Ford was at the wheel wearing overalls, Briggs beside him, French in the back. The door to the house opened, and Harold and Tony Jago emerged, came down the steps and also got in the back.

'The moment of truth, boys,' Harold said. 'Let's get to it.'

At the same time, the night security guard at the White Diamond Company, having finished his sandwiches and coffee, sat back to read the *Evening Standard*. He kept blinking his eyes, yawned a couple of times, put the newspaper down, and checked the multiple television security screens. Everything looked normal. Suddenly, he leaned over the desk, put his head on his arms, and was asleep.

In the tunnel, Ford and French, each wielding a sledgehammer, attacked the wall at the right point. The old Victorian brickwork crumbled and fell backwards in large sections into the basement.

'Perfect,' Ford said. 'In we go, gents.'

They all scrambled through. 'Now what?' Harold Jago asked.

'The tide started to come in downriver fifteen minutes ago. We're good for forty minutes. After that, the tunnel entrance will be covered.'

'Then let's bleeding get on with it,' Harold said.

Connie Briggs took an object from one of the carrying bags that resembled a television remote control. 'The Howler,' he said, and pressed a button.

'Is that it?' Tony Jago asked.

'Well, if it isn't, all hell will break loose when we go upstairs. If it works, the security system is fucked and all the doors will be open. Let's go and see.'

Dillon, the Salters, Joe Baxter and Sam Hall got out of a Transit. Baxter and Hall were carrying large canvas holdalls. Blake got out after them.

Harry Salter said, 'Look, old son, can't you stay in the Transit? You're not up to it.'

'No, it's important to me. Fox had my wife killed, Harry. I want to be there when he finally gets his. What happens now, if we succeed, will finish him.'

Strange, it was Billy who said, 'He's entitled. Let him be.'

'Well, you've changed, you young sod.'

'Damn right, Harry,' Dillon said. 'He's killed two men, and on the side of right. No going back on that.'

Salter said, 'Okay, let's get going.'

He led the way down the steps and started along the shingle to the tunnel entrance. When they got there, he turned to Billy.

'You checked with Handy. How long have we got?'

'Thirty minutes, and don't forget, when that tide floods in, it's what Handy means by St Richard's Force.'

'Right, let's get to it.'

As the Jagos and the others reached the entrance hall, they paused, observing the security guard sprawled across the desk, the security screens blank.

'There you go. Downstairs to the vault,' Connie Briggs said.

Manchester Charlie Ford laughed. 'I told you he was a genius,' and he led the way down a broad marble stairway to the vaults below.

The others, in the tunnel, had reached the grille door. Harry Salter said, 'Right, let's get on with it.'

Billy said, 'We could clobber them on the way out, Harry. I mean, twelve million.'

'Like I said, it's too much, Billy. They'd bring out the big battalions. Now, we go with my suggestion. I've never liked the Jagos, with their drugs, whores and pornography. Filth.' He turned to Joe Baxter. 'So get your gear out and let's hope the British prison system taught you a trade.'

Joe Baxter took out an oxyacetylene welding torch from his holdall. From the other bag, Sam Hall produced an oxygen cylinder.

Baxter flared the torch and started to work.

The great vault doors opened, and the Jagos and their friends were into an Aladdin's cave. They opened their canvas hold-alls, pulled out bags and poured in a stream of diamonds.

'Jesus,' Harold said. 'I've never known the like.'

There was an atmosphere of hysteria, everyone laughing, and finally, they were finished.

'Okay, let's be on our way,' Harold ordered and led the way back upstairs.

They moved down to the basement to the exit hole they'd smashed, moved through one by one.

210

Tony said, 'Christ, there's water in the tunnel.'

'Well, there would be,' Harold said. 'The tide's coming in. We've got time. Let's get moving.'

It was already a foot deep when they reached the gate, Manchester Charlie Ford in the lead. He tried to open it.

'What the hell is going on? It won't budge.'

Val French pushed him out of the way and checked it. 'Christ! Someone's welded it together.'

'That would be me and my friends.' Dillon sloshed forward in a foot of water, Blake at his side. 'Sean Dillon, and this is Blake Johnson. I'm sure you've got a mobile. Call Jack Fox and give him the bad news.'

The Jagos grabbed the bars of the grille and shook them. 'Fuck you!'

Dillon smiled. 'No, I'm afraid it's you who are fucked, gentlemen. Now, if you'll excuse me, the water's getting a bit high.'

Dillon and Blake turned and waded away, the water already two feet deep and rising. They exited on to the beach, which was already flooded. Harry Salter and the others were at the steps, waiting.

Dillon took out his Codex Four mobile phone and called Scotland Yard, using the Special Branch number.

The officer who replied said, 'Special Branch. How can I help you?'

'The Jago brothers and a hand-picked team are trapped in the White Diamond Company building at St Richard's Dock. They can't get out the way they got in underground, because the tide's rising. If you get to the front entrance fast, you'll catch them with twelve million in diamonds.'

'Who is this?'

'Don't be silly, get moving.'

In the tunnel, the Jagos and the others shook desperately at the grille together, but Joe Baxter had done too good

211

a job, and then the water rose and started to bore in very fast.

'Christ,' Harold said. 'It's that St Richard's Force thing. Let's get out of here.'

They turned and scrambled along the tunnel, the water foaming around them, got through the hole, and scrambled upstairs to the foyer and the security office.

'Listen,' Harold said, 'if that Howler works, then the front door's open.'

'That's right,' Connie told him.

'Okay, let's get the hell out of here.'

He led the way to the door, and there was a squeal of brakes as half a dozen police cars arrived outside.

Harold stood there, bitter and angry, and said to Connie, 'Close the door with your sodding Howler,' which Connie did. 'Let them wait.'

The police bunched together outside the glass doors, and Tony Jago gave them two fingers. Harold called through on the mobile to Fox at his suite at the Dorchester.

Fox said, 'Harold, how did it go?'

'Wonderful. I'm standing here at the White Diamond Company holding a bag worth twelve million and there must be at least twenty cops outside trying to get in at us.'

'What happened, for God's sake?'

Harold told him.

'Dillon?' Fox said. 'Are you sure?'

'And the American, Johnson. I think they've been on your case more than you know, Jack. The trouble is it's put them on *my* case.'

'I'll get you the best barrister in London.'

'Thanks very much. That's a great comfort, Fox. Sod you and your barrister!'

He switched off the mobile. Tony said, 'What the hell do we do, Harold?'

'Travel hopefully, Tony.' Harold turned to Connie Briggs. 'Go on, use that gadget and open the door.' Connie did, and the police rushed in and surged all over them.

Fox said, 'That bastard Dillon. He and Johnson, they've ruined the operation!'

'Signore?' Falcone said.

'God, I see it all now. It wasn't them just with the Colosseum, but Al Shariz and Kilbeg, too. And now this!'

'But how, Signore? How would they know?'

'The Johnson woman, everything flows from that. Somehow she found out and told them. God knows how.'

'So what do we do now, Signore?'

Fox turned to him with a hard light in his eyes. 'We exact revenge,' Fox said. 'That's what I want, revenge.'

'And how do we do that?'

'I'll tell you later. Right now, I want you and Russo to get down to the Colosseum and pick up Rossi and Cameci. Go on, do it now.' He was angry. 'And make it fast.'

'Signore.'

Falcone left, picked up Russo from his room, and filled him in as they went down in the elevator to get the car.

Russo said, 'He's too angry, and being too angry isn't good.'

'You don't have to tell me,' Falcone said.

In the car on the way to the Colosseum, he phoned Don Marco in New York and brought him up to date.

'Ah God, Aldo, can't he see? They're *looking* for him to come after them. He should just cut his losses, get out of there.'

'He won't do that, Don Marco. He's an angry man.'

'And insane to go after them. But then, Jack was always headstrong.'

Falcone hesitated, then said the unthinkable. 'Do you wish me to take care of him, Don Marco?'

'No, Aldo. No matter what he's done, he's my nephew, flesh of my flesh. I'm coming over there. I'll leave New York within the hour. You stay in close touch.'

'Of course.'

'Aldo. I need your total loyalty in this.'

'You have it as always, Don Marco.'

Besides the Gulfstream, the family operated a Golden Eagle twin-engine aircraft out of Bardsey Aero Club outside London. It was useful for local flights, the kind where you had to put down on short runways, so it was particularly good for Hellsmouth. Fox called the pilot now, an ageing, ex-RAF pilot named Swan, and got him at home.

'Mr Fox, what can I do for you?'

'I need a flight in a couple of hours to Hellsmouth. Can you manage that?'

'If you say so, Mr Fox. It might be a rough landing. It's pretty dark.'

'I don't care if you put us down on its belly, just so you get us there.'

'As you say, sir.'

When Dillon arrived at Stable Mews, Fox, Russo, Falcone, Rossi and Cameci were waiting in a large black van.

Dillon got out with Blake and gave him the key to the house. 'There you go. I'll be back later. I'll go and see what Ferguson wants.'

He got back into the taxi and it moved away. Blake walked slowly towards the door, and the van drove up and braked. Rossi and Cameci were out and had him in seconds. Blake tried to struggle but had little strength. Fox leaned across Russo, who was at the wheel.

'It's my turn now, Johnson. Get him in the back. You know what to do, Falcone.'

They dragged Blake in and Falcone produced a hypodermic. 'Now this will really make you feel good,' he said and jabbed it into the right arm.

Blake continued to struggle, but then everything slipped away and he was still.

Bardsey operated a twenty-four-hour service that handled the ever-increasing volume of private planes and executive jets that Heathrow didn't welcome any more. For internal flights, there was no particular security. Swan was waiting for them.

Fox said, 'We'll take off right away. I don't want to hang around. I'm a little worried about my friend here. He's had too much to drink.'

'Will there be a return, Mr Fox?' Swan asked.

'Not tonight. You wait at the airstrip for further instructions.'

Swan, only too well aware of the kind of people he was dealing with, said, 'As you say, sir,' and went and logged flight details.

Rossi and Cameci took Blake up the steps, Russo followed, and Fox turned to Falcone. 'Phone the caretaker, old Carter. Tell him I want the fireplaces lit, but I don't want him in the house. He can go home.'

'As you say, Signore.'

Fox boarded the Eagle, and Falcone got on his mobile and made the call. When he finished, Falcone followed and Swan pulled up the steps and closed the Airstair door. As he went up to the cockpit, Fox reached out to Falcone.

'Give me the phone.'

He took out a card, a digest of information Maud Jackson had given him, found Ferguson's number in Cavendish Square and dialled it.

'Charles Ferguson.'

'Jack Fox. Is Dillon there?'

'Why, Mr Fox. And how are you this evening?'

'Shove it, Ferguson. Give me Dillon.'

Ferguson handed the phone to Dillon, and he and Hannah stood up.

'Why, Jack, so sorry to hear your bad news.'

'Yeah, well, it's nothing compared to the news I have for you, Dillon. I've just grabbed Blake Johnson, and I'm taking him to hell, but not, alas, back. I saw you clear off in the cab, Dillon, and I got him before he opened the door. If you use your brains, you might come up with where I'm taking him, and that would please me no end.'

He switched off before Dillon could reply, and Dillon turned to Hannah and Ferguson. 'He's got Blake. He said he's taking him to hell but not back.' He frowned. 'Hellsmouth, his place in Cornwall, it's got to be. Let me use the phone.'

Hannah said, 'Dillon, no, it's a trap. He made it easy for you to guess, and now he'll kill you, too.'

'That may be, Hannah. But I can't leave Blake there alone.'

He dialled the Holland Park safe house and got Helen Black. 'Bad news. The bastards have kidnapped Blake Johnson. Put the Major on.'

Roper said, 'Here I am, Sean. What's the deal?'

Dillon told him.

Roper said, 'Give me a couple of minutes at my computer.'

'Good man.'

Roper was back very quickly. 'Yes, besides the Gulfstream, the Solazzo family have a Golden Eagle. You know that plane?'

'I've flown one many times,' Dillon said. 'It's excellent for short runways.'

'Well, that's what they have at the Hellsmouth estate. There's an old RAF feeder station from the Second World War. The nearest decent airfield is RAF, St Just, twenty miles away. It's an air-sea rescue set-up, helicopters, long runway.'

'Thanks, old son.'

'You're going in hard, I take it.'

'You could say that.'

'I wish I could be with you. I'll stay on the computer, in case you need me. Just a minute.' There was a pause, and Roper spoke again. 'The Golden Eagle took off twenty minutes ago. The slot booked says Cornwall, Hellsmouth, six passengers.'

'And one of those is Blake. Thanks, Roper.'

Dillon said, 'Hellsmouth, they've gone down in a Golden Eagle from Bardsey. Six passengers.' He punched another number on the phone.

'Sean, what are you doing?' Hannah said.

'Well, I'm not phoning the Cornish police. They're a fine body of men, but not for a job like this. I'm calling Farley Field.'

'What for?' she demanded.

'Because he's going after them,' Ferguson said. 'I know my Sean.'

'He said to hell but not back,' Dillon said. 'Well, I'll follow him to hell.'

A voice on the receiver said, 'Farley Field.'

'Dillon. Get me Squadron Leader Lacey, if he's there.'

'Actually, I just saw him in the mess. Hang on.'

Lacey was there quickly. 'Is that you, Dillon?'

'We're going into action, and I mean now.'

'What's the score?'

'Hellsmouth, near Lizard Point in Cornwall. It's a small airstrip, so I need a parachute landing.'

'I know that area. RAF St Just is not too far away.'

'Exactly, so you drop me, then land at St Just.'

'Jesus, Dillon, you're at it again, saving the world.'

'No, saving Blake Johnson's life. Speak to the quarter-master. Brownings, AK47s, parachutes for two. I'd say six hundred feet.'

'You're mad, Sean, but let me get on with it.'

Dillon put the phone down and Hannah Bernstein said, 'Gear for two parachutists. What the hell are you talking about?'

'Well, not the SAS. There isn't time. I've someone in mind, and I'll go and see him now. If you want to see me again, it will be at Farley Field.'

'You're just going to execute all those people, aren't you, Dillon?' she said angrily.

Dillon turned to Ferguson. 'She's a lovely woman, Brigadier, but I've had it up to here with her morality. I'm more interested in saving a good man's life,' and he turned and walked out.

Hannah turned and said, 'He's mad, sir.'

'No, Superintendent. He's Dillon.'


Harry Salter, Billy, Joe and Sam Hall were in the end booth at the Dark Man enjoying large Scotches when Dillon came in.

'Sean, my old son,' Harry Salter said. 'Did we do it or did we do it?'

'Fox has kidnapped Blake,' Dillon said. 'Flown off to this estate he has in Cornwall with four of his heavies.'

There was silence. Salter said, 'What are you going to do?'

'I can't leave it, they might chop him. I'm flying down in an hour from Farley Field. I'll drop over the estate by parachute. Try and catch them with their pants down. It's got to be a drop, the landing field there is too short for a Gulfstream. The nearest RAF base is twenty miles away.'

Billy said, 'Fox and four makes five, Dillon, and you're going in alone?'

'No, Billy, I'm going in with you.'

'You must be bleeding mad,' Harry Salter said.

Dillon ignored him. 'Billy, you've heard of Arnhem in the Second World War, all those paratroopers going in? There was one major, an army surgeon, who'd never done a jump in his life, but they needed a doctor. He survived just fine and so will you. Billy, trust me. You jump out, pull the cord at six hundred feet, you hit the ground in twenty-five seconds, and that's all there is to it.'

Salter said, 'You're crazy.'

But Billy was smiling all over his face. 'I've said it before, Dillon, you're just like me. You don't give a stuff. Just show me the way.'

'Well, if he goes, I'm bleeding going,' Salter said. 'Even if I'm only on the sidelines.'

'Right,' Dillon said. 'Then let's do it.'

# HELLSMOUTH

# 15

When Dillon, Harry Salter and Billy arrived at Farley Field, Lacey and Parry were waiting.

'Let's go into the operations room and make sure I've got it right,' Lacey said.

The quartermaster stood ready with Dillon's Brownings, two AK47s, parachutes and jumpsuits ready.

Dillon said, 'Have a word with Mr Salter, Sergeant Major, it's his first jump.'

'Is that so, Mr Dillon?' the sergeant major replied, face impassive. 'Then a word might be indicated.'

'Just show me,' Billy told him.

Dillon went to the chart table and started to check it out with Lacey and Parry. 'It's not as bad as it could be,' Lacey said. 'There's almost a half moon. One pass is all I'd recommend. There's no time for more, then we'll rush to St Just.'

'Sounds good to me.'

'The other chap,' Lacey said. 'He knows what he's doing?'

'Absolutely.'

Ferguson and Hannah Bernstein came in. When the Brigadier saw the Salters, he was astonished. 'For God's sake, what is this? You said two parachutists, and he isn't a parachutist.'

'Well, I am now,' Billy said. 'I think I've got the hang of it, Dillon. I pull this ring and that's it. The guns are pretty obvious. I managed Kilbeg, I can manage this.'

'This is madness,' Hannah Bernstein said.

'No, it's trying to save Blake Johnson's life,' Dillon said. 'I'm ready when you are, Brigadier, unless you have other ideas.'

'No,' Ferguson said. 'It makes the usual wild sense where you are concerned, so let's get on with it.'

'Harry's coming along for the ride,' Dillon said. 'I suggest you lot board, and Billy and I will change and follow.'

'As you wish.'

Ten minutes later, Dillon and Billy, in jumpsuits, flak jackets, parachutes, shoulder holsters, AKs suspended across the chest, went up the steps and took their seats. Parry closed the door.

Salter said, 'Christ, Billy, you look like you're in a Vietnam war movie or something. What are you playing at?'

Billy actually smiled. 'I'm playing at being me, Harry, and it feels great.'


Blake sat down again on the stone seat in the tunnel, waist deep in water, hugging himself and trying to keep warm. Would Dillon come? Fox seemed to expect it, dangling him as bait. It was an impossible situation, but then, Dillon had always been master of the impossible. Somewhere high above, through the thick walls of the old house, he seemed to hear a noise, far off, something like an aircraft engine, but he couldn't be sure. The rat appeared and circled, swimming.

'I told you,' he said. 'Behave yourself.'


The noise of the aircraft faded quickly. Falcone said, 'What was that?'

'It could be normal air traffic at the RAF place at St Just,' Fox said. 'And then again, it could be Dillon. We'd better get ready.'

He was standing by the fire in the great hall with Falcone and Russo. 'Get me a brandy first.'

Russo went to the sideboard, filled a glass and brought it back. Rossi and Cameci came in, holding Uzis.

Falcone said, 'Excuse me, Signore, but do you really think Dillon will come?'

'I gave him enough clues. He's smart. He'll come.'

It was Russo who said, 'But what if they send the police?'

'Dillon? No, it's too personal for that. He's not going to trust the police to do this for him.'

'But Ferguson is secret intelligence,' Falcone pointed out. 'What if he decided to use special forces, the SAS?'

'Same thing. He's operated this whole thing very close to his chest. Publicity is the last thing he wants, he won't change now. Low-key, that's the way they'll do it. Like in the bullring, mano a mano, hand-to-hand, face-to-face.'

'As you say, Signore.'

Fox turned to Rossi and Cameci. 'Get out in the garden and keep watch. Check the doors.'

They went out and he drank some of the brandy. He was right in all respects except one. Dillon was already there.

As the Gulfstream throttled back to almost stalling speed, Parry ran back, opened the door, and dropped the steps. There was a rush of wind.

Salter said, 'Christ Almighty.'

Dillon turned and grinned at Billy. 'I'm an older guy, you young bastard. I'll go first.'

'Thanks very much. Get going, Dillon.'

Billy, feeling totally insane, pushed him out and dived after him.

There was rain, light mist, and yet the moon, the house and estate were clear below. Dillon hit in no time at all, punched the quick release after a perfect landing, not even a roll, and looked around. He saw the other parachute billowing like some strange flower, ran over, and stamped on it. Billy sat up.

'Are you okay?' Dillon asked.

'I think so. Went backwards and hit my back.' He worked the muscles around. 'But it feels okay.'

Dillon punched Billy's quick release. 'Then come on, move it!'

Billy was on his feet in a moment. 'Jesus, Dillon, I can't believe this is happening.'

'Well, it is. Kilbeg all over again, except this time there are five bad guys out there waiting to pounce, so be ready.'

Dillon trawled the gardens with the Nightstalker and saw Cameci over by the terrace. 'Take a look,' he whispered to Billy.

Billy nodded. 'Can't see anything else.'

'I'll go left, you right.'

'I'm with you, Dillon.'

Cameci was by the balustrade, looking out over the moonlit garden, when the muzzle of an AK47 nudged his back.

Billy said, 'Make a sound and I'll blow your spine apart.'

Cameci said, 'Is that Dillon?'

'No, I'm his younger brother.' Billy called softly, 'Over here.'

Dillon moved out of the shadows, and Rossi, on the other side of the terrace, stood up. It was Billy who saw him.

'Dillon!' he rasped.

Dillon turned, his silenced AK coughed, and Rossi went backwards, dead.

Dillon took Cameci by the jaw. 'Tell me who's inside and tell me now, or I'll kill you.'

Cameci, terrified, said, 'Signores Fox, Falcone and Russo.'

Dillon said, 'Excellent. Now what about the American?'

'He's in the tunnel in the cellars.'

'Good. Take us there.'

Cameci led the way through the kitchen, down the stairs and into the cellar system. They arrived at an old oak door.

'That's it,' Cameci said.

'Then open it.'

Cameci did as he was told. Blake, in the water, turned, the light falling across his face, and Dillon said, 'What are you doing, taking a dip? This is no time for fun. Get the hell out of there.'

Blake stumbled up the steps. 'What kept you?'

He was shivering and very wet. Dillon said to Cameci, 'Get your clothes off. The man's freezing.'

'But, Signore,' Cameci protested.

Dillon shoved the muzzle of the AK under his chin. 'Just do it.' He pulled the combat scarf from around his neck and gave it to Blake. 'Dry yourself a little.'

Blake did the best he could while Cameci stripped. Blake pulled on the clothes. Cameci was left in his underpants.

Meanwhile, Falcone, upstairs, had opened the French windows, gone out on the terrace, and found Rossi. He was back inside in an instant to Fox and Russo.

'Rossi's out there dead. No sign of Cameci.'

'Christ,' Fox said. 'He's here, the bastard's here. Spread out.'

At that moment, Dillon shoved Cameci into the room in his underpants, and startled by the sudden apparition, Falcone turned and fired. Cameci went down, writhing.

'Hey, you got the wrong guy,' Dillon called. 'It's me, Jack. Time to pay up.'

'Fuck you, Dillon,' Fox shouted.

They crouched in the hall, the great chandelier hanging from the ceiling spreading its illumination. Falcone whispered to Russo, 'Stick with me. Let's move towards the door to the kitchen quarters.' He saw Fox moving to the right.

'There's too much light,' Russo said.

Falcone fired his Uzi up at the chandelier and brought it crashing down.

'Not any more.'

He ducked, pulling Russo with him.

The hall was a strange place now, only the light from the great log fire picking out the suits of armour, the ancient banners, the great staircase to the left. Dillon, Blake and Billy crept in and crouched behind the great central table.

'Now what?' Billy demanded.

'Just wait, Billy, always hasten slowly.' He took out his Browning and passed it to Blake. 'Just in case.'

'How the hell did you get here, anyway?' Blake asked.

'Lacey and Parry did a low pass, and Billy and I jumped.'

'Dear God, what does this boy know about parachuting?'

'A lot more than he did a couple of hours ago. Don't worry, there are reinforcements coming.'

'A special forces team?'

'No. Ferguson, Hannah and Harry Salter.'

'Christ Almighty.'

'We can make it, Blake. Cameci and Rossi are down. That just leaves Falcone, Russo and good old Jack Fox.'

'So how do we do it?' Billy asked.

'I've told you. We wait, Billy, and let them come to us.'

There was quiet. Falcone and Russo had reached the green baize door leading to the kitchen. Fox had reached another door to one side of the fireplace. He opened it and went up a spiral staircase to the landing, peered down at the hall, and saw a movement behind the table. Beneath his foot, a board creaked.

'The bastard's somewhere above us,' Dillon said. 'Slide off to the right, Billy.'

Billy moved away and Dillon called, 'Why, Jack, here we are again at the final end of things.' He pushed Blake away. 'Get over to the shadows on the other side.'

Up above, Jack Fox moved, crouching by the switches for the wall lights that normally illuminated the collection of paintings that hung on the wall. He paused and reached.

Below, Blake started to move, slipped, and cried out in pain as he fell on his arm. Dillon reached down to pick him up and Fox switched on the lights.

'I've got you now, you bastard.'

He raised the Walther in his right hand and shot Dillon twice in the back. To do it he had to stand, and so did Billy, over to the right. Raising his AK, he pumped ten rounds into Fox, driving him back across the landing. Fox bounced off the wall back to the balustrade and fell over. He lay there on the stone flagging, twitching for just a second. Then there was silence.

Falcone eased open the green baize door and said, 'We're out of here.'

'Where to?' Russo asked.

'The airstrip. We've got to get to London. Don Marco's due in, and we've got to give him the news.'

Russo said, 'Sometimes they kill the messenger.'

'Not now. This is too important.'

They slid back through the door, went down the steps and made the courtyard. A few moments later, they were driving away to the airstrip.

In the hall, Dillon had been thrown on to his face by the force of the bullets he'd taken in his back. Groaning, he forced himself up. Billy ran over, crouching.

'Dillon, are you all right?'

'Yes, thank God for flak jackets. I'll be a little sore, that's all.' He looked around. 'Anyone there?' he called.

There was silence. Blake said, 'Are you okay, Sean?'

'Yes, I'm fine. I think they've run for it. I heard a car leaving.'

He got up and walked to Jack Fox's body, and Blake followed. They stood, looking down.

'Well, there you go, Blake. He's paid the price. You've got your revenge now.'

Blake said, 'Not really. Fox gave the order, but Falcone boasted to me that it was he and Russo who killed my wife.'

'And where are they?' Billy asked.

'Come with me and I'll show you,' Dillon said.

He went and opened the front door and stood at the top of the steps, and Billy and Blake followed. A moment later, there was the sound of an aircraft engine as a plane passed over.

'There they are, Billy: Falcone and Russo getting out while they still can.'

As they turned to the door, an RAF Land Rover drove into the courtyard, Hannah Bernstein at the wheel and Ferguson and Harry Salter in the rear.

Standing by the fire in the hall, Harry Salter said, 'Are you okay, Billy?'

'He's better than okay,' Dillon said. 'Fox shot me in the back twice. Only my flak jacket saved me, and Billy blew the bastard away.' He turned. 'That's three, Billy, you're an ace.'

'So what happens now, sir?' Hannah Bernstein asked. 'Shall I notify the Cornwall constabulary?'

'I think not,' Ferguson said. 'Leave this for the caretaker to discover. Fox and these other two rogues are on Scotland Yard's intelligence information computer. This whole thing is obviously a Mafia feud, therefore it's nothing to do with us.'

'But, sir,' Hannah said.

'Superintendent, be sensible. That would be the best way of handling it, so don't let's argue. Now let's get out of here and back to St Just.'

On the Golden Eagle, Falcone called Don Marco on his mobile. The Don was about to board his Gulfstream in New York.

'Aldo, what news do you have for me?'

'Terrible, Don Marco. How can I tell you?'

Don Marco said, 'By getting on with it.'

Afterwards he said, 'Poor Jack, so stupid, so headstrong.'

'What shall I do, Signore?'

'Nothing at the moment. There is obviously a matter of family honour here, but we'll discuss that later when I'm in London.'

'As you say, Don Marco.'

On board the Gulfstream bearing Dillon and the others to Farley Field, Ferguson's mobile sounded. He hesitated, then passed it to Dillon.

'I think you need to deal with this.'

Roper said, 'I had a call from Hannah, so I know what's gone down. I'm glad you're still with us.'

'So am I.'

'I've trawled the Solazzo family affairs. The Golden Eagle just landed at Bardsey, with two passengers, Falcone and Russo.'

'Anything else?'

'Well, you'll love this. Don Marco Solazzo is en route from New York in one of the family Gulfstreams. Booked in at the Dorchester.'

Dillon laughed. 'Well, that really is going to make it old home week,' and he switched off.

# LONDON

# 16

There was fog at Heathrow airport, and Don Marco's Gulfstream was diverted to Shannon in Ireland. It was several hours before it was once again in the air. It eventually landed in the private aircraft section at Heathrow, where Falcone and Russo waited with the Don's favourite car, a Bentley.

Falcone kissed the Don's hand. 'My condolences, Don Marco. Everything that could be done was done.'

'You don't need to tell me, Aldo. Let's get going, then we speak.'

Russo did the driving. Don Marco said, 'A little brandy, Aldo.'

Falcone opened the small bar in the rear of the Bentley, found the right bottle and a glass. Don Marco sipped a little and nodded. 'Fine, so now tell me – tell me everything.'

Later, in the Oliver Messel suite at the Dorchester, he stood at the open French window, rain drifting across the Mayfair rooftops to his terrace.

'Get me a cigar,' he told Falcone. 'In the crocodile case.'

Falcone nodded to Russo, who quickly opened the case that was on the sideboard. He took out a Romeo and Julietta Havana, clipped the end, and gave it to Falcone, who warmed it with a large match and passed it to the old man. Don Marco lit up.

'Jack was stupid, Jack was greedy and headstrong, but Jack was also my nephew. Half of him was Solazzo, flesh and blood. All men are a mixture of things, Aldo.'

Rain swept across the roofs with considerable force. The curtains billowed and Don Marco nodded.

'Jack could be foolish. He was certainly a thief, whatever you mean by that. But he was also a war hero and served his country.'

'We all know what Signor Fox was,' Aldo said.

'And we all know how he ended, on his face at the hands of these people. This Dillon, Johnson, Brigadier Ferguson.' The Don turned, not even angry. 'There is a matter of honour here. A debt must be paid. Money isn't everything in this world, Aldo.'

'Of course, Don Marco.'

The old man bit on the cigar, took out his wallet, and extracted a card that carried some phone numbers.

'I think the third one is Ferguson's office at the Ministry of Defence. Try it.'


It was two-thirty at the Dark Man and they were all there in the end booth, Harry and Billy, Baxter and Hall against the wall, Dillon and Blake, Ferguson and Hannah.

Hannah's mobile rang and she answered. 'All right, tell me.' She switched off. 'Priority intelligence at Scotland Yard, keeping me informed. It seems there were three killings in Cornwall, all known members of the Mafia.'

'Well, there you are,' Dillon said.

Billy was laughing. 'Surprise, surprise.'

Harry said, 'Here now, you watch it doesn't go to your head.'

'Billy the Kid,' Dillon said. 'In the Battle of Britain, he'd have earned a DFC.'

Dora brought a bottle of Bollinger and glasses on a tray, thumbed off the cork and poured. Billy said, 'That's it, then.'

'Not really, Billy.' Dillon took a glass. 'I mean, why is good old Don Marco Solazzo flying to London? To see his doctor, to get measured for a new suit in Savile Row?' He shook his head. 'Vendetta, Billy. Kill one of our own, we kill you.'

Harry said, 'You think that?'

'I think that,' Blake said.

'So it isn't over?' Harry said.

'Last act.' Dillon shrugged. 'You'd need Shakespeare to write it.'

'He's not available, he's bleeding dead,' Billy told him.

It was then that Ferguson's mobile rang. He listened, then switched off. 'The Ministry of Defence. Don Marco Solazzo wanting a word. He's at the Dorchester.' He turned to Hannah. 'Would you mind getting him for me, Superintendent?'

Dora brought her the bar phone, and Hannah called the Dorchester and asked for the Don.

'Solazzo here.'

'I have Brigadier Ferguson for you.'

She passed the phone to Ferguson, who switched to audio so they could all listen. 'What a surprise.'

'I doubt that, Brigadier.'

'Condolences on the death of your nephew.'

'And congratulations to Dillon, I suppose?'

'Not at all. Your nephew was disposed of by an East End gangster from a family that isn't in the least intimidated by the Mafia.'

'Don't let us play games, Ferguson. This affair has gone on long enough, and my nephew is dead. I think it's time for us to meet and arrange a compromise.'

'That sounds sensible. When do you suggest?'

The old man was tranquil. 'That's up to you, but I think it should be just the two of us. I don't want Dillon and Johnson there.'

'I'll call back.'

Hannah Bernstein said, 'He's lying, sir.'

'Of course.' He turned to Dillon. 'Well?'

'He said he didn't want me and Johnson there. That means he does. If he knew Billy had killed Jack Fox, he'd want him there. This is a Mafia thing. Honour, family, revenge. He'll kill us all if he can. It's funny. We talk capitalistic values in society, but this kind of thing is the ultimate example of money being of no value.'

'So what are we talking about here?'

It was Blake who answered. 'I'd say a face-to-face meet where he'll have his people, obviously Falcone and Russo, and he'll take it for granted that you'll do the same. Not that he'll think I'm much help, but there's Dillon, and who knows.'

'There's me,' Billy said.

'Yeah, well just hold your tongue. You're getting too much of a taste for this, Billy. This isn't Dodge City,' Harry Salter said.

'It's better than Dodge City,' Billy told him.

'Fine,' Ferguson nodded. 'But what happens now?'

'You arrange a meeting,' Dillon told him.

'But where? Hardly the Piano Bar at the Dorchester. '

Dillon thought about it, then turned to Salter. 'Those boats of yours on the Thames, Harry? Something from Westminster to Chelsea or whatever.'

'The *Bluebell*?' Salter said. 'That goes from Westminster.'

Dillon turned to Ferguson. 'Choose one of the evening times. Arrange to meet him on board, just the two of you.'

Hannah said urgently, 'But he won't go alone.'

'Of course not, he'll have Falcone and Russo with him.' He smiled at Ferguson. 'He'll certainly expect me and maybe Blake.'

Blake was sweating again, his arm back in a sling. 'Not that I'm any good.'

'Yeah, well, I bleeding am,' Billy said.

'All right.' Ferguson nodded. 'So we meet and what happens?'

'He kills us if he can. It's the last act, you see,' Dillon told him.

Hannah said, 'Look, I think this is getting out of hand, sir. We've already breached all police codes by our behaviour in the Cornish matter.'

Dillon said, 'You're a good copper, and I've worked with you for some years, but we're talking about some of the worst people in the business and I want to finally put them *out* of business.'

'And I'm talking about the law,' she cried.

'Which people like Solazzo play games with. Lawyers are part of the law. The Solazzos are able to buy the best lawyers. Does that satisfy your fine moral conscience, Hannah, because it does nothing for me. I shall take those bastards out.'

There was a heavy silence. Ferguson said, 'Well, Superintendent?'

There was another pause. Blake said, 'Falcone and Russo killed my wife, and yet we'll never prove that.'

Hannah Bernstein was obviously distressed. 'I know, and it's terrible, but without the law, we've got nothing.'

'Even if they walk free?' Blake said.

'I'm afraid so.'

Dillon said, 'Well, you've got me, and I'm going to play public executioner again.'

Hannah stood up. 'I can't manage this, sir,' she said to Ferguson.

'Then I suggest you take a couple of weeks' leave, Superintendent, and I would remind you that you signed the Official Secrets Act when you joined me.'

'Of course, sir.'

'Off you go then.'

She went out, and Ferguson said, 'Now how do we handle this?'

Rain increased in force as darkness fell and the Bentley arrived at Westminster Pier and Don Marco got out and walked up the gangplank. Falcone and Russo had joined the boat on its earlier trip, dressed in jeans and reefer coats, the kind of thing crew members wore. So did Billy and Harry Salter.

The fog was quite bad and rain fell heavily. The *Bluebell* nosed out into the river, and Don Marco walked out of the saloon, where there were only two other passengers, old ladies, and on to the stern, where there was a certain cover from the upper deck. He lit his cigar, and Ferguson moved out of the shadows.

'Don Marco, Charles Ferguson.'

'Ah, Brigadier.'

Fog swirled in. There was a seaman coiling a rope at the starboard rail. 'One of yours?' Ferguson asked.

'Oh, come now, Brigadier. All I want to do is bring this whole unfortunate affair to an end. My nephew was stupid, I acknowledge that.'

'He wasn't only stupid, he was murderous,' Ferguson told him. 'Having said that, don't tell me you don't want revenge.'

'What would be the point?'

'You know something?' Ferguson said. 'The older I get, the more obvious to me it is that life's like the movies. Take this situation. It's the gunfight at the OK Corral. Earp and the Clantons. Who's going to shoot whom? I mean, my dear old stick, why would an ageing Mafia Don go to all the trouble of coming here?'

The seaman at the rail, Falcone, stood up, and another, at the port rail, appeared, Russo. On the top deck, Billy and Harry Salter looked over, Billy holding a silenced AK.

Out of the shadows, Dillon appeared, Blake beside him, his right arm in the sling, sweating badly.

Don Marco said, 'You don't look good, Mr Johnson.'

'Oh, I'll get by.' Blake turned to Falcone. 'You butchered my wife.'

'Hey, it was business.' Falcone had a gun in his hand.

'Well, this is personal.' Blake's left hand came out of his sling holding a silenced Walther, and he shot Falcone, knocking him against the rail. Falcone spun round and went over head first into the river.

Russo raised his gun to Ferguson, and Billy, leaning over the rail on the top deck, extended the silenced AK and gave Russo a burst that sent him over the rail after Falcone.

Blake was really very ill, sweat all over his face. He said to Don Marco, 'Why the hell I don't kill you, I'll never know, but we ruined your nephew, killed the bastard and his men. I think I'd rather leave you to chew on that.'

He turned, and he and Ferguson walked away. Dillon lit a cigarette. 'He's one of the good guys, Blake, wants to improve the world. Even Ferguson still tries, but not me. I've found life more disappointing than I'd hoped, so to hell with you.' He slapped Don Marco back-handed across the face, reached for his ankles, and tossed him over into the river. The fog swirled. A cigar butt floated smouldering on the water. It was over.

They were waiting for him in the Daimler on Charing Cross Pier. Ferguson said, 'Taken care of?'

Dillon nodded. 'Whichever gang took out Jack Fox and his men in Cornwall was obviously lying in wait for Don Marco here. Another Mafia execution. Very messy.'

'All in all, then,' Ferguson said, 'a satisfactory night.'

'Except for one thing.' They turned to the figure who sat slumped and ashen in the dark. Blake looked at them, his eyes burning. 'It won't bring her back.'

And to that, there was no answer.